T0284772

COLD TURKEY

COLD TURKEY

Amy Patricia Meade

**SEVERN
HOUSE**

First world edition published in Great Britain and the USA in 2023
by Severn House, an imprint of Canongate Books Ltd,
14 High Street, Edinburgh EH1 1TE.

severnhouse.com

British Library Cataloguing-in-Publication Data
A CIP catalogue record for this title is available from the British Library.

ISBN-13: 978-1-4483-0655-8 (cased)
ISBN-13: 978-1-4483-0667-1 (e-book)

All Severn House titles are printed on acid-free paper.

MIX
Paper from
responsible sources
FSC
www.fsc.org   FSC® C013056

Typeset by Palimpsest Book Production Ltd.,
Falkirk, Stirlingshire, Scotland.
Printed and bound in Great Britain by
TJ Books, Padstow, Cornwall.

Praise for Amy Patricia Meade

"A savvy and engaging amateur sleuth, Tish Tarragon and her band of eccentric friends will charm you to the very last page of this delightful cozy mystery"
Terrie Farley Moran, award-winning author of the Murder, She Wrote mysteries (with Jessica Fletcher) on *Cold Turkey*

"Will appeal to fans of foodie mysteries, such as those from Sarah Fox, Joanne Fluke, and Laura Childs"
Booklist on *Of Mushrooms and Matrimony*

"Tish is the ideal cozy heroine – clever and sensible, with just the right amount of daring"
Publishers Weekly on *Of Mushrooms and Matrimony*

"Foodies and cozy lovers will enjoy both the puzzle and the recipes"
Kirkus Reviews on *Of Mushrooms and Matrimony*

"A charming cozy with plenty of suspects"
Kirkus Reviews Starred Review of *From Ladle to Grave*

"Meade keeps the reader guessing to the end. Established fans and newcomers alike will adore this cozy"
Publishers Weekly on *From Ladle to Grave*

"Meade makes each character memorable in this layered, cleverly constructed story. Recommend Tish to fans of Laura Childs' Theodosia Browning"
Booklist on *The Curse of the Cherry Pie*

"Foodies will enjoy the cooking tips along with a tricky mystery and hints of romance to come"
Kirkus Reviews on *The Curse of the Cherry Pie*

"Delicious"
Publishers Weekly on *The Curse of the Cherry Pie*

About the author

Amy Patricia Meade is a native of Long Island, NY. Now residing in upstate New York, Amy spends her time writing mysteries with a humorous or historical bent, and is a member of Sisters in Crime and The Crime Writers' Association.

www.amypatriciameade.com

ONE

'If you can't take it down, you can always jazz it up,' Julian Pen Davis, Channel Ten weatherman and occasional human interest reporter stated as he watched Sheriff Clemson Reade endeavor to remove an enormous moose head from the space above the counter of the new Cookin' the Books café. The antlered beast was the last of several animal heads to have graced the walls of the building when it served as the Hobson Glen Bar and Grill.

'Thanksgiving is this Thursday,' he continued. 'Once the turkey leftovers are in the fridge, we'll break out the garland and Christmas balls and give him a holiday makeover.'

'And after Christmas?' Tish Tarragon, the café's owner, challenged as she held the bottom of the ladder upon which Reade stood.

'We deck him out in hearts for Valentine's Day. And then green for St Paddy's Day. And then bunny ears—'

'Jules, I'm not costuming a moose head for the seasons. This is a literary café, not the Country Bear Jamboree.'

'We could dress him as a literary character,' Celestine Rufus, the café's baker, suggested. 'And then maybe make him our mascot.'

'OK,' Tish allowed. 'Now we just need to think of a famous moose in literature.'

The question gave Celestine pause. 'Ummmm . . .'

'I know! We can call him Lenny. You know, from *Of* Moose *and Men*,' Jules offered to the sound of groans.

'Make another joke like that and I'll come down this ladder and arrest you,' Reade jokingly threatened from his lofty perch.

'That won't work, honey,' Tish admonished with a smirk. 'We're the ones who'd have to bail him out.'

'Oh, yeah. I forgot about that. There's also the matter of Biscuit.' Reade nodded toward the Bichon Frisé sniffing at Jules's feet. 'It would be a pity to take him from a good home.'

'True. Biscuit suffered enough with his previous owner.'

'Previous owner?' Celestine questioned. 'What about this one? The poor dog's forced to listen to Jules's jokes all the time.'

'Hmm, animal cruelty,' Reade pretended to ponder. 'Come to think of it, maybe I *should* arrest Jules.'

Jules folded his arms across his chest. 'Y'all are just too funny,' he sniffed. '*Too* funny.'

'Sorry,' Tish apologized with a chuckle. 'You're just too easy to tease.'

'He's always been easy to tease,' Mary Jo Okensholt remarked as she made her way downstairs from the two-bedroom apartment above the café, which she now lived in, rent-free, in exchange for her marketing and waitressing expertise. 'Nothing's changed since we were all at UVA together. What are we teasing him about now?'

'His dad jokes.'

'Oh yeah, he's telling more of them because he's rehearsing for the day he's a stepdad to Cassius.'

Jules's tanned complexion turned crimson. 'That's not true! That's . . .' He ran a hand through his chestnut hair. 'All right, maybe it's partially true. I do love that little boy.'

'You and Maurice have been datin' for three months now. Will you be seein' each other over the holiday?' Celestine asked.

'No,' Jules replied. 'He told me he's visiting his mama, so I'm visiting my mama, like I usually do, but . . .'

'But wish you could spend some time with them both?' Tish guessed.

Jules nodded. 'I didn't say anything though. I mean, maybe it's too soon to spend holidays together. What do y'all think?'

Mary Jo begged the question. 'I'm a divorcée who hasn't dated anyone in twenty years. I have absolutely no opinion.'

'Well, as a widow who hasn't dated in over forty-five years, I'm gonna answer your question,' Celestine stated. 'I think you should say somethin' to Maurice. Life is too gosh darn short to keep quiet.'

'I agree with you, Celestine,' Jules replied. 'But I don't want to scare Maurice away either. You and Clemson haven't known me for as long as Tish and Mary Jo have, but I can be overly demonstrative and even a bit dramatic at times.'

Celestine looked at Reade, who was doing his best to suppress a smile.

'You don't say?' the baker said, tongue-in-cheek.

The facetious nature of her comment completely eluded Jules. 'Yes, I know it's hard to believe, but it's true. If I tell Maurice I'd like to spend Thanksgiving with him and Cassius, he might think I'm too clingy. I don't want to risk driving him away. What do you think, Tish?'

Tish bit her lip and nervously swept her blonde hair from her shoulders. 'I'm not exactly the relationship expert, but after three months of dating, you and Maurice must feel a bit more comfortable communicating with each other than when you were first together, right?'

'Oh, talking is never a problem for us. Even when we don't see each other, we speak on the phone for hours once he's put little Cassius to bed. We talk about everything – first dates, favorite foods, our families, our pasts . . .'

'If you can talk to each other that freely and about such personal subjects, then I think you should probably talk to him about Thanksgiving. Gently, slowly. Tell him that you understand him wanting to spend it with family because you enjoy spending it with yours, but that you wish you could somehow see each other and celebrate, if just for a quiet pre- or post-holiday dinner. Be open and honest. Even if your plans can't come together in time for Thanksgiving, it gives you both a chance to discuss what you might want to do differently at Christmas.'

'Tish is right,' Reade confirmed as he shone a flashlight into the space between the moose head and the wall. 'Had she and I communicated better, we might have gotten together sooner.'

'Gee, ya think?' Celestine sassed, her laughter causing her chin-length dangle earrings to jingle against her cherry red, short-cropped hair.

'Y'all are right,' Jules agreed. 'I'll give Maurice a call when I get back to the office later. So what's everyone else doing for Turkey Day?'

'It's Clemson and my first holiday together, so I've finally gotten my grandma's china out of storage and will be using it to serve a simple, but romantic dinner for two,' Tish explained.

'For two? You're not going to be in town for the holiday, MJ?'

'Nope.' Mary Jo joined Tish at the ladder and pushed her weight against one side while Tish steadied the other. 'Gregory said he has too much studying to do to come home, so Kayla and I are going to meet him at the dorm and take him out for dinner. It's a surprise.'

'Are you sure surprising a college kid on a holiday weekend is a wise decision?' Reade questioned as he reached behind the moose head to determine how it had been fastened to the wall.

'Oh yeah. It'll be fun. Gregory has always loved Thanksgiving. A holiday committed to food and football? What teenage boy doesn't like that?'

'I was always down with the food,' Jules recalled. 'The football, not so much. I think Clemson might have a point though, MJ. Gregory just recently flew the nest. You might want to consult with him before you go swooping in and sinking your talons into him again.'

'Are you through with the bird analogies?' Mary Jo asked.

'I went a little far with the talons, didn't I?'

'Yeah, just a bit. Look, I appreciate you guys trying to keep me from being disappointed after traveling all that way, but I know Gregory. He'll be thrilled to see us! So, how about you, Celestine? Are you hosting the family this year?'

The baker shook her head. 'Nope. My daughters and daughters-in-law are doin' all the cookin'. I do, however, have dibs on the pies – sweet potato, pecan, and coconut custard. I don't let anyone else do the bakin' but me. It's my legacy, or at least I hope it will be.'

'Will it be just you and the family or will someone else be joining you?' Mary Jo cheekily asked, eliciting a punch in the arm from Tish.

'MJ, stop being so nosy!'

'I'm not being nosy . . . OK, maybe I am being nosy. But Celestine and I were roomies for a brief period before I moved in here. I was simply asking her a question – from one roomie to another.'

'In front of everyone else,' Tish argued.

'It's OK, Tish,' Celestine intervened. 'I don't mind answerin' MJ's question. Daryl will be joinin' us—'

MJ and Tish both smiled.

'—as a lifelong friend of the family,' Celestine clarified.

While MJ's smile dissipated, Tish's only broadened. Daryl Dufour had been Celestine's childhood sweetheart prior to her meeting Lloyd Rufus. It was also quite possible that Daryl was the father of Celestine's eldest daughter – although no one apart from Tish, Celestine and Daryl were privy to that fact. 'I think that's terrific, Celestine. I'm sure Daryl will enjoy catching up with the kids and grandkids.'

'Yeah, he gets a kick outta them and they like him a bunch too. He's no replacement for their Pawpaw, of course, but he's pitched in a lot since Lloyd's passin'. Both the kids and the grandkids like having an older man around to talk to and, being a librarian, Daryl loves bringin' around books and gettin' them involved in readin'. It's been good.'

'Really good?' Mary Jo pressed.

Celestine narrowed her eyes. 'Yes. In a friendly way. As my oldest grandkid would say, "I don't have the bandwidth for anything more right now." Ask me in a year or so and my story might change, but right now, I'm enjoyin' the friendship and companionship and gettin' to know Daryl again. Seems funny to say that about someone I've known my whole life, but it's true. It's been nice to reminisce, but it's also been interestin' to learn how we've both changed through the years.'

As if on cue, a man entered the café. He was somewhere between his late fifties and early sixties, of average height, with a pleasant, yet rather nondescript countenance, and hair the color of sand. 'Hey, Celly,' he addressed the baker. 'Hey, y'all. The café looks terrific! Painting over that dark paneling makes it look so much larger, and cleaner too. And I love the fact that you have room for a wider selection of books for patrons to read while eating.'

'Thanks, Daryl. We're not quite there yet, but I'm pleased with everything so far. Except this fella.' Tish pointed to the top of the ladder and then added for clarification, 'The moose head, not Clemson.'

'I'm relieved to hear that. Um, is there anything I can help you with, Sheriff?'

'Only if you've brought a construction crew with you,' Reade replied. 'This thing is bolted into the main beams of the building. Even if I managed to remove the bolts, there's no way I can get this thing down by myself. It's way too heavy. I'm going to have to call someone in.'

Tish frowned. 'That sounds expensive.'

'Not necessarily,' he assured as he climbed down the ladder. 'I know a guy in Richmond who might cut us a deal.'

'Seeing as you're a cop, the words "I know a guy" make me exceedingly nervous.'

'Oh no, this guy didn't do time or anything like that. When he lived here in Hobson Glen, I issued him a citation for operating without a license.'

'Is that all? That makes me feel *so* much better,' she wisecracked.

'He has a license now. See, he didn't want to have to pay the fees to set up a business – Virginia only licenses companies, not individuals – until I pointed out that a second citation would actually cost more than the business set-up and application fees combined. So, he took the plunge, got the license, and almost immediately found himself working on an apartment renovation project in Richmond – a project open only to licensed contractors.'

'Well, if you're confident he's right for the job, give him a call and see what he charges. I don't have a lot of cash to spare.'

'Moose or no moose, you've worked wonders with this place, Tish,' Daryl gushed. 'One would never guess that this was once the spot to grab a pitcher of beer and a plate of hot wings and watch the game on the big screen. You've made it warm and welcoming. I just hope I'm not too late to be your first customer. I tried to get here earlier, but there was a small problem at the circulation desk.'

'You're not late at all,' Tish replied. 'In fact, you're a whole week early.'

'Daryl, we open *next* Friday – the day after Thanksgivin',' Celestine explained with a heavy sigh. '*This* Friday – today – we're servin' up food at the Turkey Trot.'

'Oooooh, *next Friday*,' Daryl sang. 'Sorry, I got my weeks confused.'

'No worries,' Tish assured him. 'If I see someone camped out in his car next Friday morning, I'll know it's you.'

'To get the bragging rights of being your first customer, I very well may camp out all night,' Daryl said with a chuckle. 'Gotta say though, I'm surprised the town gave the Turkey Trot job to y'all, what with Tish's history with Mayor Thompson.'

Prior to being elected mayor of Hobson Glen, Schuyler Thompson was Tish's boyfriend and landlord. Months after their breakup, he evicted her from the building she rented from him, forcing her to find a new home – the bar and grill building now being renovated – for the café.

'Mayor Thompson,' she replied with clear disdain, 'had no say in the matter. Nor did the town council. The Interfaith Center asked me if we'd donate the food and our time. The Turkey Trot benefits their food shelf, so I immediately said yes – even before consulting Celestine, I'm sorry to say.'

'No problem, sugar,' Celestine responded with a wave of her hand. 'I would have done the same thing. It's a darn good cause.'

'That it is,' Tish agreed with a nod. 'It also gave me a chance to come up with a menu that pays tribute to Thanksgiving without taking away from the day itself.'

'How'd you do that?' Daryl asked.

'With a little help from Louisa May Alcott's *An Old Fashioned Thanksgiving*.'

'Is that the short story where two teenage girls decide to cook Thanksgiving dinner for their family after their parents are called away to care for their grandmother?'

'One and the same. It's a bit saccharine at times, but the food descriptions are brilliant – well, the food that's cooked properly anyway. Certainly not the half-burnt turkey. Since there's great talk in the story of Mrs Bassett's applesauce, I have Brie and apple chutney on a baguette. Inspired by the older brother's lunch of cold, leftover pork, I created a ham sandwich on cranberry pecan bread. And, finally, in honor of the root cellar vegetables served at the dinner – the two things that turned out successfully – there's roasted root vegetable soup and classic onion soup. Oh, and because they're mentioned nearly a dozen times in the story, I'm offering both regular and vegan doughnuts dusted with cinnamon sugar as a sweet treat.'

Daryl rubbed his hands together eagerly. 'It all sounds delicious. And perfect for autumn.'

'I think so. I only hope everyone else agrees,' Tish said. 'Hey, Celestine, why don't you take Daryl to the kitchen and let him choose from what we're bringing over to the Turkey Trot? He shouldn't have to go without lunch just because we're not open for business yet.'

'That's very kind of you, Tish. I'll pay you for the sandwich,' Daryl offered.

'No need, Daryl, but I *will* accept a small donation to the food shelf.'

The head librarian reached into his wallet and handed her a ten-dollar bill.

Tish stretched it between both index fingers and gave it a good snap. 'Congratulations. This makes it official. You're our very first customer, and you didn't need to arrive here at the crack of dawn on Black Friday to do it.'

After selecting a ham sandwich on cranberry pecan bread and a cup of root vegetable soup, Daryl left Celestine, Tish, and the others to load her van with the various foodstuffs to be sold at the Turkey Trot.

'I'm so glad you're able to help us today, Jules,' Tish said appreciatively as she loaded a platter of sandwiches into the van.

'Of course. What would a Cookin' the Books function be like without your beverage guy? Besides, I've been waiting for a chance to "trot out" my famous warm cranberry apple cider.'

'Again with the dad jokes,' Reade remarked with a shake of his head, while busying himself by loading a gas generator into the back of his SUV.

'Sorry,' a self-conscious Jules apologized. 'Anyway, when I'm not serving beverages, I'll be covering the event for Channel Ten, so it's an all-around win for me. I've been looking forward to it for weeks.'

'I'm sorry I won't be able to help,' Mary Jo lamented as she loaded an industrial-sized slow cooker of soup onto one of the van's many shelves and anchored it in place with a bungee cord. 'Why the high school scheduled an early dismissal for teacher development less than a week before Thanksgiving break is beyond me.'

'We'll be fine,' Tish assured her. 'You're taking Kayla for her driver's test after school, aren't you?'

Jules gasped. 'Kayla's getting her driver's license?'

'Yes,' MJ replied. 'She took a driver's ed class this semester and, even though she still has a couple of weeks of class left, the teacher already told her she's passed.'

'How exciting!'

'Yes, it is – for her. For me, it's a bit depressing and more than a bit nerve-racking. If you notice my hair suddenly going white these next few weeks, you'll know why. Anyway, Kayla's exam isn't until twelve thirty. I can help you unload and then, when her test is done, I'm happy to come back here and help for an hour or so, if you guys need me.'

Tish refused the generous offer. 'Thanks, sweetie, but you're already keeping Biscuit at your place while Jules serves beverages today. That's enough help. I also think we have it covered. In addition to me, Celestine, and Jules, Opal Schaffer' – Hobson Glen's resident romance novelist and organic gardener – 'and Clemson have both volunteered to lend a hand.'

'I volunteered to help in between checking in with Officer Clayton,' Reade amended, loading in a giant coffee percolator filled with Jules's cider. 'I've never put him in charge of traffic control before and, although I have no doubt he's ready for the task, I still might be needed should an issue arise.'

'So long as Enid Kemper stays off the road, all should be fine,' MJ said.

Eighty-year-old Enid Kemper, the town eccentric, was known for wandering about town with her beloved green conure bird, Langhorne, on her shoulder. She was a frequent guest at Tish's café before it was forced to relocate.

'Enid?' Reade repeated, his finely chiseled face a question. 'In all my years with the sheriff's department, I've never known Enid Kemper to drive a car.'

'She used to, but that was over forty years ago,' Celestine replied. 'Before her parents and sister passed away and left Enid to hole herself up in that big ol' house of hers.'

'Why is she looking to drive again at this point in her life?'

'Because of the new law handed down by the town council and "Lord King Mayor,"' MJ said, her voice dripping with sarcasm. 'Effective immediately, only dogs are to be considered support animals – that means Enid can no longer bring Langhorne on the bus, to the library, to this café . . .'

'Jeez, that's right,' he said with a sigh. 'The council sent me the paperwork yesterday. It's disastrous for Enid, poor woman. She's not about to go anywhere without that bird of hers. As for the sheriff's department, if the council and the mayor think we're going to issue citations to citizens who need the comforting presence of an animal companion in order to venture out into the world, they're sorely mistaken. If a private business owner doesn't welcome animals, that's their right, but why should anyone else care if Enid – or any other resident of this town – travels with a bird on their shoulder, or a cat in their handbag, or a lizard in their pocket, so long as the animal isn't a threat to public safety?'

'They shouldn't,' MJ rejoined. 'This new ordinance is just an act of cruelty. That's all there is to it. Everyone knows that Langhorne's the only thing keeping Enid Kemper from becoming a total recluse.'

Jules, placing a box of napkins and recycled bamboo utensils in the back of the van, spoke up. 'According to my sources, the ordinance was passed because of the proposed housing and shopping mall project. Apparently the developers couldn't find high-end shops willing to reserve mall space with the old regulations in place.'

'As if Enid would ever step foot in one of those places,' Tish scoffed.

'As if any of us would step foot in those places,' Celestine added. 'How the heck did this upscale housin' and mall idea even become a thing? What we need are more affordable homes so our young folks don't move outta town to raise their families. That would be the death of Hobson Glen.'

Reade pulled his phone from the rear pocket of his jeans.

'Who are you calling?' Tish asked.

'The office. I'm sending a car over to check on Enid and see if she and Langhorne want a lift to the Turkey Trot.'

'What about the ordinance?'

'The Turkey Trot is outdoors. There's nothing prohibiting Enid from attending with her pet.'

Tish gave him a kiss on the cheek. 'You're awfully sweet.'

'Thanks, but it's also a matter of public safety. You know, just in case someone in town is crazy enough to loan Enid their car . . .'

TWO

Colonial Springs was, as the name implied, an area of lush, spring-fed beaver ponds and wetlands that were first discovered around the time of the American Revolution. After centuries of private ownership, the land was ultimately purchased by the town of Hobson Glen for the purpose of establishing a nature preserve and recreation area. Now boasting a three-and-a-half mile trail consisting of wooden boardwalks and well-maintained dirt and gravel paths, Colonial Springs was a favorite of local joggers, ardent birdwatchers, and out-of-town history buffs.

Tish and company, aided by Officer Clayton, set up a pair of sturdy tables and a gas generator to power their slow cookers, electric cooktop, and coffee percolators in a clearing thirty yards from the parking area and just at the start of the trailhead.

'Thanks for the help,' Reade acknowledged his junior officer. 'How's the detail going?'

'Super mellow. I remember last year's event – the whole road was blocked by cars trying to get in here.' He shook his head. 'Not this year. It's been a trickle of vehicles coming here and no traffic on the road at all. I opened the overflow parking area down the road as per protocol for Colonial Springs events, but I've yet to send anyone over to patrol. When this lot starts to fill up, I will, but we're a long way from that point.'

Reade nodded his approval. 'The race starts in twenty minutes. If you haven't used the overflow by now, odds are, you probably won't. Sounds like you're doing fine, but if you need me—'

'I know where you are, sir.' Clayton finished Reade's sentence with a small salute before returning to the parking lot.

'I love walking on this trail,' Tish remarked as she draped a neatly pressed red cloth over the two tables and attached the café advertising banner to it, 'but what with the move and the new place, I haven't been down here in ages. It looks so different now than it did back in June.'

'It looks very different, I'm sure. Not only are the leaves off the trees, but we're now in the "rainless" period which lasts until mid-March,' Jules replied, unknowingly adopting the voice he used when giving the Channel Ten forecast. 'This year's "rainless" period is coming after an unusually rain-free October. Typically, we receive three-point-six inches of rain in October, but this year we only got one-point-eight. If we don't get rain soon, the county will declare a drought.'

'Yeah, Clayton and I came down here yesterday to scope out the traffic and parking situation,' Reade responded. 'The beaver pond looks more like a beaver puddle. I saw a snowy egret wading in it, looking for a fish, but the water barely covered its feet. I've been here for several events and I've never seen it as dry as this.'

As Jules dispensed cider for two early arrivals, the quartet was joined by a woman on a bicycle. She was in her late sixties, with flowing gray hair that had been pinned into a partial bun, and was dressed in a broomstick skirt in a paisley pattern, a heavy, high-necked cable-knit sweater, and a well-worn pair of Granny boots. 'Hey, y'all!' she greeted as she dismounted. 'I hope I'm not late. I was thick in the middle of edits when I realized what time it was.'

'You're not late at all, Opal,' Tish assured the author. 'Everyone is just starting to arrive.'

'Including his nibs.' Celestine hiked a thumb toward the figure of Mayor Schuyler Thompson, who had traded his usual 'power ensemble' of dark suit, white shirt, and solid tie for a gray quarter-zip fleece sweatshirt, black track pants, and a pair of brightly laced running shoes. Although a passerby might have mistaken Schuyler as an experienced athlete, his fair hair had been perfectly trimmed and styled and it was apparent that his outfit, including the spotlessly clean sneakers, had been purchased specifically for the event.

He was soon joined by Deputy Mayor Royce Behrens. Dressed in a similar get-up to Schuyler and sporting the same Ivy League haircut and pasted-on smile, Behrens might have been a clone of Mayor Thompson if it weren't for his dark hair.

'Hmph,' Opal grunted as they walked past the group and to the front of the clearing, where a podium, microphone – and Turkey Trot signage – had been erected. 'Do you know I can no longer sell my sex bombs because of those two?'

'What?' a surprised Tish asked. Opal had created her sex bombs (herbal scented, salt-based bath bombs), massage oil, and body lotion from the herbs and flowers that she grew in her own garden. Although they had started life as author swag – little extras a writer might send to bloggers and faithful readers in return for their loyalty – as Opal's career as a novelist grew, so did the demand for the products she claimed had aphrodisiacal properties. Before Tish was forced to close her café, she was selling ten to fifteen bombs a week, mostly to travelers who stopped in for a bite to eat on the way to or from Richmond. She could only guess that they were selling equally as well at other shops in the area.

'It's true,' Opal asserted. 'Three weeks ago, I received a cease and desist letter from the council, stating that my sex bombs were in violation of town decency laws and that if I didn't stop selling them, I'd be fined and possibly jailed. I called the mayor's office thinking maybe Schuyler could make the council and the deputy mayor see some sense – I mean, they're just fizzy bath bombs, for crying out loud!'

'I'd ask what Schuyler said, but I can probably guess. He upheld the council's and deputy mayor's decision, right?'

'He did. He said that young children shouldn't see a product labeled as a sex bomb in our local shops. Can you believe it? The massage oil is probably the most provocative of the three, but no one says anything because I called it "bath oil."' Opal shook her head. 'In any event, I offered to change the name of the bombs to something less . . . suggestive, but Schuyler still said no. He said that everyone recognizes them as sex bombs and it was far too late to change them.'

'I'm sorry, Opal,' Tish apologized.

'Yeah, I am too, but it's not your fault. It's not either of our faults.'

'I don't know. Schuyler might be going out of his way to punish people who are my friends.'

'No, I don't think that's the case,' Opal maintained. 'Schuyler and the town council seem to be punishing anyone who's decent.'

'That sure is true,' Celestine agreed. 'My one son-in-law works for town maintenance and do you know that the council is talkin' about makin' everyone part-time instead of full-time so that they don't need to provide health insurance?'

At this revelation, everyone gathered tightly around the table, their jaws agape.

Celestine nodded. 'My daughter and grandbabies need those full-time wages and the insurance. If the town doesn't provide it, my son-in-law will have to look for work elsewhere. Times are hard . . . and the council is just makin' it harder.'

'They are. After I spoke with Mayor Thompson, I called Edwin Wilson,' Opal stated. 'Remember, he was elected to the council last year? Well, he's just beside himself with the direction the town council is heading. He's been voting against the new legislation – which includes a decrease to the library budget, which, since his wife, Augusta, is head of the board would be most distressing, as I'm sure it is to Daryl. But Edwin's in the minority – not just as the only black council member, but as one of the few council members who still has any sense of decency. If the face of the council doesn't change, Edwin says he's not going to seek re-election.'

'That would be a shame,' Tish noted. 'He's a good man. If anyone could turn things around, he could.'

'Hear, hear,' Jules seconded. 'Ooh, there's a bunch of cars entering the parking lot right now and I think I see my crew. Tish, you mind if I dash out to meet them so they know I'm here?'

'Not at all.'

'Cool. I'll be back before most of the hungry hordes descend upon us.'

Jules was true to his word. He returned approximately three minutes later to find a queue of spectators ordering soup and hot beverages to keep warm on a chilly race day. Included in the group were Augusta Mae and Edwin Wilson.

'Hi y'all,' Augusta Mae greeted. She looked chic in a long camel coat and a cream-colored cashmere hat and scarf set. 'Good to see everyone.'

Edwin gave a silent wave.

'Good to see you too,' Tish replied. 'I didn't know you'd be here.'

'We didn't either until a few minutes ago,' Augusta Mae conceded. 'Old grumpy pants here didn't want to come to the Turkey Trot, but I convinced him that people need to know there's at least one councilman on their side.'

'Not that he can do very much,' Edwin lamented.

'Still, it's good for people to know there's a sympathetic listener in their local government. Someone who understands.' She slid her eyes toward the two men at the podium. 'Especially when others don't.'

The words had only just left Augusta Mae's mouth when the quiet atmosphere was interrupted by the feedback of a microphone. 'Good, um, good afternoon,' Mayor Schuyler Thompson greeted the crowd. 'Welcome to the Thirty-First Annual Colonial Springs Turkey Trot. Thank you all for joining us and a special thank you to our contestants for taking the time to compete today. Deputy Mayor Behrens and I both understand that this event has traditionally been held on the Saturday after Thanksgiving, but I appreciate your willingness and the . . .' Schuyler shuffled through his notes, '. . . the Interfaith Center Food Pantry's willingness to trade days with the Rod and Gun Club whose annual autumn sporting event takes place next Saturday.'

Schuyler's mention of the change of day elicited groans from the contestants and audience, including a disgruntled Edwin Wilson, who said in a voice just loud enough for those in his immediate vicinity to hear him, 'As if we had a choice in the matter. And now look, just a third of the people who usually come to this thing have turned out. It's a disaster.'

Ever image-conscious and seeking approval, a flustered Schuyler endeavored to speak over the crowd but failed. 'Yes, um, thank you for your understanding. Next Saturday is bound to be the best one yet. We have some serious marksmen and anglers arriving from Richmond and the DC area to compete in a wide range of sporting events—'

'Is this why we had to move the Turkey Trot?' an unknown woman shouted from the back of the crowd. 'To accommodate wealthy people from the city?'

Her remark drew applause from those around her.

Schuyler did not acknowledge the woman or her remarks. Instead, he continued with his prepared speech. 'Um, so I, um, I encourage you to come out next weekend and cheer on our contestants. And now, a few words from our deputy mayor.' He hastily passed the microphone to Royce Behrens.

Royce was completely unfazed by the negative sentiments of those gathered at the Turkey Trot. Rather, he seemed amused by them. 'Good afternoon,' he hailed. 'Thank y'all for taking the time to turn out for our little race today.'

That the 'little race' and, indeed, the presence of Tish's food stand, had been arranged to benefit the food pantry was clearly secondary to Royce's agenda, for he immediately recounted the town council's 'successes' since Schuyler Thompson had been sworn in as mayor: lower crime (not that it was high in the first place), a streamlined budget, and, the jewel in the crown, a high-end housing development and shopping center to be built on the edge of town.

'We're excited for the future,' Behrens said to an audience that was less than enthusiastic. 'We look forward to welcoming a new neighborhood into our community: the beautiful, vibrant, luxurious Hobson Meadows, the perfect American town.'

Tish's eyes narrowed. *The perfect American town?* What about Hobson Glen? What about the food pantry? What about the people in the town they currently governed who needed them?

Angered by their apathy toward the day's event – and the people of Hobson Glen in general – Tish stepped toward the podium. She wasn't one for public speaking. In fact, she had once been so rattled by a televised Christmastime interview with Jules that she almost didn't notice that the pompom of his elf hat had been ignited by a nearby holiday lantern. However, Behrens's tone and the disrespect the town council had shown for its constituents caused a reaction in Tish that was far stronger than fear. 'Deputy Mayor. I'd like to add a few words about today's event, if I may.'

'No one invited you to speak,' Schuyler retorted, prompting a round of boos.

'The food pantry folks did,' Celestine challenged, joining Tish at the front of the clearing. 'When y'all switched the date of this race, you switched it to senior grocery day. The food pantry folks are busy handing out essentials to low-income senior citizens and can't be here right now. That makes Tish their de facto spokesperson.' To Behrens's surprise, Celestine wrestled the microphone from his hand and thrust it at Tish. 'Go on, honey. Speak on the food pantry's behalf, 'coz these two sure ain't gonna do it.'

'Umm.' Tish licked her lips nervously. 'Hello, everyone. Thank you for coming out here today. I-I simply wanted to say that today's turnout isn't what we might have enjoyed in the past, but we can still try to do our part. I'm here – rather, Cookin' the Books is here – with soup, sandwiches, hot and cold beverages, and a few sweet

treats for carnivores and vegans alike. What's more, every cent of
your purchase goes directly to the Interfaith Center Food Pantry.'
This announcement garnered both applause and cheers.

'If you're not hungry now, not to worry,' Tish continued. 'We
have recyclable, microwaveable containers so you can take some
soup back to your desk or even back home for dinner tonight. We'll
all be doing plenty of cooking soon enough, right? Our soup is
freezable, so you can tuck some away for an evening when you're
busy holiday shopping and need a speedy meal. At our table, you'll
also find a list of the food pantry's most requested items. I encourage
you to take a copy and carry it with you when you do your grocery
shopping. It's set to be a tough winter, so let's all be thankful for
what we have and let's help each other as much as possible. Thank
you.'

Tish passed the microphone back to Celestine who, in turn, handed
it back to Royce Behrens, but not before stating into it, 'Here ya
go, fellas. It's just about time to start that "little race," isn't it?'

Her comment prompted cheers, laughter, and whistles from those
assembled at the trailhead. However, the mayor and deputy mayor
behaved as if the crowd reaction was for them.

Were they being willfully obtuse? Tish wondered. *Or were they
actually so detached from reality to believe that they, and their
policies, were popular?*

'Thank you,' Behrens replied as Schuyler held his hand aloft and
smiled. 'Thank you. And now to start a new Turkey Trot tradition.
Here's Mayor Thompson to tell you all about it.'

Schuyler accepted the microphone from Behrens. 'Thank you,
Royce. Yes, a brand-new tradition begins today. As a symbol of our
leadership and our willingness to take this town in new directions,
Deputy Mayor Behrens and I are going to lead off the race. We
won't be competing with y'all. We're not in as good a shape as
those who train for this all year, but once Senior Councilman Tripp
Sennette fires his handy starter's pistol, we're going to head off
down the trail. Tripp will pass that pistol to Royce's mother, the
honorable Annabelle Behrens – whom y'all know and love from
the time her father was mayor of Hobson Glen – and, once we're
clear of the starting line, she'll signal the official start of the race.'

'Looking for a photo op,' Edwin Wilson accurately surmised
as photographers and camera operators from various local news

agencies took shots of the two men posed at the start of the trail. When the paparazzi had finished, Tripp Sennette – a heavyset, balding man with thick-rimmed glasses – fired the pistol and Schuyler set off down the trail, followed several seconds later by Royce Behrens.

'I hope people still want to eat after that little display,' Jules said quietly to his friends once the two men had disappeared from view. 'Because I, for one, feel nauseous.'

'Yeah, that was quite the dog and pony show,' Tish concurred.

'With the emphasis on dog. You, however, did incredibly well,' Opal told Tish. 'Your words were probably the sincerest ones spoken today.'

'Apart from Miss Celly's verbal hand slap, that is,' Reade added with a satisfied grin.

'Hey, someone had to let them know it's not all about them,' Celestine said with a chuckle. 'Not sure it made one bit of difference, though.'

The group settled down and waited for the second shot from the starter's pistol which would, once the contestants departed, prompt spectators to make food and beverage purchases to enjoy while waiting for runners to complete the three-and-a-half mile loop.

Shockingly, instead of a starter's pistol, Hobson Glen residents were confronted by the sound of rifle shots in the woods just beyond the clearing.

'Get down! Everyone get down!' Reade ordered at the top of his lungs, desperate to be heard over the panicked screams and sound of heavy footfall.

The majority of spectators and participants had already heeded Reade's orders, dropping to the ground and scrambling to conceal themselves behind bushes, trees, and even the speaker's podium. However, a handful of individuals, deeming it – perhaps unwisely – safer to run than to shelter in place, decided to flee to the parking lot.

As they ran away from the trailhead, Officer Clayton bolted toward it, a bulletproof vest in one hand, a gun in his other. He tossed the vest to Reade who donned it in record speed and the pair set off on the trail with their weapons drawn. Within moments, the other officers who had been on parking duty – all now armed – followed them.

Tish crouched down on the ground and watched helplessly as Reade sprinted down the trail and into imminent danger. She knew it was his duty to protect the community, but that knowledge didn't make it any easier to see him go. As her eyes welled with tears, she felt an urgent tugging at her coat sleeves.

'Tish! Tish, get under here,' Celestine frantically urged as she and Opal pulled her beneath the folding tables where they, Jules, and the Wilsons had taken refuge along with a mother and her two young sons.

'But I-I can't see Clemson from here . . .' Tish half-heartedly argued.

'Can't see him from out there either. Just makes you a sittin' duck,' Celestine whispered.

Tish knew Celestine was right. Glancing at the faces around her, she drew a deep breath, blinked back her tears, and steadied herself. She wasn't about to break down and cry in front of children who were, without question, more terrified by the situation than she was. She also realized it wasn't precisely a ringing endorsement of Clemson's abilities as sheriff if his girlfriend appeared less-than-confident in his safe return.

'We were here to see my husband race,' the mother explained breathlessly to those gathered around her. 'I don't know where he is. We haven't seen him. We don't know—'

'Shhh.' Jules crawled to her side. 'You got separated in the crowd, that's all. You'll find each other again. I'm sure of it.'

As the mother gathered her sons close to her, Jules wrapped an arm around the woman's shoulder and pulled her closer to him, using his body to shield the family from the menace that lurked outside. Beside Jules, Augusta Mae and Edwin embraced each other tightly, their eyes wide with horror. Tish, trying her best to suppress the traumatic memory of the last time she'd encountered gunfire in a public place, closed her eyes, braced against the chill slowly encompassing her body, and reached to either side for Celestine's and Opal's hands. They eagerly obliged and the three women, hand in hand and with arms entwined, waited in the enveloping silence for whatever might come next.

With the tablecloths obscuring all but the ground within an inch of the perimeter of the table, it was impossible to tell whether the gunman had left his previous position along the trail and entered the trailhead area, or if any member of the police had returned to protect the people assembled there. The only thing that those gathered beneath the table knew was that the sound of rifle fire had ceased, leaving the Springs in eerie stillness.

THREE

After what felt like hours, the sound of police cars and ambulances cut through the crisp, late autumn air, bringing with it the hope that life in Hobson Glen might soon return to something approaching normal. Several minutes later, that hope was borne out as Sheriff Clemson Reade's voice issued an all-clear.

After sharing elated hugs with her tablemates, Tish rushed from her hiding spot and into Reade's arms. 'I'm so glad you're safe!'

'I'm fine. I'm fine,' he assured, while holding her tightly and nestling his face in her hair. 'How are you?'

'Shaken, like everyone else, but otherwise OK.'

'You sure? What with your shooting, I was worried . . .'

'I'm OK, sweetie. Really. Oh! I just remembered. Enid Kemper isn't here, is she?'

'No, the officer who went to check on her heard the call and wisely decided that Enid should stay put.'

Tish was elated. 'Thank heavens! So, what happened? Was there a hunter in the area?'

'Yeah, a hunter of human beings. Deputy Mayor Behrens is dead.'

Tish pulled away from Reade in astonishment. 'Dead?'

'Dead? Who's dead?' Ever the reporter, after ensuring that the mother of the two boys had been reconnected with her husband, Jules made a beeline for Reade for the scoop.

'Royce Behrens,' Tish replied.

'Shot in the chest with an automatic rifle,' Reade described. 'The only question, apart from who might have done such a thing, is whether or not Behrens was the intended target. He and Schuyler were jogging fairly close together when the gunman attacked, plus the two men are of the same height and build and were dressed alike.'

'Yeah, but Schuyler's hair is blond and Behrens's was dark,' Jules pointed out.

'That's an awfully big mistake to make in broad daylight,' Tish noted.

'Well, I did say that Schuyler was in close proximity when Behrens was shot,' Reade reiterated. 'The shooter might have missed the intended target.'

'It *does* seem more likely that the shooter would have been targeting Schuyler, doesn't it?' Tish stated.

'It figures you'd think that,' Jules quipped.

'I don't think Schuyler's the target because he's a jerk who evicted me. I think it's more likely he's the target because he's the face of our town government. If someone has a beef with town policy, they're going to go after the mayor. Besides, if I recall correctly, I'm not the only one who's ever had words with the man.' She slid her eyes toward Jules.

'The only nasty thing I've ever said to Schuyler Thompson was that his shoes were ugly.'

Tish folded her arms across her chest and glared at him.

'All right.' Jules capitulated. 'I said his shoes were as ugly as his dark, twisted little soul, but that was right after the two of you broke up and it doesn't mean I think someone should take a shot at the man.'

'I never said I wanted someone to take a shot at Schuyler. I said that it's more likely that someone would *want* to take a shot at Schuyler.'

'I agree with you, honey,' Reade said. 'It does seem more likely that Schuyler's the intended victim, but we need to look at both men carefully.'

'What does Schuyler have to say about it?'

'He says he has no enemies—'

'No enemies?' Tish and Jules both guffawed.

'—but he's also in a state of shock right now.'

'Is delusion a symptom of shock?' Jules asked with a laugh.

'Speaking of shock, Annabelle Behrens has been taken to the hospital by ambulance,' Reade announced. 'She started experiencing chest pains shortly after the shots were fired. EMTs took her away before I could even tell her the news about her son. We'll have to question her once she's stable.'

'Poor thing,' Tish said, with a click of her tongue. 'I hope she's OK. If she's having chest pains now, I can't imagine how she'll react to Royce's death.'

'This was a traumatic event. That's why I've required everyone to check in with the paramedics before they're cleared to go home. That includes the two of you.'

'But we're fine,' Jules argued. 'I mean, we were terrified for a little while there, but . . .'

'Which is precisely why everyone involved needs to be seen by a healthcare professional. Once again, this was a traumatic event. It can have a major impact on your mental and physical well-being.'

'OK, but I need to do a segment with my crew first.'

'Segment? And just who are you planning to feature in this segment?'

'Um, you. Hopefully.' Jules flashed a bedazzling smile.

Reade raised an eyebrow. 'You know I always give you first crack at interviews, but there's not much I can say right now.'

'That's fine. Just a few words will do.'

'Sure, but afterwards you need to be tended to by the emergency health workers.'

'OK, OK,' Jules agreed. 'Wait one minute . . . it looks as if my own personal emergency health worker has just arrived.'

Tish and Reade followed Jules's gaze to the parking area, where Maurice Joseph, a reporter for Richmond's National Public Radio station WCVE-FM, had alighted from his vehicle and was rushing toward the trailhead.

'Maurice,' Jules shouted, hastening to meet him.

'Julian,' Maurice replied. Unlike Tish and Mary Jo, Maurice always called Jules by his given name. 'Julian, my God! I heard on the police scanner that there was a shooting. Are you OK?'

The two men embraced.

'Yes, I'm fine,' Jules assured, as tears welled in his eyes.

'And Tish and Celestine? And everyone at the café? No one was hurt, were they?'

'No, no. They're all OK.'

'Oh, thank heavens,' an elated Maurice responded. 'I was on my way to cover an event in Ashton Courthouse when I heard the police say there was a shooting. I drove straight here. I was so afraid I'd never see you again.'

'I know. The whole time we were hidden from the shooter, I kept thinking of you and Cassius. I prayed that I'd be safe so that we could all spend time together again. I also – and this might not be the right time to tell you, but I'm so grateful to still be here.' Jules took a step back and clutched Maurice's hands in his. 'I'd like to celebrate Thanksgiving with you and Cassius somehow. I'm not asking you to cancel plans with your mama – I wouldn't dream of such a thing – but maybe before you travel or after you get home, we could have a special dinner, just the three of us . . . so I can give thanks for having found you both.'

'I'm grateful that you found us too, Julian. Your idea is very sweet. *You're* very sweet – it's just one of the many things that drew me to you – but I think I need some time to process everything that's gone on today. I think you do, too.'

'Yeah, you're right, of course. My brain isn't entirely together yet, what with a gunman being on the loose and Royce Behrens's fatal shooting.'

'Wait a minute. The deputy mayor is dead?'

'Yes, whether his death was the result of a random shooting or if he was the intended target all along, no one knows, but I have an interview with Reade in a few minutes. You're welcome to tag along on behalf of NPR if you'd like.'

Considering how protective Jules was of his 'exclusives,' it was an exceedingly generous offer.

'You're giving me first crack at your scoop? Must be the trauma talking,' Maurice teased.

'Nah – well, maybe – nah, with you, I'd share anything.'

'Thanks. That's kind of you and I really appreciate the sentiment, but this isn't my story. I passed another crew from the station in the parking lot.'

'Oh, they can schedule their own exclusives – my offer only stands for you,' Jules explained with a laugh and a playful slap on Maurice's arm.

Maurice smiled. 'Are you sure you're up to working right now?'

'Positive. I feel as though I've been given a new lease on life. Probably because I have.'

'Well, take it easy. You've had a *day*, you don't want to overdo things.'

'Have you ever known me to overdo things?' Jules joked, prompting Maurice to shake his head.

'Are you OK getting home?'

'I'll be fine. My car's at the café and we drove here in Tish's van – I can get a lift if need be.'

Maurice nodded. 'I'll check in with you later to see how you're doing.'

'I'd like that.' Jules gave Maurice a quick embrace before saying goodbye.

As Maurice walked back to his car, he passed Celestine stepping out of the back of one of the ambulances assembled at the scene. Daryl Dufour held her by one arm to steady her as she alighted.

'Hey, Miss Celly. Are you doing OK?' Maurice questioned, lending Daryl a hand by taking hold of Celestine's other arm.

'Thank you,' she replied. 'Twisted my back a little squeezin' underneath that table, but overall, I'm just happy not to be Swiss cheese.'

'I think everyone's grateful that the situation wasn't as bad as it could have been. I know I am.'

Daryl nodded solemnly. 'I'm also grateful to you for getting me in here. The police were only allowing the media and family members into the parking lot,' he explained to Celestine. 'Maurice here got me in under his press pass.'

'Not a problem. You and I were on the same mission,' a humble Maurice replied. After ensuring Celestine was solidly on her feet, and with a fist bump to Daryl, he set off for his car.

'I'm glad Maurice got you in to see me. I know Opal is just over there in the next ambulance and Tish and Clem and Jules are nearby, but I was feelin' a bit vulnerable,' Celestine said appreciatively.

'That's to be expected after what you've been through. What you've all been through.'

'It's true what they say about your life flashin' in front of your eyes when you're about to die. I know I wasn't injured or anythin' like that, but I was prepared to go. I wasn't about to let Tish or Jules or that mama with her babies take a bullet – not while I had air in my lungs. So, I waited – I waited for that shooter to come for me. And while I waited, I got to thinkin' about my life and how lucky I've been. Good kids, good husband, good friends, good health . . . and then there was you.'

Daryl smiled. 'Surely I fit into the "good friends" category.'

'Do you? Sometimes maybe you do, but there have been times when you've been much, much more. When I got to thinkin' about it, I realized that if I died under that table where I was hidin' that I'd die without ever tellin' you how much . . .' Celestine blinked back tears. 'How much I do care for you.'

'Now, Celly,' Daryl soothed. 'You're very emotional right now.'

'I am,' she confessed, 'but that's got nothin' to do with what I'm sayin'. There was the time when we were datin' back in school, of course, but even while I was married to Lloyd, you were always there to support me or lend a helpin' hand. When Lloyd was outta work because of his back, you bought the kids their school clothes and arranged to pay for my groceries. When Lloyd's foot slipped with that office woman he'd hired, you could have been grinnin' from ear-to-ear like a Cheshire cat tellin' me he was a no-good cheat and "I told you so" for leavin' you in the first place, but you didn't. You let me bawl my eyes out and confide in you. And, now, since Lloyd has passed, you've become a valued companion to me – a rock, really. I know lots of folks use that word, but you're the real thing. You always have been and I want you to know how much I appreciate that – how much I appreciate *you*.'

'I care about and appreciate you too, Celly. That's why I'm always around. That's why I'll always be around.'

'Yes, I'm finally beginning to understand that,' she said with a smile. 'Do you, um, do you think maybe we can go to the town Christmas tree lighting next Sunday?'

'I'd love to! You know, that was our very first date way back when we were in middle school.'

Celestine smirked. 'Why do you think I suggested it?'

'Too bad that ice-cream parlor we went to after the tree lighting is no longer around.'

'Tell you what. How about I save us two pieces of sweet potato pie from Thanksgiving dinner and we can eat them on a bench on the town square.'

It was Daryl's turn to smile. 'Why, Celestine Rufus, I do believe you have yourself a date.'

FOUR

As Tish emerged from the back of one ambulance, having been deemed healthy enough to be discharged from the shooting scene, the body of Royce Behrens, zipped into a bright blue bag, was loaded into the back of another.

'Have you been able to get in touch with anyone in his family?' she asked of Reade who was waiting for her.

'I have. His wife is on her way here. I was hoping she'd meet me at headquarters, but she was already in her car when I called her. What about you? You OK?'

'Yep. I got a clean bill of health and I'm available to help you apprehend whoever did this,' she proudly boasted. 'I mean, if you want my help, that is.'

After Tish had assisted the sheriff's office in solving several puzzling cases, Reade had made the move to hire her to work in an official consultant capacity. Honored to be both recognized and compensated for her sleuthing work, Tish readily accepted the position. The time commitment required for the job was sporadic. When there were no new, interesting cases, Tish carried on with life and her business as if the consulting position never existed. But when, as Sherlock Holmes might say, "the game was afoot," Tish found herself frantically juggling catering and café work with an active police investigation.

'Is Schuyler still around?' Tish asked, assuming Reade would automatically approve her request to be put on the case. 'I think we should talk to him again. He might be able to remember a bit more, now that he's had some time to calm down.'

'Hon, as much as I love having you on my team as a consultant, I don't think this case is for you. First, your new café is opening in one week—'

Tish dismissed his concerns with a wave of her hand. 'Not a problem. The opening is completely under control.'

'But just last night, you mentioned having to proof and print menus, place supply orders, and a myriad of other tasks.

I don't want this investigation to get in the way of a successful opening.'

'It won't,' she promised. 'If I need time, I'll let you know. That's our arrangement, isn't it?'

'It is. There's also the matter of your background . . .'

'You mean my links to Schuyler?'

'I mean your *history* with Schuyler. I know we were laughing about it earlier, but the fact that he evicted you puts you in an awkward position. I know I can trust you to remain professional as we look into who might have tried to kill him, but people in this town might question your objectivity.'

'Meaning that some folks would say I have no place investigating a crime that I might have wanted to commit myself?' she guessed.

'To put a finer point on it, yes.'

'But I have no reason to want Schuyler Thompson dead. I mean, he's not my favorite person in the world, but I broke up with him, not the other way around. That breakup left me available to pursue a healthy and wonderful relationship with you.'

'For which I thank God each and every day,' Reade interjected.

'And the eviction, although difficult at the time, led me to securing the bar and grill building, thereby increasing the number of patrons I can serve. So, ultimately, my *history* with Schuyler Thompson – as you put it – was a positive thing.'

'I don't think most people would view it that way.'

'Hmph,' Tish grunted. 'Need I remind you that you're not exactly without motive either? First, Schuyler evicted your girlfriend from her café and left her and her cat homeless. Your love, your queen, your sweetie-pie—'

'I get it.' Read responded with a roll of his eyes. 'And you weren't homeless. You moved in with me.'

'I did, but not immediately. There were several weeks where I didn't know what I was going to do. I was fraught with despair, uncertain what to do and where to go—'

'Yes, I know you were. However, by your own account the end justifies the means.'

Tish bit her lip. 'OK, you got me there, but you're forgetting the second and most important motive – Schuyler Thompson threatened to have you fired if you didn't drop the Honeycutt case.'

Reade fell silent. After several seconds had elapsed, he conceded, 'You're right. Maybe I should take a backseat on the investigation and let the deputy sheriff and Clayton lead.'

'Uh, yeaaaah,' Clayton sang from a spot nearby – he had clearly been listening in on their conversation. 'I wouldn't count on the deputy sheriff to take over this case. She and the mayor went on a few dates not too long ago. I'm not sure what transpired exactly, but the last time I mentioned Thompson's name to her, the deputy called him an "arrogant, power-hungry loser."'

'Glad to know I'm not the only one to have made that assessment,' Tish remarked.

'Yeah, no. If we asked around, we'd find hundreds more people who agree with you. In fact, we may have to go to Richmond to find someone who didn't have an axe to grind with Schuyler Thompson.'

'Richmond isn't far enough,' she deemed with a shake of her head. 'Schuyler has law partners there. I bet they don't like him either.'

'So, you too?' Reade asked the officer.

'A parking ticket thing,' the young uniformed officer explained. 'I took my own car on an emergency call and placed my permit on the dashboard so it could be seen through the windshield. You know, like we usually do. I came back to find my car had been towed. Had to pay five hundred dollars to get it back. I took the matter to the town council who, in turn, referred me to Mayor Thompson. He was a complete . . .' Clayton breathed in sharply. 'He was less than helpful. He basically said I shouldn't have been driving my own car for police business.'

'Did you tell me about this?'

'No, I tried to handle it myself. And failed miserably.'

'When things settle down, I'll take your case to Thompson myself. In the meantime, we'd better go and question him again. As Tish said, he might remember something valuable now that he's had a chance to calm down.'

'We're not calling in another officer?' a puzzled Clayton questioned.

'No, I'd like to know what we're dealing with first. Besides, even if we did call in another officer, it would be hours before they arrived here. I doubt "his honor" wants to stick around that long.'

'Since you quoted me, am I to assume I'm included?' Tish asked. 'Or am I still considered police-work poison?'

'No more than the rest of us outlaws,' Reade replied with a smile. 'If you don't mind hanging out with Sundance and me, we'd love to have you.'

'I think I could slum it for a little while,' she joked before following them to the trailhead. 'Before we speak to Schuyler, I'd like to see the spot on the trail where Behrens was shot, if that's OK with you.'

'Yeah, absolutely. I have to warn you, the killer used an AR-15. There's a good deal of blood.'

Tish felt a wave of nausea pass over her, but she wasn't about to back down. She knew that the only way to understand the events of that day was to attempt to visualize what might have happened. The only way to do that was to visit the scene of the crime. 'It's all right, Clemson. I understand.'

Reade and Clayton led Tish along the gravel path, through a section of trail heavily shaded by a stand of eastern white pines and into an area known by local hikers as 'The Cathedral.' Named for the canopy of interlacing holly branches that resembled the skeletal supports of a Gothic church ceiling, 'The Cathedral' was enclosed, on either side, by columns of tall yellow birch to form a sort of outer sanctuary.

On the trail, the dappled, tree-filtered sunlight shone upon the vast pool of dark red blood that marked the spot where Royce Behrens drew his last breath.

Tish gazed at the scene, her reaction a mixture of wonder and horror. She had no idea how much blood she had lost when she was shot at the Christmas Fair – she knew she had required a trans-fusion, but that was the extent of her knowledge. If she had lost even half of what had accumulated on the trail or splattered onto the trees, she was certain she'd no longer be alive. 'Behrens didn't stand a chance, did he?'

'Not against an AR-15, he didn't. Few people do,' Reade replied. 'Should we head back to the trailhead or . . .?'

'No. No, I'm OK. Tell me more.'

'Obviously, Behrens was jogging away from the trailhead when he was shot.' He pointed toward the east. 'Given the location of the wounds, we believe the shooter was hidden behind that copse of young eastern hemlock just a few yards ahead.'

'Hemlock trees?' Tish gave a sardonic laugh. 'Not too much symbolism going on, is there?'

'What do you mean?'

'Holly is the symbol of eternal life, hemlocks signify sorrow, and yellow birches represent rebirth – a renewal after purification. Then there's the whole "Cathedral" setting. It's a made-to-order spot for a murder, isn't it? In a spiritual and literary sense.'

'Do you think the killer might have understood the symbolism too?' Clayton asked. 'Maybe that's why he or she chose this location.'

She shrugged. 'Could be. It's certainly not exclusive knowledge. The symbolism of trees dates back to Norse, Celtic, and Native American mythology – anyone who reads could know about it.'

'Or anyone who attended scouts as a kid,' Reade reasoned. 'Mythology aside, it's also a made-to-order spot because of the vantage point.'

Tish moved behind the trees and took the view of the killer. 'It's a terrific hiding spot and an even better position for a shooter. He or she would have had a perfect view of Schuyler and Royce's faces. Although, given the slight bend in the path, if the two men were jogging one closely behind the other, it's possible the killer might have missed the intended target.'

'Can anyone really miss with an AR-15?' Clayton asked rhetorically. 'If you don't hit your target on the first try, you just keep blasting holes in things until you hit it.'

'You're not far from the truth there, Clayton,' Reade was loath to admit. 'Royce Behrens had been shot more than once. Hard to believe the killer didn't adjust their aim.'

'Unless they weren't familiar with using that kind of weapon. It's possible someone purchased it for the purpose of killing the mayor or deputy mayor, but didn't get much practise time. Everything else, though, indicates that this was a premeditated attack. Not only does this spot offer the killer access and camouflage, but just beyond those hemlocks is a footpath that links to the overflow parking lot.'

'Leaving an escape route,' Tish noted. 'But wouldn't using the overflow lot be risky?'

'In the middle of a work and school day in late November?' Reade challenged. 'Not really. I told Clayton to open the gate on that lot this morning because it's part of protocol for this event, but we all knew it probably wasn't going to be used. Also, anyone who's been to the Turkey Trot before knows that the police don't even bother patrolling that lot until the main parking area is nearly full.'

'So, the shooter could have parked in the empty lot, come up here, hidden behind the hemlocks, and, when Behrens and Schuyler came by, took their shot.'

'Let's not forget that the shooter also had another escape route,' Clayton pointed out. 'He or she could have easily tracked through the woods and back to the trailhead. It's not very far and the hunters always mark the trees.'

'You've done this before? Backtracked through the woods?' Reade asked the officer.

'Many times. Usually during summer when the trail is a little crowded and I really don't want to talk to anyone during my run. It messes up my stride,' he explained, aside to Tish, his youthful countenance turning a deep pink color. 'Ahem, there are a couple of routes back there that follow close to the trail, but are far enough that you're not seen by those out here hiking or jogging. They're surprisingly easy to navigate – even more so now the leaves are off the trees.'

'This route that tracks back to the trailhead,' Reade started. 'Can you show us where it comes out?'

'Sure, although it doesn't take you exactly to the trailhead,' Clayton explained as he turned on one heel and led the way back. 'It swings north and leads to the other side of the clearing where we were assembled today.'

Tish and Reade followed the officer along the gravel path, back through the cluster of eastern white pines, past the trailhead, and to a small gap in the trees far to the left of the speaker's podium. 'Here,' he said as he indicated a narrow passage across the clearing from Tish's catering table.

'We were all gathered on the other side of the clearing, in front of the trailhead, when the shots rang out. Then mass confusion ensued as we all scrambled to escape or hide,' Tish recounted. 'While our attention was focused elsewhere, the shooter could have easily snuck back here and taken cover with the rest of us.'

Clayton nodded toward the parking lot. 'The killer may even have been treated in one of those ambulances before being set loose.'

'If the shooter was discharged by the medics, then we'll have his or her name. We'll also have a detailed physical description,' Reade calmly reasoned. 'What we need to do is determine which, if any, of the two escape routes the killer might have used. Clayton, show the forensics team the two trails and tell them to search for anything that might link to the killer.'

With a single nod, Clayton retraced his steps across the clearing and back down the trail.

'We haven't had rain in over two weeks, so I'm fairly certain they won't find prints,' Reade explained to Tish once Clayton had gone. 'But there could be hair or clothing fibers present on the trail that the killer unknowingly left behind.'

'While the forensics team does its work, should we interview Schuyler?' Tish suggested.

'We should. He's probably getting restless right about now.'

'Really? Seeing as he's mayor, you'd think he'd stick around until Royce Behrens's widow arrived, wouldn't you?'

Reade pulled a face. 'If I were mayor, I would. So would you. But Schuyler . . .?'

'Excellent point. We'd better hurry.'

Tish and Reade were just about to enter the ambulance where Mayor Schuyler Thompson waited, swathed in a blanket and sipping a cup of American Red Cross-issued tea, when a woman came running across the parking lot and toward the trailhead.

She was petite, blonde, well dressed in a purple quilted coat, and highly distraught. 'Sheriff Reade! Sheriff Reade! I'm Amanda Behrens.'

Reade gestured to the uniformed officer securing the trailhead from the public to allow Mrs Behrens admittance. A tall, adolescent male, approximately seventeen years of age, lagged behind her, his handsome young face turned downward. He was wearing gym shorts, a T-shirt, and an unzipped black puffer jacket.

Reade stepped forward to receive the pair. 'Mrs Behrens,' he addressed the woman as he extended his hand. 'And this is—?'

'My eldest son, Chase,' she replied distractedly. 'We-we were in the car. Chase had just finished his practice. I-I got here as quick as I could. What's going on here? You told me my husband – that

. . . that Royce is dead. That can't be, Sheriff. That simply can't be. You must be mistaken. You simply must be . . .'

As Amanda's voice broke into sobs, Reade waved to an emergency health worker to signal that Mrs Behrens might need some assistance. 'I'm afraid I'm not mistaken, ma'am. My consultant, Ms Tarragon, and I are terribly sorry, but your husband, Royce, was shot and killed this afternoon.'

'Shot? How? Who . . .?'

'Your husband was jogging along the trail with the mayor when the shooter opened fire. He sustained a massive gunshot wound to the chest and died on the scene. No word on the identity of the killer or motive, but we're investigating.'

'No word? You have no word? I need answers, Sheriff! I need to know who did this. I need to know who killed . . .' Amanda Behrens brought a gloved hand to her head and stumbled backward. 'Oh, my God, this is a nightmare!'

Reade leapt forward and caught the woman before she could fall. Meanwhile, a uniformed medic wrapped her in a brown wool blanket and placed an opened bottle of water to her lips. Amanda drank greedily and then, after a deep breath, said, 'I'm sorry, Sheriff, but I can't . . . I can't believe he's gone.'

'I understand,' Reade assured her. 'Now, the EMT is going to bring you to the ambulance and check your vitals. When you're feeling better, we'll talk.'

'No,' Amanda insisted, clutching at Reade's arm. 'No, I want to talk to you now. I need to talk to you. I need to know more about my husband's death.'

'I don't have much more to tell you, Mrs Behrens. We're not even sure if your husband was the intended target.'

'Oh, but he was. I know he was!' she asserted, much to Tish and Reade's surprise.

'Had your husband been receiving death threats?'

'No,' she answered reluctantly, all the while glancing in Chase's direction. 'I just need to talk to you, Sheriff. I need to talk to you about my husband. Please?'

'All right.' He capitulated. 'But we'll talk in the ambulance. If there's any serious change in your vitals or you begin to feel unwell, then the discussion is over until you've recuperated. OK?'

Amanda nodded her consent. 'And my son?' she whispered. 'I don't want to talk in front of him, but I don't want him to be alone.'

'I'll have one of my officers stay with him,' Reade promised. She responded with alarm. 'Your officers? I don't know how Chase will react to questioning. He hasn't said a word since it happened. Oh! Maybe I should call my therapist and see if—'

'My officer would be acting in a custodial, not an investigative, capacity,' Reade explained. 'Chase will be offered a hot drink, a warm blanket, and anything else he might need.'

This answer seemed to appease Amanda, for she relaxed slightly. 'Yes – yes, I guess that'll be OK. Chase,' she called to the teen. 'Chase, Mom needs to speak with Sheriff Reade. Someone will keep you company while you wait, but I'll try not to take too long.'

Amanda's tone and phrasing was that used by a mother speaking to a young child, not a nearly six-foot-tall teenager. In different circumstances, Tish might have reacted negatively, however, it seemed reasonable that a woman, having just lost her husband, might become overly protective of her children – even to the extent of babying them.

Chase, meanwhile, was less forgiving. 'Mom,' he urged through clenched teeth. 'Stop. I'll be OK.'

Amanda swallowed her tears and, with a vigorous nod, allowed Reade to lead her into the ambulance, where the medic helped her onto a table and took her blood pressure. 'I – I don't like to talk around my boys, but my husband . . .' she started, as the cuff of the sphygmomanometer tightened around her forearm. 'Royce wasn't very well liked by some of the people in this town.'

'Oh?' Reade asked, although the statement did not surprise him.

'Yes, he . . .' Amanda shivered. 'Do you – do you think Chase is all right? Do you think he's all right out there on his own?'

'Chase is in good hands,' Reade promised.

Amanda's nervousness briefly subsided. 'Royce – Royce was supposed to be mayor. He'd worked for his grandfather, the past mayor, as a boy. He ran for town council right after passing the Bar exam and became its youngest member. The job of mayor was supposed to be his – not Schuyler Thompson's.'

'What happened?' Tish asked as the medic announced Amanda's blood pressure reading.

'Ninety over sixty,' the health worker said aloud. 'Ma'am, I need you to lie down and take some deep breaths.'

'I would – I would breathe easier if I knew my boy – Chase – was all right,' Amanda stated between gasps for air.

'Would you like me to go out and check on him?' Tish offered.

'Oh, would you?' Amanda nearly leapt from her seat, prompting the medic to hold her in place. 'You have no idea how much that means, Ms Tarragon.'

'Ma'am,' the physician shushed. 'Quiet, please.'

'I'll go, if you promise to lie down and listen to medical advice,' Tish stipulated.

'Yes, yes,' Amanda replied hastily. 'You will report back to me, won't you? And let me know he's OK?'

'I will,' Tish swore before stepping out into the cold, autumn air. As befitting a day of tragedy, the sun had disappeared, replaced with a dense layer of clouds. She spotted Chase standing a few yards away from the ambulance. To his right stood a uniformed female police officer. To his left a Red Cross volunteer. Although both were speaking to him, Chase remained emotionless.

It was only as Tish approached that the teen showed any interest in his surroundings. 'How is my mother?' he asked, snapping to life. 'Is she OK?'

'She's agitated and anxious. I'm not a doctor so I can't really say more than that, apart from the fact that she's worried about you.'

He sighed heavily. 'I told her I'd be OK. She should worry about herself or who's going to pick up Ladd from school.'

'Ladd? Is that your brother?' Tish asked.

Chase nodded.

'And you usually pick him up from school?'

'No, I don't drive yet.'

Tish wondered if she'd overestimated Chase's age. Most teenagers couldn't wait to get behind the wheel of an automobile. *Perhaps he had taken the test and failed*, she assumed.

'I get out of class early so I can train. Track,' he went on to explain. 'Mom picks me up from school and takes me to the rec park so I can run. Then, when I'm finished, we pick up Ladd.'

'We could send a car,' the officer suggested. 'But it might be easier for him if he was met by a friendly face instead of a patrol car.'

Tish nodded in agreement. 'How old is your brother?'

'Fourteen.'

'Is there a friend he could go home with and maybe stay there until you and your mom get home?'

'No. Ladd and I kinda keep to ourselves, you know,' he replied awkwardly.

Tish was sorry she had asked the question. 'Are there any family members or family friends nearby who could pick him up?'

'Our neighbors, the Fairchilds. I think they're on the school emergency contact list.'

'Good. Do you happen to have their number?'

'Yeah.' Chase rummaged through the pocket of his shorts and extracted his cell phone. 'In contacts under "F."'

'Is there a password?' Tish asked, while taking the phone from Chase's hands.

'Nope. Parental controls.'

'Ah. Are you certain the Fairchilds aren't here today? I mean, this is an annual event, your dad was speaking, and you're all friends . . .'

'I'm sure they're not here. They're retired, so they have plenty of time and all, but they hate my dad as much as everyone else does.'

'Oh, I'm so glad your friend is checking in on Chase!' Amanda exclaimed after Tish had left the ambulance. She seemed slightly less agitated, but was still ill-at-ease. Reade wondered if all her nervousness had been caused by the loss of her husband or if she was naturally prone to anxiety. 'I worry about him so,' she went on. 'He's so serious all the time. He'll think of himself as the man of the house now that Royce is gone. He already acts it sometimes.'

'I'm sure with some family and grief counseling, you'll both be able to move through this. It will take time, of course, but it will happen.'

'Oh, I hope so, Sheriff. I do hope so, but everything is so fresh now – so – so – ugh, it's all such a mess! How can anything ever be the same? How could it, with some murderer running free!'

'Yes, going back to that . . . you said your husband had enemies.'

'I-I'm not sure I'd call them enemies, but – but yes, there were many people who didn't like him. You need to understand that Royce was different from most people in this town. He was the type of man who made things happen.' She stared up at the ceiling, as if recalling a distant memory. 'If he wanted something, he pursued it, no matter the cost.'

Reade watched as her nervousness gave way to wistfulness and then back to anxiousness again. 'Sounds like a trait the council would have appreciated,' he remarked.

'Not here.' Amanda folded, unfolded, and refolded the tissue in her hands. 'Not in *this* small town. Royce wanted Hobson Glen to be more than just an exit off the interstate. He – he wanted it to become a tourist destination.'

'Hence the new housing and shopping development,' Reade guessed.

'That was just one part of it. R-Royce's plan was to add golf courses, theatres, opera halls, and upscale restaurants. He wanted to give Richmond a run for its money. That's how he put it – g-giving Richmond a run for its money.' She laughed nervously. 'R-Royce never was much of a wordsmith. Ch-Chase is much better in English than his father was. Thank goodness!'

'Would you say Royce's plans were unpopular?'

'Wi-with the less forward-thinking members of the council, yes. Edwin Wilson and Leonard Pruett were against anything Royce had to say, so of course they found fault with his plans.'

That Amanda would single out the council's only non-white and non-Christian members was interesting. 'Mr Wilson and Mr Pruett were at loggerheads with your husband?'

'Always. They never liked Royce. He – he was a Behrens, one of the oldest families in town. Edwin Wilson was always going on at Royce about his privilege. As if he had a choice which family he was born into! It absolutely infuriated Royce. After all, Wilson isn't exactly living in a shack!'

Royce Behrens didn't get to choose which family he was born into, but he did have a choice as to how to use his position on the council, Reade reflected. Building a luxury apartment complex when many of Hobson Glen's residents were in need of affordable housing options showed that Behrens was either out of touch with his constituency or that their needs were not at the top of his agenda. 'Any of the other council members balk at his proposals?'

'Y-yes, Judson Darley. He's so old and crotchety, I suppose he hates everything, b-but he especially hated Royce. As the longest-serving council member, he felt that he should have been mayor – or at least deputy mayor.'

'Then he would have held a grudge against Mayor Thompson as well,' Reade presumed.

'Y-yes, yes, I suppose he would.'

'Is there anyone else you can think of who might have had an axe to grind with your husband?'

Amanda replied with her usual nervous stutter, but she replied quickly. 'F-Faye Wheeler.'

'And Ms Wheeler is?'

'The old cow who used to work at the town clerk's office. She's been trying to cause trouble for Royce for months now.'

Reade recalled reading about a town clerk who had been fired over some internal council issue, but he couldn't remember anything about the case except it was the subject of an ongoing internal investigation by the town council. 'Trouble?'

'She had it out for my husband. She-she wanted to ruin him.'

'Why?'

Amanda threw her hands in the air, allowing the tissue she had been folding to drift to the ambulance floor. 'Who knows why? She's – she's a spinster and a lifelong civil servant. She was probably jealous that Royce had what she didn't: a marriage, children, and a successful career. You know how nasty older women can be!'

'No, actually I don't. It's not a subject with which I have experience, but then again I try not to lump people together by age, gender, religion, ethnicity, or any other number of attributes,' Reade firmly dismissed.

Amanda's eyes grew wide with surprise.

'What about Mayor Thompson?' the sheriff continued. 'Did he and Royce get along?'

'Y-yes. Mayor Thompson had no reason at all to dislike Royce. He brought a g-great deal of experience to the position of deputy mayor. Royce was an asset.'

'How did Royce feel about Mayor Thompson?'

'What? Well, y-you know. Royce thought Schuyler was an OK guy and a decent attorney, but he didn't have the experience Royce did. It was a disgrace, actually, that the council endorsed Schuyler for mayor over my husband during the election. A disgrace!'

FIVE

Tish and Reade convened in the area between the parked ambulance that contained Amanda Behrens and the spot near the podium where Chase waited with the uniformed police officer for the arrival of his younger brother.

'How'd it go?' he asked.

'Good . . . strange . . . awkward . . . but fine in the end. How was your conversation with Amanda?'

'Nervous . . . strange . . . awkward . . . but informative.'

'Yes, I got a bit of information as well, even though I didn't ask for it,' Tish announced with a gleam in her eye. 'Get this—'

'Everyone hated Royce Behrens,' Reade and Tish said in unison.

A disappointed Tish groaned. 'Here I thought I had a scoop.'

'Sorry, Jules,' he teased. 'From the sound of it, just about everyone on the town council had an axe to grind with Behrens.'

'What about Schuyler?'

'Schuyler had no beef with Behrens, but Behrens apparently wasn't very fond of the mayor.'

'Someone didn't like Schuyler? Now there's a plot twist,' she deadpanned.

'Yeah, hardly the case-breaking info we're after,' Reade remarked. 'However, it seems Behrens didn't like Schuyler because Behrens himself thought he should be mayor.'

'Hmm, what if Schuyler was wise to the fact that Behrens was gunning for his job? Oops! Um, sorry – pun not intended.'

'Excused. It happens in this business. If Schuyler felt threatened, it gives him a fairly good motive for murder.'

'It does. And with his law firm income and mayor's salary, he could easily have afforded to pay someone to do the dirty work for him,' Tish said with a frown. Schuyler was many things, but she found it difficult to think of him as a murderer. Still, he was relentless in his pursuit of success. Considering he pushed Tish and her needs – indeed their entire relationship – to the wayside during the mayoral election, what might he do to retain his position?

Reade must have read her mind. 'I'm having a hard time processing it, too, Tish. I mean, he's an elected official. The majority of this town put their faith in him to do the right thing, but from what we've seen of his performance . . .'

Tish nodded. 'Yeah, I know. It's hard not to go there.'

'Exactly. So, let's go question him and see where he stands and what he has to say and let's take it from there.'

Tish smiled. She was grateful to have Clemson as her partner. 'Oh, hey, did Amanda mention her younger son, Ladd, during her interview with you?'

'No, why?'

'Well, when I went out to see Chase, he was concerned about who was going to pick up his younger brother from school. We sorted it all out. The officer you put in charge called the Behrens's neighbors. I just thought it strange that Amanda didn't say anything about it.'

'You saw Amanda. She was in too much of a state to think about anything apart from what was right in front of her,' Reade said.

'Of course,' she agreed with a sigh. 'Do the EMTs think she'll be OK?'

'There are no plans to take her to the hospital right now and, at the end of our interview, her blood pressure started to rise a little, so I think so.'

'Good. Sorry if it seems I'm looking behind glass doors for something sinister, but I just . . .' She shrugged.

He wrapped an arm around her and pulled her close. 'Hey, it's OK. It's difficult to maintain perspective in these situations. And sometimes we have to look behind glass doors even though we may think we know what we see behind them.'

She gave him a kiss on the cheek. 'Thanks for always making sense.'

'Remember that statement the next time I make household repairs and you spy me doing my best to avoid getting the ladder from the back of the garage,' he half-joked.

'Are you trying to tell me that you're a living, breathing "this is why women live longer than men" meme?'

'Possibly,' he conceded.

'Sounds like I'd better keep my phone on me at all times this spring.'

'To call nine-one-one?'

'No, to call the handyman you recommended earlier.'

'Wise woman,' he said with a smile as he escorted Tish to the Red Cross tent, where Schuyler Thompson, draped in a wool blanket, sat in front of an electric space heater. He was dictating notes into the voice recorder app of his phone and, at Reade and Tish's entrance, raised a hand to request their silence until he had finished.

'I'm not speaking to her,' Schuyler said once he'd switched the recorder off.

'Ms Tarragon is assisting the sheriff's office on this case,' Reade stated.

'Someone took a shot at me and the most likely suspect is assisting the sheriff's office?' the mayor questioned angrily.

'I'm not the most likely suspect,' Tish replied. 'But it's nice that you acknowledge that I have an excellent motive. The first step in self-improvement is admitting when you've made a mistake.'

'The only mistake I made was ever getting involved with you.'

'I'd second that statement, except that hiding out in the Red Cross tent while your deputy mayor's widow is treated for shock and his eldest son waits outside in the cold isn't exactly a genius move.'

'I wouldn't be hiding if the sheriff's office did its job and apprehended the killer before he could get away. Instead, I'm left wondering when and if the shooter might come back to finish the job.'

'Yeah, about that,' Reade prefaced, 'it's looking more likely that Royce Behrens was the killer's intended target.'

'Royce? Why would anyone want to kill him?'

'That's why we're here – to review your original statement and see if there's anything else you might remember.'

Schuyler rose from his chair and warmed his hands in front of the heater. 'Not sure I have anything to add. Royce was my deputy mayor, but we weren't friends. Apart from the fact he had a wife and two kids and was the grandson of a former mayor, I knew nothing about him or his personal life. We each had our respective offices and got down to business each morning – we didn't socialize or chitchat.'

'And how was business for the deputy mayor?' Tish asked.

'I thought I established that I wasn't talking to you.'

'Fine. Have it your way. I'm sure the Hobson Glen residents

you've been avoiding, even though they could use some strong leadership and reassurance at the moment, would love to hear that you've kicked the sheriff department's most successful consultant off the case. And I'm sure Amanda Behrens will be delighted to know that you've taken resources *away* from her husband's murder investigation rather than adding them.' Tish turned on one heel as if to exit the tent.

As she had expected, Schuyler stopped her. 'Wait!'

She stood in the entrance of the tent, but didn't turn around to face him.

'Why do you always have to . . .?' He slammed his cell phone down onto a nearby folding table and drew a deep breath. 'Fine. OK. You win. I'll answer your questions.'

Tish sat down in the chair Schuyler had just vacated. 'Describe what happened this afternoon.'

'I've already told Sheriff—'

Reade interrupted him. 'Yes, and I want you to tell us again, in detail, in case you remember something new.'

Schuyler sighed again. 'It was a busy morning. My staff was making certain that everything was in place for today's Turkey Trot while simultaneously planning next week's Rod and Gun Club event.'

'Whose idea was it to move the Turkey Trot to the Friday before Thanksgiving and give its traditional post-holiday slot to the Rod and Gun Club?' Tish asked.

'It's was Royce's. It was brilliant, really. By switching the two, we were able to attract wealthy gun owners to town for the holiday weekend. It should give a nice little boost to our local economy.'

'Were either you or Royce aware of how unpopular that decision was?'

Schuyler glanced at Reade imploringly. 'What does this have to do with—?'

'Just answer the question, Mr Mayor,' Reade insisted.

'Yes, we were both aware that certain, er . . . *parties* weren't exactly pleased with the decision, but we opted to go ahead because it's expected to be a highly profitable event for the town. Both of our hotels are full. So is Glory Bishop's B and B. Even your café should benefit,' Schuyler appealed.

'Yes, I know just how much my livelihood concerns you,' Tish said sarcastically. 'These "displeased" parties you mentioned – was there anyone who was more vocal than the others? Possibly more aggressive?'

'Connie Ramirez,' he replied without hesitation. 'She's the head of a local anti-gun group. They're always protesting outside the State Supreme Court in Richmond and bogging down traffic.'

Tish suppressed a weary sigh. Schuyler would, of course, paint Ramirez's organization as a public nuisance.

'From the day the Rod and Gun Club event was announced,' Schuyler continued, 'Ramirez has either been standing outside the deputy mayor's office or calling his office asking him to reconsider.'

'So she knew that the event was Royce's brainchild,' Tish presumed.

'Only because I told her,' he replied with a laugh. 'The minute she called my office, I decided to nip it in the bud. I didn't need that kind of craziness wasting my time and that of my employees.'

Leave it to Schuyler to throw someone else under the bus. 'Was she at the office this morning?'

'No, but Royce wasn't either. I didn't see him until he showed up here just before the Trot was to begin.'

'Do you know if Ms Ramirez was here at Colonial Springs today?' Reade asked.

'She and her group were at the entrance to the parking lot when I drove in. Royce must have seen them, too – he arrived just a minute or two after I did. I sent someone from my office to deal with them. I don't know what happened to them after that. For all I know, they may have asked for help from one of your officers,' Schuyler told the sheriff.

'No formal complaint was registered, but that doesn't mean one of my people didn't act in an unofficial capacity,' Reade noted as he scrolled through the files on his iPad. 'Tell us what happened once you arrived here.'

'Nothing. I mean, nothing you both don't already know about. You were both here before Royce and I even arrived.'

'Tell us anyway.'

'Again?' Schuyler paced impatiently. 'We said hello to each other, reviewed our speech notes to make sure we covered the key points we wished to make, and then it was showtime. I gave my speech,

Royce gave his, Tish grandstanded' – he directed a nasty look toward the caterer – 'and then Tripp Sennette fired his pistol.'

'What happened on the trail?' Tish asked.

'We weren't on it for very long before all hell broke loose. Felt like we'd only just hit our stride when the shots rang out and Royce fell down in front of me.'

'Wait,' Reade interjected. 'What did you just say?'

Schuyler's face was a question. 'What?'

'You said that Behrens fell down in front of you.'

'That's right.'

'But when you took off down the trail, he was behind you.'

'That's right. We were a couple of yards in when he dashed ahead. Royce was always competitive. I guess he wanted to look like the hero by completing his lap before I did.'

'You didn't tell us this earlier.'

'Didn't I?' Schuyler asked absently. 'I suppose I didn't think of it until now.'

Tish examined Schuyler's face for a trace of deceit. She found none. 'Is there anything else you remember? Sounds, smells – anything.'

'Smells? Really, Tish?' the mayor sneered.

'Yes, really, Schuyler. Royce Behrens – a public official – is dead. It might seem like a stretch, but even the scent of the killer's aftershave or tobacco brand might be helpful. We need you to think back to what happened.'

With a few shakes of his head, Schuyler opened a nearby folding chair, sat down, and closed his eyes tightly. Several seconds elapsed before he spoke. 'Just before Royce dashed ahead of me, I could have sworn I saw something moving in the trees further along the trail.'

'To your left?' Tish asked, recalling the spot where the shooter had hidden.

'No, to the right,' he replied, his eyes still shut.

Tish fired a questioning glance at Reade. It was not the answer they had anticipated. 'You're sure it was on the right?' she asked the mayor.

'One hundred percent certain. I don't know what it was – a bird, a squirrel, a rustling tree limb. All I can tell you is that I saw *something*. I was watching it when Royce pushed past me and jogged ahead. Then I heard something – leaves rustling and twigs snapping in the woods near where Royce was jogging. The shots rang out shortly after that and I watched as he fell. Before he could even hit the ground, I ducked and covered and escaped, praying that the shooter wouldn't follow. He didn't.' Schuyler opened his eyes. 'That's it. I've told you everything I know.'

'Which way did you escape?' Reade questioned.

'What do you mean?'

'Which direction did you move – to the left or the right?'

'To the rear. Back toward the trailhead.'

'You're positive?'

'Yes, I remember it vividly now. The shots themselves were a surprise at the time, and Royce getting hit was an absolute shock, but the thing about the situation that put me in a complete tailspin was that the shots didn't come from where I expected. Seeing something or someone moving in one spot, hearing something moving in another spot, and then hearing shots from yet another – it was confusing.'

'So confusing that you forgot it until now?' Reade challenged.

'Look, I probably should have said something earlier, but I knew something was wrong about the shooting. I just didn't know what it was until now. Had I told you something was wrong, but then couldn't tell you what it was, you'd have thought me suspicious for that too,' Schuyler argued.

Reade typed notes into his iPad rather than counter Schuyler's ridiculous argument. 'Were you aware that Royce Behrens wanted to be mayor?'

'Everyone knew that,' Schuyler dismissed with a humorless laugh. 'Royce would have sold his own mother if it meant an increase in the polls. Unfortunately, that wouldn't have been a smart move – Annabelle is far more popular than he was.'

'"Sold his own mother?" Sounds like he was pretty ruthless.'

'When it came to success, he was.'

'And he was looking to take over your job. How did that make you feel?'

'I was elected to office. This town gave me a mandate to govern. Behrens couldn't take that away from me.'

Mandate? Tish winced. Winning an election by a slim, three-point margin could scarcely be considered a mandate. 'I'm not sure if you saw the memo, but like any other federal, state, or local official, you can be impeached.'

'Not without good reason.'

Tish thought about the new mall and housing development scheme, the switch of the Turkey Trot from a lucrative holiday Saturday to a Friday workday, the new companion animal legislation, and the other myriad of complaints that had reached her ears in recent days. 'You wouldn't exactly be named the most popular mayor in Hobson Glen history,' she stated delicately.

'What does it matter?' he scoffed. 'Once Hobson Meadows is built, people will see things differently. The naysayers will be surprised by job growth, less crime—'

'Um, you mean apart from the brutal murder of the deputy mayor?' Tish interjected.

Schuyler ignored her. 'And a coffer full of taxes to spend on improvement projects for the town. Now that the Hobson Meadows project is in my hands, it will be perfectly executed. Absolutely down-to-the-letter perfect.'

SIX

Annabelle Behrens sat upright in her hospital bed. Although connected to a heart monitor and receiving an intravenous drip of an unidentified substance, her color was good and her silver hair was still piled elegantly, and meticulously, on the top of her head. 'Royce was, in every sense of the phrase, his father's son,' she said with a soft Virginia drawl. 'Passionate, reckless, impulsive, yet at the same time calculating and cold. They were both ridiculously handsome, with thick, dark hair and eyes as blue as the Mediterranean Sea. Neither one of them could keep their hands to themselves when it came to the opposite sex.'

The directness of her statement gave Reade pause. 'Ah, um, ma'am, can you, um . . .'

'Sorry for being candid, Sheriff. I've never been much for pretending the men in my family were anything other than what they were. My father, God bless him, was the best in the bunch. We'll never see the likes of him again. My father lived to serve this community. Royce and his daddy, they lived to serve themselves.'

'But Royce was on the town council. He was deputy mayor,' Tish argued.

'Only because Royce wanted so desperately to walk in his grandfather's shoes. When he graduated from law school, Royce was going to run for mayor on his grandfather's name alone. He thought the mayorship was his birthright,' she said, her face a blend of exasperation and amusement. 'But I set him straight right away. I told him how hard his grandfather worked to gain the people's trust – to become the best name on the ballot. Royce wound up running for a town council spot instead. Won it, too – became the youngest councilman this town's ever had.'

'Did Royce often come to you for career advice?' Reade asked.

'No. I wish he had, but that was the only time he sought my guidance. Royce had very clear ideas about what it meant to serve the public. Those ideas were similar to those of his father. My late husband, Wade, ran the savings and loan over in Ashton

Courthouse. It was the only bank in the area for a time. What with his exorbitant fees and penalties, Wade must have stolen from just about every member of the community over the years. Royce would have too, if given the opportunity . . . and had he lived long enough.'

'"Stolen from the community?"' Tish questioned. 'How?'

Annabelle waved her hands dismissively. 'Oh, don't ask me how, but he would have found a way. It was in his blood – in his nature.'

'So your son had enemies,' Reade surmised.

'Enemies?' she repeated with a snort and a whistle. 'A better question is whether he had any friends.'

'Can you think of anyone in that group of enemies who may have wanted your son dead?'

Annabelle shook her head. 'I tried not to interfere in Royce's life. Not because I wished to avoid being the overbearing mother – although that was a consideration – but because it hurt too much to know all the ugly details of his existence. Still, I have a broad circle of friends and a busy social life, so I had more than an inkling of what he had been up to, and there were moments when I needed to act to protect his family. Suffice to say, between the jealous husbands, the jilted lovers, the political enemies, the embittered business partners, and the disenchanted townspeople, I'm sure someone felt they had a very good reason to end Royce's life.'

'And you? How did you and Royce get along?'

Annabelle stared at a spot on the thin sheet that covered her legs and lower torso. 'Royce was my only child. I had tried for a baby for so very long that I'd just about given up on motherhood. I was forty when Royce came along. He was such a beautiful boy that I spoiled him terribly. There was nothing he wanted for, nothing I wouldn't do for him. It's probably why he turned out the way he did. He was so accustomed to getting his own way.

'I loved my son, Sheriff. I loved him desperately, but I didn't like the man he grew to be. I never wished him ill, mind you. I only wished that he'd come around and realize how many people he'd hurt, how many people he was still hurting. I invited him to attend my charity luncheons and to join me on *Habitat for Humanity* building projects. I suggested he bring his boys along – my grand-sons – so they, too, could learn the benefits of kindness. I so wanted Royce to be a good example to them, unlike his own father, but he wasn't about to change his ways.'

Annabelle heaved a weary sigh. 'So, the care of my grandsons has fallen primarily on their mother. Amanda enrolled them in private schools, ensured they participated in the debate team and piano recitals, and has shuttled them to endless sporting events. With the emotional absence of my son, she's focused all her energy on raising those boys and, in turn, has become overprotective of them. That's not at all a complaint – it's an observation. I couldn't have chosen a better wife for Royce or a better mother for my grandsons. Amanda's a Coker, you know.'

At Tish and Reade's blank stares, Annabelle explained, 'The Cokers are an old Virginia family – descendants of William Coker, who served in the Virginia House of Burgesses, back when we were just a colony. There's been a Coker on the board of just about every museum and university in the state. Poor Amanda's family was nearly wiped out in the crash of '87, but they didn't let it take them down. They're tough and well thought of, which made Amanda a perfect match for Royce. She possessed the strength and respectability that the Behrens name lacked. I just wish her life with him had been different. I wish all their lives could have been different.'

SEVEN

'Councilmen, mistresses, cuckolded husbands, duped businesspeople, and Burgesses. When was the last time you even thought about Burgesses? Fifth grade maybe? Your last visit to Colonial Williamsburg?' Tish mused aloud as they crossed the hospital parking lot to Reade's waiting SUV. 'So, where do we go next?'

'Back to Colonial Springs.'

'Back? What about the leads we've gotten? The councilmen, the cuckolded husbands, the duped businesspeople, the – oh, I suppose we can't include the Burgesses – but what about all those other people?'

'We'll talk to them soon. I'd like us to have a little more information before we start questioning everyone who might have had something to do with Behrens's death.'

'But what about the anti-gun activists? What about the other councilmen?' she argued. 'Shouldn't we be speaking with them now?'

'We will,' Reade explained, as he held open the passenger side door of the SUV for Tish. 'We've gotten the preliminary statements of nearly everyone who was at the Turkey Trot today,' he continued upon entering the driver's side of the car and positioning himself behind the steering wheel. 'Once I review those with Clayton – and you, if you're up for it – we'll devise a list of suspects to question and a list of what we need to ask them.'

Tish stared silently out through the windshield.

'I also need to verify with ballistics that the weapon used was, in fact, an AR-15 and I need to check in with forensics to see if they might have discovered anything of significance at the crime scene or along the trails.'

Tish remained silent.

'Look, honey, I understand you want to catch this person. I do, too – not just for what they did to Royce Behrens, but for what they did to this town, for what they did to you. However, I still need to approach this as I would any other case. I need to have whatever evidence we can find before I start leveling questions or allegations.'

'I understand, Clemson. Really, I do. I just feel like we need to *do* something.'

'And I understand your frustration in waiting, but when we catch this person – and we *will* catch them – we need to make sure our investigation is watertight. Now, do you want to join Clayton and me?' Reade asked tentatively. 'We've collected a lot of statements, which means a lot of reading, which you normally enjoy, but I could also drop you back at home if you'd prefer.'

'As much as I could do with some kitty snuggles right now,' Tish replied, referring to their cats, Tuna and Marlowe, 'what I want most is to pack up my table and gear and bring everything back to the café.'

'Sure, but you don't necessarily need to do that right now if you don't feel up to it. Colonial Springs is closed to the public. I'll have officers there all night – your things will be safe.'

'The food won't. It's been cold at night, but not that cold. I can't let it all go to waste, Clemson. If I bring everything back to the café, maybe we can feed the Red Cross and emergency workers, or maybe even hold an open house where people can buy the food they might have purchased today – that way the food bank doesn't completely lose out.'

Reade pulled her close and kissed her on the forehead. 'Both are wonderful ideas, hon, but promise me you won't bite off more than you can chew. Even you, my Wonder Woman, need some time to rest today.'

She flashed a weary smile. 'I will – eventually – but I can't think of sitting still right now. Besides, I'll rest easier tonight knowing I don't have to step foot in Colonial Springs again – at least not for a very long time.'

Reade and Tish arrived at Colonial Springs twenty minutes later to find that the rank of ambulances had diminished to just one and that the flood of cars in the parking lot had shrunk down to a small handful.

An eager Clayton awaited them. 'How's Annabelle Behrens?'

'Stable and sharp as a tack,' Reade replied. 'I'm a little over half her age and I wish I were as lucid as she is. What's going on here?'

'Just getting statements from the last of the attendees. Amanda and Chase Behrens are still here. They're waiting for Amanda to be cleared by the medical team, but that should take place any minute now. I've arranged for one of the uniforms to give them a ride home, but Amanda is insisting on driving, so he might follow her home instead.'

'That's fine. We'll lock down the area and post officers on watch duty overnight to prevent the media and other lookie-loos from stumbling around. Any new reports?'

'Ballistics confirms that Behrens was killed by an AR-15. Three shots to the chest. So far there's no evidence that any other rounds were fired. Apart from the three bullets that killed Behrens and the three cartridges found in the small copse of trees where the shooter hid, there were no other bullets or cartridges found on the scene.'

'So it would appear the killer *was* a good shot,' Reade noted. 'Which only reinforces the theory that Behrens was the intended target and not Thompson.'

'Dr Andres stopped by – he's been assigned as the ME on the case. He's going to try to rush the tox screen, but until that comes through, a search of Behrens's car turned up four different prescription drugs, all filled within the past month or two.'

'Four?' Tish repeated.

'That's right. The dude who told people to give up their support for animals and reach within themselves to find their hidden strength was on Adderal, Ritalin and Librium.'

'Uppers *and* downers. Impressive,' Reade quipped. 'What was the fourth prescription?'

Clayton slid his eyes toward Tish self-consciously. 'Umm . . . male . . . um . . . male enhancement drugs.'

'That's not too surprising, given the other drugs. He was a pharmaceutical yo-yo.'

'And yet very surprising given his relationship with his wife,' Tish stated. 'According to Annabelle, Royce and Amanda were living separate lives, leaving Amanda to lavish her affections on her sons.'

'Annabelle also said that Royce, like his father, had an eye for the ladies,' Reade added.

'Yes, but which of those ladies had he been with most recently?'

Reade raised his eyebrows while Clayton registered his disgust.

'I know we're talking about a potential murder suspect here, but ew.'

'Don't start with the whole "old people" thing, Clayton,' Reade warned. 'Royce Behrens was the same age I am.'

'Oh? OK . . . well, erm, moving on, then . . .' It was clear that Clayton still had no interest in hearing about the love life of Royce Behrens, Reade, or any individual over the age of thirty-five. 'I tried to contact the deputy mayor's office to obtain a list of Behrens's appointments and correspondence these past two weeks to see if there was anything unusual.'

'And?'

'And I was met with both a pre-recorded phone message and an automated email response stating that, due to the death of the deputy mayor, the office was closed and wouldn't open until sometime next week.'

'But Behrens died just a few hours ago,' Tish exclaimed. 'Did you try Schuyler's office?'

'Same thing. Closed in deference to the passing of the deputy mayor.'

'Both offices?'

Clayton nodded and looked to his superior for a reaction.

'I never disclosed the identity of the victim,'. Reade said, clearly surprised that he had been 'scooped.' 'I was saving that for a press conference later this evening.'

'It's a small town,' Clayton offered as an excuse. 'News travels fast.'

'No, Clayton. Rumors and gossip travel fast. The truth tends to take a more circuitous route,' the sheriff corrected. 'How long ago did you make those phone calls?'

'I made those calls immediately after we learned about the anti-gun protestors, so maybe two hours ago?'

'That's far too quick for anyone to have deduced the victim was Royce. Someone must have leaked the news.'

'The only people who knew were Behrens's immediate family, the team working the case, and Julian Davis.'

'*And* Schuyler Thompson,' Tish added. 'He was there, remember?'

'That's a pretty short amount of time in which to shut down the town offices, isn't it?' Reade questioned.

'Schuyler would pull any strings to preserve his image. He must have called his office right after the shooting and then they spread the word to Behrens's team.' She pulled a face. 'The real question is did he close the offices because of how it might appear if he kept them open, or because he didn't want you or anyone else calling over there?'

'He was on the phone when Clayton and I first interviewed him and he was working again when you and I questioned him for the second time. I understand that his office needn't have been open for him to be working, but it does suggest that someone, somewhere was receiving his directives.'

'Which makes my question even more relevant. Why go through the motions of "closing" the office if his staff was working anyway? Was it to ensure that no one was there to answer our questions?'

'Yeah, but whatever information his employees have today, they'll still have on Monday morning,' Clayton argued.

'Not necessarily. There might be something in the office that Schuyler doesn't want people to find,' Tish countered. 'Something that he'll make sure disappears over the weekend.'

'Do you really think Mayor Thompson would . . . um . . . oh.' Clayton's voice trailed off as he obviously recalled Tish and Schuyler's relationship.

'I know firsthand that Mayor Thompson is willing to sacrifice just about anything for the sake of his career.'

'We'll be sure to ask about the office closure in our next round of questions,' Reade assured. 'Got anything else, Clayton?'

'Fibers,' the officer replied, pulling his phone from the inside pocket of his navy blue down parka and opening a photo showing a piece of material measuring approximately one half-inch long and one quarter-inch wide. 'Forensics found a fragment of water-repellent fabric caught on the branches of a tree on the south side of the path, just beyond where Behrens was killed. The sample is fresh – torn within the past twenty-four hours.'

'Corroborating Schuyler's account of seeing something or someone farther along the path and to his right, just before Behrens was shot.'

Tish gazed at the image on Clayton's phone. 'Is the color of this photo accurate?'

'Oh yeah, this is the iPhone 14 Pro Max with a forty-eight

megapixel camera fed by . . .' Clayton turned red as Reade glared at him. 'Yes, that's the color of the fabric.'

'Winter white,' she mused aloud.

'Winter white?' Reade repeated. 'My grandmother used to mention that color, but I never knew what it was. All that fuss about not wearing white after Labor Day, but then being able to wear it as a different shade in winter never really made sense to me.'

'Because unless you summer at your "cottage" in Newport before returning to the grime of a turn-of-the-century city, it doesn't make sense at all. What *does* make sense, however, is that the thing Schuyler saw further down the trail was most likely a woman.'

'A woman?' Reade and Clayton voiced simultaneously.

'Well, I don't know of too many men's outerwear labels that offer winter white as a colorway, do you?'

The two men glanced at each other and shook their heads.

'That is what we're talking about here, isn't it? Scraps from a water-resistant winter jacket.'

'Most likely, yes,' Reade replied. 'Are you certain about the winter white thing?'

'Positive. In fact, I guarantee that if you Google "winter white outerwear," predictive text will add the search term "women's" to the end of it.'

Clayton typed into his phone and then nodded. 'She's right. Not only did the search engine want to add "women's" to the search term, but the shopping results for "winter white outerwear" show only female models.'

'Put out a statement that we're looking for a woman dressed in a winter white jacket who was in the vicinity of the shooting today. Make it clear we have no reason to suspect this person of anything, but they might have information vital to the case,' Reade ordered. 'And, um, good work, Clayton.'

'Thanks, sir,' he replied before striding off to the Red Cross tent to make some phone calls.

'I'll meet you in a few seconds to review security for this evening,' he shouted after his officer before turning to Tish. 'And you did some great work, too.'

'Just using my minimal fashion knowledge for good rather than evil,' she dismissed.

'Don't downplay it. We don't know yet what this mysterious

white-jacketed person might reveal. I'm going to join Clayton and make sure we have a plan to lock this place down tonight. Would you like to join us? The sun's starting to go down, it would be warmer in there. You can also go home if you'd like. If you're not up to the drive, I can have a car take you and we can pick up your van tomorrow.'

Tish suppressed a chill. As much as she would have loved to go home and sit by the fire, she wanted – and needed – to be busy; to control some small corner of her world. 'No, I really want to pack up and get everything back to the café.'

'OK, forensics did a thorough examination of your table and the immediate surrounding area. They've picked up anything of interest from the ground – you'll notice that the circle surrounding your serving area looks tidier than the rest of the trailhead. Everything on the periphery is to remain untouched until forensics can do another sweep. Do you need a hand with anything?' he asked as she donned a pair of blue plastic shoe covers.

'No, I should be all right with the packing up. When I'm ready to load things into the van, I'll call you.'

'I'll check in with you before then,' he promised.

She leaned forward and kissed him. 'See you then.'

Reade walked across the clearing to the tent, leaving Tish to tend to the food and refuse left behind at her catering table.

She stared, bewildered, at the scene. As Reade described, the grounds surrounding her table had been swept clean, but it was an oasis in the center of chaos. Encircling this oasis, hats, gloves, napkins, cups, and straw wrappers were all scattered across the ground. Some blown and scattered by the wind, others dropped in a panic. A half-eaten sandwich in its foil wrapper abandoned by an eater caught unawares. A full cup of coffee left undrunk. A pastry partially consumed.

Life interrupted.

Fighting the urge to retreat to her van and sob, Tish went to the box beside the till and extracted a pair of blue latex gloves. Donning them, she set about sealing the hot beverage carafes and slow cookers full of soup and repacking the sandwiches in their insulated coolers. As she worked, the sun sank below the horizon, casting Colonial Springs and its environs in a purplish glow.

Tish looked up to see a figure in silhouette rushing across the parking lot and heading directly toward her. Despite the considerable police presence at the Springs, she watched the figure in fear. Who or what could it possibly be? And what could they possibly want?

Seeing no law enforcement officers in the immediate vicinity, she stepped back against the table, grabbed the knife she'd brought along for the purpose of cutting sandwiches, and deliberated whether or not she should cry for help.

'Tish! Tish are you OK?' the figure shouted.

Recognizing the voice, Tish allowed the knife to fall from her fingertips. 'Oh, MJ. I'm so sorry I didn't call you,' she cried as she ran toward her friend.

'Don't be sorry, duckie,' MJ, in her maternal tone, excused. 'I'm just happy to see you.'

The two women embraced.

'Kayla was taking her test when I heard the sirens go off. I thought there was an accident on the interstate. It wasn't until we were driving back to town when I heard the news. I tried calling you, but there was no answer, so I called Celestine and Jules. They both assured me you were fine, but then I got to thinking about the van and the gear and the food and thought I should just get my butt down here to help you. Kayla dropped me off.'

'Wait. *Kayla* dropped you off?' Tish repeated, recognizing the significance of the statement. 'She passed?'

'With flying colors! The moment she pulled over to the side of the road to allow the emergency vehicles the right of way, the instructor gave her a passing grade. Which, between you and me is a lucky thing, because if she'd had to parallel park . . .' MJ held her head in her hands.

'Oh, that's right. She took the side mirror off Celestine's car while practicing last week, didn't she?'

'Yeah. Celestine laughed it off and had her son-in-law fix it, but I notice since then that she's started parking behind the café instead of in the parking lot.'

'Oh, that's terrific news about Kayla. But shouldn't you be celebrating with her?'

'Celebrating? She borrowed my car and is driving to meet her friends to share the news – and gloat, most likely. I made her promise that she and her friends would hang out at one of their houses and not go to any shopping centers or movie theaters. What with some crazy killer on the loose . . .' She shook her head as if to dispel her concerns. 'I'm going to check in on her later to make sure she listened. Until then, let's get to work. The sooner we clean this place up, the sooner we can get you home where it's warm.'

The prospect of hearth and home appealed greatly to Tish. With the darkness had come a bone-chilling cold and she was certain that they'd see, if not a freeze, certainly a thick frost overnight. She buzzed along with her tasks, happy to have a second pair of hands to help.

When all the food, signage and tablecloths had been packed, Tish and MJ got to work disassembling the tables.

'You want me to get rid of this trash?' MJ asked, holding a white garbage bag aloft.

'What's in it?'

'Some napkins that have gone damp and the few sandwiches and doughnuts that have been lying unwrapped on the table all afternoon.'

'Ick, yeah, we probably should. I'm not sure where to take it though. This area's been given the all clear by forensics, but the rest haven't.'

'We can take it with us in the van.'

'Err, I'm not sure about that. I'm also not supposed to take anything other than my gear out of the Springs.'

'Maybe give Reade a call and ask?' MJ suggested.

Tish shook her head. 'I don't want to bother him over something as trivial as this if I can avoid it. There's a trashcan over there by the streetlight. Dump it in there. If the contents of the can have already been checked, then it will go out with the next trash pickup. If not, worst-case scenario, forensics analyzes it again when they go through the contents of that can.'

'Perfect. This way we're not taking anything out of the park either.' MJ wandered over to the trashcan, bag in hand, expecting the bin in question to be full. 'Hey, Tish, maybe this isn't a good idea after all. Looks like the can is empty. Maybe forensics was already here?'

'Oh, that's possible. Maybe I should call—'

'Wait,' MJ instructed as she shone the light from her phone into the black abyss of the can. 'I was wrong. It's not empty. There's some sort of rag in here. It's black with white lettering of some kind. Hey, it's an old rock T-shirt and – oh, Tish! Call Clemson.'

'What? Why?'

'Because the front of the shirt is splattered with what looks like blood.'

EIGHT

'Dr Andres has the shirt,' Clemson Reade announced upon arriving home with Clayton in tow. 'He'll give us a match on the blood just as soon as he can.'

'It's good to see you too, honey.' Tish, freshly bathed and dressed in a pair of red satin pajamas and white fuzzy slippers, greeted him dryly. She was on the sofa, in front of the fire, with a cat resting on either side of her lap.

'Sorry. Still in police mode,' he apologized, before bending over and planting a kiss on her forehead. 'You look cozy.'

'Following nurse's orders.' Tish pointed a manicured finger at the kitchen door.

As if on cue, MJ emerged from the room in question carrying two open bottles of beer. 'Because you, Tish – yes, even you – need looking after on occasion. Supper will be ready in a few minutes,' she announced, handing the beers to Reade and Clayton and disappearing back into the kitchen.

'Thanks.' Clayton sat down in one of two wood-frame mid-century modern club chairs that flanked the fireplace and took a swig. 'So, do I need to update my bulletin to state that we're looking for a female in a winter white jacket *and* a male in a Nirvana T-shirt?'

'Why a male?' Tish challenged.

'Because the T-shirt was a men's size medium.'

MJ reappeared with a glass of white wine for Tish. 'Back in the day, we wore lots of men-sized shirts over leggings.'

'Remember we bought those matching Depeche Mode *Violator* tees?' Tish recalled. 'Those were sweet!'

'Depeche who?' Clayton asked.

'Depeche – never mind. Our point was that the wearer of that shirt could have been female.'

'OK, I'll update the bulletin to say "individual," even though the fashion trend you're describing was eons ago.'

'If you use the word "eons" to describe our youth again, there will be no soup for you,' MJ threatened. 'What's more, I'll have you know that the oversized shirt trend is still popular. Kayla and her friends all wear oversized band T-shirts over skinny jeans and cut-off shorts.'

'Was she joking about the soup?' the young officer asked after MJ had returned to the kitchen in a huff. The fact that she was quoting a Nineties sitcom had completely eluded him.

'Let's just say that I've had a bath and I'm in my pajamas and it's not yet seven o'clock,' Tish offered as proof of the earnestness behind MJ's threat. 'The woman means business.'

Clayton's eyes widened. 'OK, so a female in a jacket and an *individual* in a Nirvana T-shirt. I've gotta say this doesn't make much sense to me. How did we not see someone taking off a T-shirt and tossing that shirt in the trash?'

'People were in a panic,' Reade replied, taking the seat next to Tish. 'Rushing to the parking lot, to the trail, to the woods in order to hide. You'd be surprised what can go unnoticed in that type of situation.'

'And the person going topless afterward? I mean, if we're looking for an *individual* and not just a guy . . .'

'It's late November. Whoever took off that shirt probably had a jacket with them.'

'Then why take off the shirt?' Tish reasoned. 'Why not put on the jacket, zip it up, and get out of there without anyone noticing them?'

'Because they didn't want to risk being caught covered in Behrens's blood.'

'So you think the shirt belonged to the killer?'

'Actually, no. We need the lab results, of course, but in my opinion those splatters are more consistent with someone who got caught in the crossfire.'

'OK, then, if you're not guilty, why ditch the shirt?' Tish emphasized. 'Why not report what you've seen to the police? Why not tell them everything you know?'

'Because they don't want the killer to come after them next,' Clayton suggested.

'Or because they weren't supposed to be there,' MJ ventured, as she placed a stack of bowls on the coffee table in preparation for supper.

'This is what I've missed,' Clayton exclaimed, before taking another swig of beer. 'I mean, not that I don't enjoy working with you, Sheriff, but during the Bake-Off case, we'd all meet up over dinner every night and share our discoveries and toss around theories, just like we're doing now. It was an awesome case! All we're missing is—'

The doorbell rang, spurring Tuna and Marlowe to leave their comfortable spots near Tish and hide upstairs.

'Jules,' MJ and Tish declared in unison.

Reade got up and answered the door. There, standing on the doorstep as expected, stood Jules. 'Hi, Clemson, I'm not bothering you, am I?'

'No, we were just about to have some of Tish's soup and sandwiches for dinner. You're welcome to join us.'

'Oh, no. I don't want to impose,' Jules stated, all the while removing his scarf and undoing the front buttons of his black overcoat.

Reade took Biscuit's lead and, to prevent any canine/feline altercations, put him in the office and closed a metal baby gate behind him. 'You're always welcome here, Jules.'

'Thanks, Clem. You're a gem.' He dumped his outerwear into Reade's waiting arms and went into the living room.

'Hi, Jules. We've been expecting you,' MJ greeted.

'Really?'

'Yeah, it's suppertime.'

Jules laughed. 'You're such a card, MJ.'

Tish pointed to the stack of five bowls on the coffee table. 'Nope, she was expecting you.'

Jules pleaded his innocence. 'I had no idea it was dinnertime.'

'It's six o'clock and dark outside,' MJ countered.

'OK,' Jules said with a sigh. 'I was lonely. Maurice got called to cover an accident in Richmond so he'll be working late and can't come over and I . . . I was afraid to be alone.'

Tish stood up and she and MJ gathered him in their arms. 'You're never alone, Jules.'

'As I said when you arrived, you're always welcome here,' Reade told him.

'I was only joking about dinnertime,' MJ offered as an apology. 'Partly.'

Jules laughed. 'You're not wrong. I do sort of sync my visits with mealtimes, except tonight I have something to offer in exchange for my dinner – a scoop!'

'That's exactly what we were talking about when you arrived,' Clayton explained. 'How you, MJ, Tish and I used to share food and information during the Bake-Off case. Good times.'

'Yeah, apart from me being assaulted by a psychotic killer, it was a real hoot,' Tish deadpanned as she sat back down on the sofa.

'I understand what Clayton is trying to say. There was a terrific synergy created by us sharing a communal meal and the day's discoveries.' Jules plopped down in the spot Reade had recently vacated. 'And my discovery is sure to lend some vigor to the investigation. With the information I have, I may just earn myself a surf-and-turf dinner.'

MJ, bearing a stockpot and a trivet, glared at him.

'However, I'm completely fine with soup and sandwiches,' he was quick to amend. 'And possibly your sofa. I just can't be alone in my apartment tonight. I know I have Biscuit to protect me, but he's not much of a guard dog. If the UPS man knocks on the door, he runs under the bed and pees on the carpet.'

'No sofa. You and Biscuit can have the pull-out bed in the office with pillows, clean sheets, and plenty of extra blankets,' Reade stated as he handed Jules a glass of wine and sat down in a chair he had brought from the kitchen. 'Now, what's the scoop?'

As MJ passed the platter of sandwiches and ladled up some soup, Jules related his story. 'Well, like everyone here I was shaken by what happened this afternoon, but when I calmed down a little bit, just a little, I started to remember something that was in the news just a few weeks back. So, after I collected Biscuit from the café – thanks, Mary Jo—'

'No problem. I was out most of the time he was there,' she dismissed, settling into the club chair opposite Clayton's.

'After I collected Biscuit, I stopped in at the newsroom and started searching for previous broadcasts. It took some doing and I nearly gave up, but I finally found it!'

'What was it?' Clayton asked.

'A little news story about a planning commission meeting with a hot microphone.'

'That's it!' Reade exclaimed. 'That's what I was trying to remember when I questioned Amanda Behrens this morning.'

'Then listen up.' Jules's audience sat, plates on laps, in rapt attention as the newsman described the events of June twenty-ninth of that year. 'First up, y'all have got to understand that no one on the town council really liked Royce Behrens. It's common knowledge in the newsroom that even some of the councilmen who were his political allies actually hated his guts. Behrens was the young, rich kid who lied to get his position and that didn't set well with the other members. Behrens ran on the same platform as his granddaddy – that's how he got people's trust – but, once he was on the council, he failed to deliver. I'd actually go so far as to say he went out of his way not to deliver.'

'I remember when he was elected,' MJ recalled. 'I was pregnant with Gregory and Glen and I had just moved into our house. Jules hadn't arrived in town yet and I don't think you had either, Clemson.'

'No, I took the sheriff's office job several months after Behrens joined the council,' Reade replied.

'Wow! That's like eighteen years ago. I was, like, seven years old,' Clayton gleefully remarked.

'We know,' Jules, Tish, Reade and MJ responded in unison.

'So, as the new kid in town, I'm in the dark about something. Behrens was elected because he lied to voters, but how did he keep getting re-elected once they knew what he was about?' Tish asked.

'Because he made sure his donors became wealthy . . . er – wealthier than they already were,' Jules explained. 'And he kept voters on the line by breeding fear, although it wasn't enough. Behrens's goal was to become mayor, but he didn't have the public support, so he rose as high as he could – to deputy mayor – a position that doesn't rely upon a public vote, but is appointed by the council itself.'

'So what *is* this hot mic incident all about again?' an impatient Reade quizzed.

'The planning commission held a meeting the evening of June twenty-ninth regarding the ordinances surrounding Hobson Meadows. The meeting went as expected. Gavin Sheppard, the developer behind Hobson Meadows, gave his pitch about how a luxury housing development and adjacent upscale shopping and entertainment complex would drive tourism and create jobs. He left out the part where the only jobs given to locals are the ones that pay minimum wage and offer zero chance of advancement. That's what happened in my hometown,' Jules told Reade and Clayton. 'The die-and-tool company where my father was shop steward was sold to a multinational company under the condition that the staff was kept on the payroll. The buyers kept their promise, but demoted the existing staff and replaced the higher-ups – including my father – with those who had graduated from the corporate management-training program. The old employees could no longer support their families, so those who could find other jobs left in droves and those who were older gave up. My father was one of them. A year after the company sold, he left town. Two years after that, we learned that he was dead. Self-inflicted bullet wound to the skull.'

Reade and Clayton both expressed their condolences. 'That really stinks, man,' Clayton professed.

'It was rough at first, but my father wasn't a kind person. He was a jealous man who verbally abused my mother and, had he been around, would never have approved of my coming-out. My sister is younger and doesn't remember half of what my father did, so she still worships him, but my mother and I – well, we wouldn't be the people we are today had he stuck around.'

'And we wouldn't be treated to your fabulosity,' Tish declared, instantly lightening the mood.

'Your lives *would* be a lot quieter,' he admitted with a laugh.

'And a lot less fun,' MJ added, holding her glass aloft.

Tish mirrored the gesture. 'Hear, hear.'

Reade lifted his bottle of beer. 'Cheers. And I'll give another toast when Jules finally finishes his story.'

'Haha! You know I love a bit of drama, but for your sake, Clem, I'll cut to the chase,' Jules stated. 'As I said, the planning commission meeting went ahead without any fuss or trouble until, at the end, Town Clerk Secretary Faye Wheeler forgot – I'd draw air quotes if I didn't have a sandwich in my hand – to switch off the microphone. As a result, Behrens's attempts to reassure Sheppard that the plans for Hobson Meadows would be approved were amplified throughout the meeting room for all to hear. During this exchange, Behrens told Sheppard' – he retrieved his phone from the end table and read from it – '"I have them looking at the shiny red ball – hey, look over here! – when the real issue is over there. Just wait a few weeks and I'll get you what you need. When people are fat, dumb and happy, they don't care what's going on outside the walls of their property."'

Tish's jaw dropped. 'Wow! How did everyone react?'

'Everyone? First of all, no one attends planning commission meetings unless they absolutely have to. They're so boring that we don't even cover them – we send the local public access station to record them and then upload them directly to YouTube.'

MJ nodded. 'Glen and I attended one to get a permit for our fence. Ours was the last petition to be heard and I thought I'd fall asleep waiting through that meeting. I think Glen actually did fall asleep, but then again he was half-asleep at our wedding, so . . .'

Jules cleared his throat. 'Second, it was a beautiful summer evening. I checked – highs in the low seventies, a light breeze from the northeast. Perfection. So everyone left in a hurry to go out and enjoy what was left of the day. The only people still in the room apart from Behrens and Sheppard were Councilmen Leonard Pruett and Edwin Wilson. They immediately reported it to the council and the press, which is how we got the story.'

'Why don't I remember all the details of this story?' Reade questioned.

'Because our local government is a coalition of chaos. As soon as one story breaks, there's another one to replace it. The day after the hot mic story aired, Schuyler Thompson announced the new Main Street parking regulations.'

At the mention of parking regulations, Clayton snarled.

'The day after that, it was the new vehicle registration fees,' Jules continued. 'The news cycle never comes full circle. They never allow it to. It's like the shiny red ball Behrens was talking about.'

'What happened to Faye Wheeler?' Tish asked.

'Don't know. She no longer works at Town Hall, but I'm not sure if she was fired or forced out or if she resigned. I asked around my office and everyone seems to think she was laid off, but no one is one hundred percent sure.'

'Sounds as if we'd better put Faye Wheeler at the top of our interview list,' Reade announced. 'If she left that microphone on intentionally, it's because she knew Behrens was up to no good. It would be interesting to find out what else she might know about him.'

Clayton drank the remainder of his beer with a satisfied sigh. 'I love it! The team's together again. So awesome.'

NINE

Tish spent a fitful night, tossing, turning, pulling the covers up to her chin one minute, kicking them off the next. The few times she did manage to drift off to sleep, she would awaken with a start and the distinct feeling that someone was watching her, hunting her. As the clock registered five, Tish surrendered to the fact that she would be spending the day in a sleep deficit and slid into her slippers and tiptoed out of the bedroom, past the fleece-lined beds containing the croissant shapes of a snoozing Tuna and Marlowe, and downstairs into the kitchen, where she found Jules ensconced at the vintage enamel-top table.

'Hey, is everything OK?' she asked, yawning and stretching.

'Oh, yeah. The bed, the pillows, the comforter you gave me – everything is great. Which is why Biscuit is still asleep, oh, and snoring.'

Tish smiled. 'Ditto upstairs. To be clear, the cats are snoring, not Clemson – well, at least he wasn't when I got out of bed.'

It was Jules's turn to smile. 'No, that little office of yours is a lovely haven. The source of my sleeplessness was me – every noise, every creak, every gust of wind outside the window set me on edge.'

'That's precisely how I felt – on edge. I was hot, I was cold, I couldn't get comfortable, but the trouble wasn't my body, it was my mind. I simply couldn't relax. I kept imagining someone watching me and the house, wanting to get inside.'

'Same. At one point during the night, Biscuit burped. Honey, just the sound of it made me jump so high, you practically had to scrape me off the ceiling.'

Tish's smile turned into a laugh. 'I'm sorry for laughing. I'm also sorry you slept so badly.'

'I'm sorry *you* slept so badly. Although I wish I'd known sooner that you were awake. I spent my time finishing up some work and then doom-scrolling social media. Have you heard of this chip challenge thing that teens are doing? They find the hottest chips they can find and consume them in one go. It's absolutely insane! I swear with the damage those kids are doing to their upper GI system, their next challenge is going to be chugging a cocktail of Mylanta and Gaviscon with a twist of lime.'

Tish wrinkled her nose. 'Now there's a TikTok video I never want to see.'

'Oh, speaking of gastrointestinal issues, I made some coffee. Decaf, but strong. Very strong.'

Tish glanced at the French press on the counter. 'I think I'll make a fresh pot.'

Jules nodded. 'Mind making some for me? This has an awful lot of lead for unleaded.'

'Sure,' she complied with a chuckle.

'Social media is kind of anxiety-inducing.'

'Kinda?' Tish poured Jules's attempt at coffee down the drain and rinsed the carafe.

'OK, quite anxiety-inducing. You know what I was thinking about? When you used to be stressed about exams or generally not feeling well, you used to watch those cooking shows.'

'And you and MJ would balk,' she recalled as she put the kettle on to boil. 'But then you'd both end up watching them with me and we'd make popcorn and all eventually fall asleep with the television on.'

'I love my life now and wouldn't trade it, or Maurice or my job or Biscuit, for anything in the world, but there are moments when I wish we could go back for even just a few minutes. Life seemed so much simpler.'

'Or maybe we didn't worry as much because we thought we were indestructible.'

'Probably a bit of both. You, um, you don't happen to have any of those videos available to watch right now, do you?'

'As a matter of fact, I do. Come on,' she replied before leading him into the living room.

Tish climbed into the passenger seat of Reade's SUV clutching an insulated travel mug of coffee. 'Don't tell Jules, but your coffee is far better than his.'

'I learned from the best.' He slid behind the driver's wheel and started the engine. 'Hey, I'm sorry I woke the two of you in the living room earlier. Had I known you both had such a rough night . . .'

'It's fine. I'm glad you woke us. Jules had to be at the station and I didn't want to miss our investigation this morning. Besides, that ninety-minute-long nap I got helped quite a bit.'

'Well, next time you can't sleep, let me know and we can talk or I can make you tea or something.'

'So that way we can both be bleary-eyed the next morning?'

'It would be worth it.' He leaned across the center console and kissed her.

'Thanks, sweetie.' She kissed him back. 'However, I still contend that one of us should be lucid before we question people. Speaking of which, what's our schedule today?'

'We're starting with Faye Wheeler, so we can hear her version of the hot mic story. Then we're moving on to Tripp Sennette, Leonard Pruett, Judson Darley, Edwin Wilson. And, finally, we'll pay a visit to Gavin Sheppard.'

'Five politicians and a sleazy land developer. You know how to show a girl a good time,' she joked.

'Yeah, I thought about that. How about when we're done for the day we drive down to that little market in Richmond you like so much and shop for our Thanksgiving meal?'

'Really?' she asked excitedly.

'Yep, I know how you love menu planning and shopping. I thought it might be a nice break from everything that's gone on. I also don't want to lose sight of the fact that this is our first holiday together.'

'I don't either. I feel lucky to have found you, but after yesterday and how close we came to . . . well, I feel even luckier.'

'Same here.' He clutched her gloved hand. 'So, I probably shouldn't even ask, but have you given any thought to the menu?'

'You know I did. How about a starter of warm brie with a compote of figs and pears?'

'Ooh, sounds delicious. Are you going to use those red pears you've been buying?'

'Yes, they're beautiful, aren't they?'

'Yeah, I had one with my lunch every day last week.'

'I noticed they disappeared rather quickly. For the main course, there's a spiced Cornish game hen recipe I want to try. It's served on a bed of couscous studded with dried apricots, golden raisins and pomegranate seeds. I'd serve that with a side of roasted Brussels sprouts.'

'Hmm, I've never had game hen before.'

'They're like tiny chickens,' she explained. 'But what's nice is there's just enough meat on one of them for one person, so we won't have a refrigerator of leftovers.'

'No leftovers?' An awkward silence descended over the SUV.

'You're right, that doesn't work, does it?'

'No, no . . . I was just thinking out loud. Your menu sounds delicious and elegant.'

'And not like Thanksgiving at all. I mean what is Thanksgiving without that late-night leftover turkey sandwich with cranberry sauce?'

'And stuffing. I add stuffing to mine,' Reade mentioned.

'OK, I'll save the Cornish hens for New Year's Eve.'

'Perfect.'

'And I'll get a small turkey breast for Thanksgiving which I'll make with my great-grandmother's bread, onion, celery and sage stuffing.'

'Wait? You have an heirloom recipe for stuffing and I haven't heard about it until now? Stuffing is the perfect holiday food. I have terrific memories of helping my grandmother crumble up the stale bread while watching *Charlie Brown's Thanksgiving* on TV. She'd save up supermarket coupons to get a free turkey. It was always tiny, but she made it taste great and, to help fill me up, she'd make a double batch of stuffing.'

'That's a sweet memory,' Tish said with a smile. 'Should I make a double batch for us?'

'No. Although my affection for it has remained the same, my metabolism hasn't.'

She laughed. 'OK, single batch it is. Are the sprouts good with you?'

'Oh yeah, it's isn't the holidays without them.'

'I feel exactly the same way. And for dessert, I was going to make pumpkin mousse.'

Reade nodded. 'Yeah, yeah, I could do that.'

'But, pumpkin pie is *the* pie for Turkey Day, isn't it?'

'It's also the breakfast of champions the next morning. A hot cup of coffee, a slice of pumpkin pie with a dollop of whipped cream – heaven.'

'But don't you find your energy levels crash before noon?'

'Yes, but that just means I'm ready for another turkey sandwich.'

'Well, you sold me. We'll do an old-fashioned Thanksgiving, just the two of us.'

Faye Wheeler lived in a Craftsman-style cottage just a few blocks away from Town Hall at the end of a tree-lined cul-de-sac. Reade parked the SUV along the curb and, with Tish at his side, ascended the front steps to the porch and rang the doorbell. After several seconds elapsed, a woman peered through the sidelights. She was about fifty years of age with shoulder-length blonde hair and glasses.

Reade held his badge aloft, prompting the woman to open the door and step outside.

The sheriff introduced himself and Tish. 'We're here to ask you some questions about Deputy Mayor Royce Behrens.'

'I'm not sure what I can tell you, Sheriff. I haven't worked at Town Hall in months.'

'We understand that, but you did work with the deputy mayor for a number of years, didn't you?'

'I didn't really work "with" him. I was an administrator, a pencil-pusher. I worked for the council and the town clerk. The mayor and deputy mayor have their own staff, but I'd pitch in whenever an extra pair of hands were needed.'

'Still, you knew him in a professional capacity, did you not?'

'Y-y-yes, I suppose so.'

'Then we need to speak with you.'

Faye glanced up and down the block nervously. 'All right, but we'll have to go around back. My mother is in the living room watching TV right now. She's immunocompromised, so I don't like to have too many guests around her.'

'We understand completely. We can even talk out here, if you'd prefer,' Reade offered. 'If you want to go get your coat—'

'No,' she insisted, scanning the neighborhood. 'No, let's go around back to the kitchen.'

She stepped off the front porch and cut across the now-brown front lawn of the cottage to the driveway, where she led them past the ten-year-old car parked there to a metal storm door. Pulling it open, she waved them inside.

The cottage kitchen was older – possibly original to the house

– with vintage wood cabinets and a scalloped wood valance over the sink and window, but the sunshine-yellow color of the walls and the pristine white floor tiles kept it light, bright and welcoming.

Once they were all inside the house, Faye visibly relaxed. 'I really don't know what to tell you about Mr Behrens. Have you spoken to his wife? Or his mother, Ms Annabelle?'

'We have, but we need your perspective on things. We know about the hot microphone incident after the June twenty-ninth planning commission meeting.'

Faye's demeanor quickly grew frosty. 'I'm afraid I can't tell you anything about that.'

'If you refuse to talk to us, we'll just come back here with a subpoena, Ms Wheeler,' Reade threatened.

'You don't understand. I *can't* talk to you about that. I signed a non-disclosure agreement with the council prior to retiring. If I talk to you or anyone else about what happened that day, I'll lose my pension, my insurance, everything. I have a sick mother and a kid who just started college. I can't afford to be cut off without a cent.'

'They can't cut you off, Ms Wheeler. Non-disclosure agreements don't cover conversations with law enforcement. Also, that pension money is yours – they cannot legally touch it. Nor can they touch your health insurance – it's protected by the COBRA act. So long as you continue to pay the premiums, it cannot be revoked by your former employer.'

A dubious Wheeler folded her arms across her chest.

'I know a labor attorney. If the council tries to take anything away from you after speaking with me, she'll help you sue them.'

Wheeler glanced at Tish, as if for confirmation that Reade would keep his word.

Tish nodded. 'We won't let them bully you.'

'All right, I'll talk to you,' the woman agreed. 'But first, I need to get my mother back to her room. She's overdue for her last morning pill and a nap.'

'May I lend you a hand?' the sheriff asked.

'No, I couldn't. You're not here for that.'

'No, but I've been trained for these kind of things.' He pulled a surgical mask from the pocket of his black Carhartt jacket. 'I did a year of pre-med before switching to criminal justice.'

'In that case, come on then.' She led him into the living room.

While Reade and Faye Wheeler helped Faye's mother back into bed, Tish perused the array of postcards and photos that festooned the refrigerator. There were photo Christmas cards soon to be replaced by a new batch of seasonal greetings, snapshots of Faye and her mother – prior to her illness – on vacation at the beach and in New York City, and shots of Faye, her mother, and a good-looking, dark-haired boy, posing and smiling for the camera. The same dark-haired boy, at different ages, appeared in photos that lined the living-room walls.

'That's my boy, Ethan,' Faye explained upon her return to the kitchen.

'He's a handsome young man,' Tish complimented.

Faye appeared discomfited by the remark. 'Better than that, he's kind. He's a good boy, my Ethan. Never once gave me a moment of trouble, even though he could have given—' She paused abruptly. 'He's at Old Dominion University on a full scholarship. Full for this year, anyway, but it means the student loans will be minimal. There's still room and board and books and a car to pay for, though. He works part time to help, even though I told him not to.'

'You must be very proud of him,' Reade said.

'He's the one thing in my life that I actually got right,' she said ruefully.

'I'm sure that isn't true,' Tish insisted.

Faye merely raised her eyebrows and then stared down at the floor.

'So Royce Behrens?' Reade prompted.

'Royce was first elected to the council nearly nineteen years ago. He was so different from the other councilmen. He was young, bright, energetic. He promised to bring back the policies that had made his grandfather the best-loved mayor in our town's history and, what's more, Royce seemed to possess the get-up-and-go to actually do it. He honestly seemed too good to be true.' She gazed off into the distance.

'May we sit down?' Reade asked, seeking to wake Faye from her fugue state.

She jumped back to life. 'Oh! Oh, yes. We can move into the living room now that my mother is back in her room. I should probably go check on her, too.'

As Tish and Reade took their places on an overstuffed blue sofa,

Faye peeked in on her mother. 'She's asleep,' she announced upon her return. 'She usually gets up between four and five and then falls asleep after her morning meds. When that happens, she's out until one o'clock, but there are times when she becomes agitated. An interruption in sleep patterns is a common problem for patients with Lewy Body Dementia.'

'Do you have any help?' Tish asked.

'No. When I was working for the town, I could afford a part-time nurse to come and bathe and watch her during the mornings, then I'd work from home during the afternoon.'

'Sounds like a good arrangement.'

'Yes, Councilman Darley came up with the idea. He's an old curmudgeon, but he's always been fair to me. He's always been fair to everyone, actually. He should have been mayor, if you ask my opinion,' she said with a sniff. 'But folks would never have voted for him. They never could look beneath that grumpy exterior, you know?'

'So you think Councilman Darley should have been mayor instead of Schuyler Thompson?' Reade questioned.

'Mr Thompson just says "yes" to everyone in order to keep his job. He's not in charge – he's governing by the council's edict. Or should I say, the council as led by Royce Behrens. Now that Royce is gone, maybe Mr Thompson will grow a backbone and govern the way he sees fit, instead of being afraid the council will try to force him out. If he did that, he might just be OK.'

At the prospect of Schuyler being an effective mayor, it was Tish's turn to sniff. 'And Royce Behrens? Did he have what it takes to be a good mayor?'

'I once believed he did. We all believed it, but it eventually became clear that it was all a lie. Royce had absolutely no intention of helping working families. He only sought to help himself.'

'When did you begin to understand that Behrens wasn't what he originally touted himself to be?'

Faye drew a deep breath and flopped into the plaid wing chair adjacent to the front window. 'It wasn't anything sudden. It was more of a gradual realization. A vote against a law that might make things easier for the average taxpayer. A brand-new, expensive suit and a pair of Italian leather shoes. Meetings with land developers looking to build in towns outside of Hobson Glen.'

'You mean Gavin Sheppard?'

'Among others. Gavin just happened to be the one who took the bait.'

'So Behrens was shopping this town to developers?'

Faye nodded. 'As if Royce didn't already have enough money. Money to him was power, I think. I'm guessing, of course. I have not the slightest idea what made that man tick, apart from self-preservation. His mother, Ms Annabelle, once told me that he was exactly like his father and, although I don't doubt it's true, it saddened me. There comes a time in one's life, don't you think, when someone can overcome their nature – when a person should try to do better.'

Tish thought of her own father – his affairs, his lies, even while her mother was on her deathbed. 'Yes, but sadly, there are times when instincts are too strong.'

'Maybe, but I believe that with proper support and awareness one can overcome instinct,' Faye insisted.

'So, the night of June twenty-ninth,' Reade interjected. 'Was that you trying to do better? Did you decide to leave the microphone on as a way to warn others?'

'I don't know. I can't remember thinking to myself that I'd leave it on. It just . . . happened. I set up for the meeting just as I always had, and then, because Ethan was home with my mother, I waited the meeting out in my office. When I heard the meeting wrapping up, I went back out to the meeting room to tidy up and switch off the sound system, only I never switched it off. I stared at it for a good amount of time while I deliberated my next move. I knew that leaving it on and capturing something might result in my being fired, but I wanted – I needed – everyone to see through the façade, the lies. Royce had lied to everyone. He'd cultivated public fear so that he could stay on the council, and then, from the council, he'd become mayor, and from the mayorship, congress, and from there maybe even the White House. That was his plan, that was his goal, and he'd hurt anyone who got in his way. Anyone.'

'What happened afterward?

'The council met with the town clerk and it was decided that since I'd been an ideal employee for so many years, I should take a week off, with pay, to gather my thoughts and get a rest. Royce had other ideas. He wanted me to pay for what I did. He spoke with Tripp Sennette and insisted that my position be terminated. It was

Councilman Darley who suggested that I resign and take an early retirement; that way I didn't lose my income. Before I could retire, Councilman Sennette and Royce Behrens worked together on the non-disclosure. They presented it to me on my last day of work and warned me not to speak to anyone.' Faye broke down in tears. 'I've been so afraid . . . so afraid to talk to anyone, so fearful I'd lose my earnings, my house, how to pay for my son's books, my mother, the medical bills. God, I hope you're right about the non-disclosure, Sheriff, because Royce Behrens would take anyone down who stood in his way. He might be dead, but the man knew nothing of mercy. Nothing at all.'

TEN

R eade pulled the SUV into the Town Hall parking lot in preparation for their next interview.

'Didn't Clayton tell us that all town offices were closed out in deference to the passing of the deputy mayor?' Tish questioned.

'Yep,' Reade confirmed. 'I also received an email about the closure late last night. But this is where Mr Sennette said I could find him.'

'Maybe it's quieter than his house,' she suggested as she opened the passenger side door of the SUV and stepped outside.

Reade followed her lead and exited the vehicle, locking it behind them. 'Whatever his reason for meeting here, I'm sure we're about to find out.'

'I'm afraid I don't have much time for questions, Sheriff,' Tripp Sennette warned from Royce Behrens's desk and office chair as he logged onto a laptop computer. 'I need to catch up on the late deputy mayor's work, so this town of ours doesn't grind to a halt.'

'Are we to assume that you're set to become the new deputy mayor?' Tish asked.

'No, as senior councilman, the duty falls upon me to take over the position in an interim capacity. However, I'm reasonably certain that the appointment will become permanent just as soon as our next business meeting takes place,' he stated, smoothing the lapels of his dark blue suit jacket with his fingertips. 'It leaves a council seat open, but it's the only move that makes sense.'

'Do you happen to know who shut down the town offices yesterday?'

'I did. With Royce Behrens's death, our staff needed time and space in which to collect their thoughts and grieve and pray.'

'That's some pretty quick thinking on your part,' Reade said admiringly.

'We strive to be efficient,' Sennette bragged as he took off his thick-rimmed glasses and cleaned them on his bright red tie. In addition to his presence in Royce's office, the bright nature of his attire made it clear that the 'Town Hall Day of Mourning' did not extend to him.

'So efficient that your shutdown preceded my official statement.'

'I was there at the Springs yesterday, Sheriff. I fired the starter's pistol. The only person not to walk away from the event was Royce Behrens. Didn't take a brain surgeon to figure out he was dead. All you did was make his death official.'

'Exactly. As interim deputy mayor – and de facto mayor while Schuyler Thompson was temporarily unavailable during his medical treatment and subsequent questioning – one would have thought you'd have spoken to me before issuing such an order to your staff. I'd have also thought that you'd have spoken to me for an update regarding any possible lockdown and shelter-in-place orders for the town since there was a shooter on the loose.'

'Why complicate matters? If you needed me, you would have found me. I thought it best to let you do your job while I did mine.'

'Speaking of jobs, how did it come about that you were chosen to start the race?'

'Tradition has it that a member of the council fires the starter pistol. I did it last year, so someone else should have taken over this year, but everyone was too busy to go down to the Springs on a Friday afternoon.'

'Hmm, that's strange. Edwin Wilson was there,' Tish pointed out.

'Yes, well.' He looked away with a chuckle. 'Edwin's not a senior member, so that wouldn't have looked right.'

Tish wondered if it was Edwin's lack of seniority or his skin color that 'wouldn't have looked right' in Sennette's eyes. 'I don't know. Edwin's a good man and very popular with the townspeople. I think he would have been great.'

'Ms Tarragon, the Turkey Trot has been a tradition in Hobson Glen for nearly fifty-two years. There are certain proprieties that need to be followed.'

Proprieties? Tish folded her arms across her chest. No, the trouble with Edwin Wilson wasn't his newbie status, but the fact that he looked different than the other councilmen. 'It's still surprising he wasn't allowed to participate. It's also surprising that Judson Darley wasn't available – he's retired, isn't he? And, technically, the most senior member of the council as he is the oldest.'

'He's the oldest, yes, but I'm *the* senior councilman in organizational terms – meaning I run meetings and call votes – so naturally I would be first choice. In addition,' he began laughing, 'Darley's probably so slow on the draw we'd still be waiting for him to start the race.'

Ageist and racist. Lovely.

'What occurred after you shot the starter's pistol?' Reade asked.

'You know what happened, Sheriff. You were there. Behrens and Thompson took off down the path. A few moments later, a rifle fired.'

'And you? What did you do?'

'As a public servant, my instinct was to run toward the shots to see what I could do to help—'

Tish suppressed an urge to roll her eyes.

'—but then you stepped forward, Sheriff, and told everyone to stay put and hunker down.'

'Did you?'

'Yes. I found a thicket of shrubs to the right of the podium and ducked behind it.'

'Was anyone with you?'

'No, I was alone. My wife doesn't typically join me on council business. She doesn't follow politics much. She prefers to get her news from me and focus her efforts on her women's clubs, knitting, and maintaining our restored Colonial on the edge of town.'

And misogynist, Tish added to her mental tally of Sennette's flaws.

Reade glanced at Tish. It was his way of asking if she'd like to jump in on the questioning. Fearful of what she might say at that particular moment, she wrinkled her nose and shook her head.

'Was anyone near you?'

'No, everyone else stayed to the other side of the podium, closer to the trailhead.'

'What happened after you hid?'

'Nothing. I remained hidden until you gave the all clear. Then I gave a statement to one of your people, got checked out by one of the medics, and was discharged around four. Your officer has my story,' he said, obviously hoping that the words would result in Reade and Tish leaving him alone and going on to question someone else.

'Yes, I reviewed your statement yesterday evening,' Reade acknowledged. 'What was your relationship with Royce Behrens like?'

'Amicable. We enjoyed a solid working relationship – didn't socialize much away from council, but neither of us were really interested in pursuing a friendship.'

'So you had no issues with Behrens? Nothing that might have hindered that solid working relationship?'

'No, no issues at all.'

'Then you agreed with all his policies,' Reade presumed.

Sennette chose his words carefully. 'I – didn't *dis*agree with him, but I didn't always agree with him either. There were some bills he advocated that I believed were too strict or too lenient, but we always worked together to find common ground.'

'And the Hobson Meadows development – was that something about which you agreed?'

Sennette fell silent. 'I, um, I wholeheartedly believe that such a development will greatly benefit our community.'

'*Such a* development?' Tish parroted. 'But not necessarily the Hobson Meadows development?'

'You're putting words in my mouth, miss,' he snapped. 'If the plans for Hobson Meadows were to pass council scrutiny and receive town approval, I'm sure it would be quite successful.'

'*If* it passes?'

'Yes, the people of Hobson Glen need to have their say. I can't predict their response to the proposal as it currently stands. There may be requests for modifications. It might be voted down. I have no idea of knowing.'

'I thought Royce Behrens was ensuring the Hobson Meadows plans were approved,' she asserted.

Sennette's face grew red. 'I'm not sure what you're talking about.'

'Behrens planned to distract the electorate. While they were "looking elsewhere," he planned to pass whatever legislation was required to proceed with the development.'

'I know nothing about this,' the councilman insisted, pounding on the laptop keyboard, although it was clear from his reaction that he did.

'"Keep people fat, dumb, and comfortable enough and they don't care what happens beyond their own walls,"' Tish paraphrased.

Sennette finally broke down. 'Those were Royce's words, not mine!'

'Ah, so you do remember them,' Reade said with a grin.

'I do, but that silly newswoman took them out of context.'

A news*woman. Of course*, Tish thought to herself. 'Out of context? I'm not sure in what context those words could ever be considered positive. Besides, there were witnesses present.'

'Edwin Wilson and Leonard Pruett heard Behrens boasting to Sheppard. He had a tendency to boast – most of what he boasted about wasn't true. It was a quirk of his, that's all.'

'I'd consider that more of a character flaw than a quirk,' Reade asserted.

'You sound like Wilson and Pruett. They never liked Behrens. His bragging, his attitude . . . they always had a beef with the guy. They disliked him so much that that they were always the dissenting votes on the council. They were never willing to compromise.'

'If I were faced with a deputy mayor who thought the towns-people were livestock, I wouldn't compromise either,' Tish stated.

'Like I said, those comments were taken out of context. Wilson and Pruett heard them and they made the whole thing political. Things were bad enough between them and Behrens without it being plastered all over the news. And it was all that damn stupid woman's fault for leaving the microphone on.'

Reade seized the opportunity to confront Sennette with the truth. 'And so you made her sign a non-disclosure agreement and then forced her to retire.'

A crimson stain crept up Sennette's sinewy neck, into his face, and the entirety of his bald head. 'You . . . I . . . That . . .' He snorted and sputtered. 'We couldn't – we couldn't just let her go around town telling lies about the deputy mayor!'

'Lies or her misinterpretation? I thought you said his words were being taken out of context?'

'They *were* taken out of context, but we couldn't let the public get wind of the fact that councilmen were at odds with each other.

People need to have confidence in their government. They can't think that they're at each other's throats.'

'At each other's throats? Are you trying to say that Wilson and Pruett both hated Behrens enough to kill him?'

Sennette mopped his forehead with the handkerchief in his suit pocket and straightened his tie. 'As the future deputy mayor, it would be both unseemly and irresponsible of me to put forth such a statement, but from one man doing his job to another, I sincerely think your office should explore the possibility.'

ELEVEN

'Ugh. How can people like that be on our town council? It's depressing, disgusting, and disappointing. I mean, who voted for him?' Tish complained from the passenger seat of the SUV while Reade pulled to a halt outside Leonard Pruett's split-level home in Hobson Meadows's most populated neighborhood. It was already their third interview of the day and it was just going on eleven thirty.

'What? You don't envision the day when you give up the café and throw yourself into women's clubs and remodeling our house instead of helping me with my "business?"' Reade teased.

'Keep talking like that and you can kiss that Thanksgiving stuffing goodbye,' she threatened.

'I was joking! Joking,' he nearly shouted.

'Are you saying that because you were, in fact, joking? Or because I threatened to take away your favorite part of the holiday dinner?'

'Honestly? Both.'

'OK, I believe you. Stuffing is back on the menu,' Tish said, opening the passenger side door of the SUV. The moment her foot hit the pavement, a pumpkin came hurtling through the air, smashing at her feet.

'Sorry! I didn't see you there until it was too late. It didn't splatter you, did it?' A bearded man in his mid- to late fifties jogged out to meet the couple.

'Nope, just missed me. Had I known this was a flying squash area, I might have worn a helmet,' she joked.

'I'm so sorry. I was just giving the garden a good clearing out before the ground freezes, and I tossed out one of the rotting pumpkins for the birds to feast on. Hey, you, um, you run the café in town, don't you?'

'Yes, I did. I mean, I do, once it reopens.'

'Day after Thanksgiving, right?'

'That's right. We'll be open bright and early for breakfast.'

'Now that's a Black Friday line I won't mind waiting in. You know, I have a glut of turnips and parsnips from the garden this year. Care to take any off my hands? My freezer is already full.'

Tish awkwardly shifted her weight from one foot to the other. 'You, um, might want to hold off on offering me homegrown produce until you find out why I'm here,' she cautioned.

Reade held his badge aloft. 'Leonard Pruett? I'm Sheriff Clemson Reade.'

Pruett nodded. 'You're here about Royce Behrens, aren't you? Come on back into the garden.'

To call the side yard of Pruett's oversized corner lot a garden was misleading. It was, indeed, a space for growing things – dozens upon dozens of vines, bushes, plants and trees appeared to have thrived there during the warmer months. However, nothing had been planted or arranged in any discernible order and any spaces between the fruit or vegetable-producing flora was filled with what appeared to have been tall grass and weeds.

'I strive to keep my property as a "wildscape" rather than a traditional garden,' Pruett explained. 'I propagate wildflowers and native plants to grow alongside my food crops, and plant peas and beans with the corn so that the stalks serve as living trellises. Although I do prune back some of the wildflowers so they and the food-bearing plants don't vie for resources, I don't do much except water, which I do by collecting rain in barrels. I've successfully attracted bees, rabbits, deer, and eleven different kinds of songbirds to this yard over the years. Unheard of for a suburban garden.'

'Impressive,' Tish remarked.

'Thanks. It doesn't look like much, I know, but it provides enough veg to last me the entire year, with preservation and freezing – plus I'm helping our ecosystem.'

'It's amazing, Mr Pruett,' Reade said.

'Leonard,' he corrected. 'Now, what do you want to know?'

'What did you think of Royce Behrens?'

'He was a despicable human being without any moral compass whatsoever. If he couldn't count it and put it in his bank account, it held no interest for him.'

'That's pretty . . .' Tish struggled to find the appropriate word.

'Harsh? Yes, but it's true. I'll have been with the council for eight years next month. During that time, I tried to pass several new bills to help save our citizens and the environment on a local level. I tried to institute a law that requires residents to compost food waste, the compost of which would be used on the field and plants at the rec park. Shot down. Cordon off a section of said rec park for a garden where local schoolchildren can learn where their food comes from and then donate the harvest to the local food shelf? Shot down. Ensuring our drinking water and the pipes that carry it are free of lead and toxins? Shot down. Offering a local sliding scale property tax reduction for working parents and seniors? Shot down. Offering a tax reduction to homeowners who install solar panels on their homes? Shot down. Passing a bill that ensures our children – all our children – have access to healthy school lunches featuring fresh local produce? Shot all the way down. Do you need more of a profile?'

'No, that's probably enough.'

'The bills you mentioned,' Tish ventured, 'they would have been voted on by the entire council, not just Royce Behrens.'

'They never made it to a vote, because Behrens argued that they would cost the town too much money. Even though I found a way to fund each and every one of them, and fund them in a manner that would actually reduce taxes. I put forth an idea for a community green-up day, where everyone pitches in and removes the trash from the side of the roads and in our parks and green spaces. Behrens, instead, hired a buddy of his who runs a sanitation company to do the job. It cost Hobson Glen tens of thousands of dollars, but he got accolades for cleaning up the town.'

'How did that make you feel?' Reade asked.

'How do you think it made me feel? About what a man who has let his garden become a nature habitat despite the condemnation of the neighbors should feel – upset, angry, at times even furious. Actually, I was furious most of the time. Until Edwin Wilson was elected to the council, I also felt completely helpless. I wondered all these years if *I* wasn't the problem. I wondered if my ideas were just far too progressive. I even wondered for a time if I was completely nuts. I mean, didn't anyone else see Behrens the way I did? Didn't anyone else realize he was a charlatan and a liar? Edwin has been a valuable addition to the council. He and I are still outnumbered, but he's well-educated, well-respected, and we see eye-to-eye on most issues. He doesn't let his garden run wild,' Leonard said with a smirk, 'but I don't hold that against him.'

'There was a meeting a few months ago which ended with you and Edwin Wilson overhearing a conversation between Royce Behrens and Gavin Sheppard,' Tish prompted. 'Can you tell us what happened?'

Pruett nodded again. 'I remember it vividly. It was a planning commission meeting to discuss Hobson Meadows. Not only is Hobson Meadows a bad deal for the residents of Hobson Glen in that it will drive home prices and property taxes sky high, but the plans for the development places it adjacent to tidal wetlands. When I asked Behrens about permits during the meeting, he dodged the question completely. Probably another case of him "knowing a guy" who'd fix the problem.

'As if all of that wasn't enough of a news story, after the meeting, Edwin and I overheard him telling Sheppard that he was essentially going to rig things so that the plans would pass no matter what.'

'Do you know how he would have done that?'

'I took it that he'd pass some legislation that would appease everyone and make them less likely to balk over the plans. Like a small property tax break to offset the rise in gas and electric rates, for instance. While everyone's happy with the couple of hundred dollars they saved during the year, they vote to approve the Hobson Meadows plans, only to discover years later that it's a big mistake. That's not to say the electorate of this town aren't smart – quite the contrary – but it's tough to make the best decisions when your wallet is being squeezed from several different directions.'

'What happened next?'

'Edwin and I reported it to Sennette and, when he told us we were overreacting, we contacted the media. I'm sorry we did that. If the story hadn't made it on to the local news that night, Faye Wheeler might still have a job.'

'At least she wasn't fired,' Tish noted.

'True, but she's still forced to live on a fraction of what she was earning. Plus she's left to care for her mother on her own, now that her son's gone off to school. She can't afford to hire a nurse, which is what she'd need to do to hold down a part-time job to help make up the difference. There also aren't many places in town who will hire her, poor thing. I know Edwin and I offered to give her refer- ences, but without the council's endorsement as a whole, she's in a real jam. I bring her vegetables, honey, local cheese and eggs every other week under the false pretense that I have more than I can possibly consume, but I think she might be on to me,' he said with a gentle smile.

'So it's safe to assume that you disagreed with the council's action against her,' Reade put forth in an effort to test the man's temper.

'Disagreed? I thought it was a disgrace. With everything on that woman's plate, it's no wonder she made a mistake. And, if leaving that mic on wasn't a mistake, she deserved a raise – maybe even a medal. But Behrens was after blood and, as per usual, he got what he wanted.' Pruett scowled. 'I love life. I love living things: animals, people, plants, insects. Behrens was a plague on this town. Whoever bumped him off did the world a favor. Perhaps now, balance can be restored.'

'Where were you yesterday around noon?'

Pruett's mood lightened. 'I suppose I just gave myself a motive, didn't I, Sheriff?' he noted with a smirk. 'Sadly, I don't have an alibi. I was on a video call until eleven thirty with clients in Arlington who have since hired me to design a sustainable garden with a water feature. After that, I was in my kitchen, blanching an abundance of kale and late spinach for the freezer. The cooler weather has them growing like wildfire. And, no, no one can substantiate my alibi. However, in my defense, you'll find I'm one of the few people in town who neither owns a gun nor has the remotest idea of how to fire one.'

'Filth!' Judson Darley vehemently declared. 'Royce Behrens was nothing but filth, just like his daddy before him.'

Although only a mile away, Judson Darley's tired-looking Dutch Colonial home stood in stark contrast to Pruett's split-level property. In lieu of a lush, verdant garden, Darley's house was surrounded by a landscape of white rocks and asphalt – an obvious attempt to keep maintenance to a minimum for the septegenarian. And light years from being 'green,' Darley's house itself was clad in red asbestos shingles and boasted ancient, energy-sucking appliances.

'What made Behrens filth, sir?' Reade questioned as he spied Tish in mid-yawn. It was a little after twelve and her sleepless night was clearly catching up to her.

'He had no respect for anything or anyone. Not our town, not our institutions, not even his own wife and family. No wonder he was shot.' Darley leaned back in his kitchen chair and placed his heads behind his head.

'Mind if we ask where you were yesterday?'

'Don't mind at all. Was walking ol' Montogomery over there.' Darley nodded toward the elderly black Lab asleep on his dog bed a few yards away. At the mention of his name, Montgomery looked up, but upon the realization that no treats were being distributed, he settled back down to his nap.

'Did anyone see you?'

The gray-haired man shrugged. 'Don't know. Neighborhood's quiet at that time of day. Kids at school. People at work. Then there was the event at the Springs. Didn't see anyone or talk to anyone, if that's what you're asking.'

'Going back to Royce Behrens . . .' Reade prompted.

'Royce was a wild one from way back. Gave Ms Annabelle a heck of a time. Never listened. Never minded her. He even got physical with her more than once. She talked about sending him to a military academy for a time, but she never went through with it. She was always too soft with him. Way too soft. But she was pretty much on her own in raising him. His father was useless. That's why I give Faye Wheeler so much credit. She's raised that boy of hers, Ethan, all on her own. He's turned out to be a fine boy. Fine boy.'

Darley's comment about Faye provided the perfect opening for questions. 'How do you feel about Faye being forced into retirement?' Tish asked.

'A cryin' shame. A real cryin' shame. Faye's a lovely woman. Good at her job, too. It was absolutely unfair what the council did to her. She was with us for years, but the moment her foot slipped, Behrens was ready to toss her to the curb. And her with a sick mama and her boy heading off for school. Behrens and Sennette wanted to fire her. I tried to reason with them. Tried to get them to let her stay on, but they wouldn't listen. They just wouldn't listen. I was eventually able to sell them on the idea of her retiring. Told them how women that age get crazy and forgetful and all that.'

Tish wrinkled her nose.

Darley stared over the top of his bifocals, his brown eyes fixed on Tish. 'I didn't like saying that, Ms Tarragon – nor do I believe it. But they were convinced that Faye left that microphone on deliberately. I even wondered about it myself. But I didn't want Faye to lose everything for what she did. She didn't deserve it. Took hours of flattery, wheedling, nonsense and needless talking, but it worked. Faye got her retirement, but little else.'

'Did you know that Tripp Sennette and Royce Behrens made Faye sign a non-disclosure agreement as a condition of her retirement?' Reade questioned.

Darley's already weathered countenance hardened. 'No. They forced her to sign something away?'

'Only if she broke the agreement. She wasn't permitted to speak about the meeting night and what transpired afterward. If she did, she'd lose her income and insurance.'

Darley appeared genuinely flabbergasted. 'I had no idea. Poor Faye. How? Why? How could they do such a thing?'

'Legally, they can't,' Reade explained. 'It's a bullying tactic intended to keep Faye from talking.'

The older man sat upright. 'I had absolutely no idea. If I had any inkling, I'd have fought it with everything I had.'

'Well, you'd said earlier that Royce Behrens has no respect,' Tish reminded.

'Yeah, but this is a new low. Running around on his wife and family with that lawyer lady is one thing, but crushing a decent, hardworking woman into the ground and threatening to leave her with nothing, just so his reputation remained intact, is another.'

Reade spoke up. 'What's this about a lawyer lady?'

'Her name's Lucy something-or-other. Lucy . . . that's it! Lucy Van Gorder. She has an office in Richmond and another one in Petersburg. Behrens's personal lawyer, but he brought her in to meet the council with the thought that she might become our consultant. Sennette refused to even bring it to a vote. Behrens already held a lot of sway over the council. Bringing in his own personal attorney to oversee council matters would have given him even more power – particularly an attorney with whom he had more than just a professional relationship.'

'Why did he want to bring his own attorney into council proceedings?'

'He said he wanted someone he trusted to review the paperwork for the Hobson Meadows development. Why he suddenly didn't trust the lawyer who worked for the council for forty years, I don't know. I'm just repeating what he told us.'

'That's interesting, considering what was overheard by Councilmen Pruett and Wilson, don't you think?'

'I don't follow you.' Darley leaned back in his chair again and blinked several times.

'According to Pruett and Wilson, Behrens was playing the old shell game to get the Hobson Meadows development plans to pass a public vote. You think Behrens might have wanted his personal attorney involved to protect him from potential fallout?' Reade ventured.

'Now wait just a minute. Behrens's words were taken out of context during that whole incident. Senior Councilman Sennette said so. Behrens was always bragging and boasting. It was no different this time around.'

'Yet you yourself called him filth,' Tish was quick to point out. 'You also were against Faye Wheeler being forced out of her job.'

'I was against how the council treated Faye Wheeler. Still am. But that was more about trust and loyalty than anything Behrens said or did that night. He completely overreacted to the situation, but it could be argued that if you can't trust your secretary to do her job, she shouldn't be doing it. And part of her job is to be discreet. After all, the first part of the word secretary is secret,' he said with a self-satisfied grin.

'You maintain that view despite Behrens's character?' she challenged.

'I do. Behrens was filth – I don't take that back for a second – but he was a good politician. A horrible, no-good human being, but an excellent politician.'

Tish was incredulous. 'What?'

'It's true. He could outmaneuver just about anyone. I'm no genius, but I've been in local government in one form or another for fifty years and he even outsmarted me. I made him a deal when he was first elected – he put my name up for deputy mayor and, when the time came that I was elected to mayor, I'd do my best to ensure he became deputy. He never did put my name up for deputy mayor. Instead he rose through the ranks, campaigned for the position himself, and won. No, Behrens was a brilliant politician . . . didn't make me hate him any less, but he was brilliant.'

TWELVE

'Royce Behrens operated on a platform of fear,' Edwin Wilson said as he offered his guests refreshments at his reserved table at the nineteenth hole of the Hobson Glen Community Golf Course.

Tish, chilled by the sudden damp turn in the weather, ordered a decaf coffee, although given her long, sleepless night, she'd been half-tempted to order a double shot of espresso. Reade, meanwhile, settled for water and, it being lunchtime, a club sandwich which he planned to share with Tish.

'Not fear *of* him,' Edwin went on to clarify. 'Fear of not voting for him. Fear of not supporting him and his ideas. Fear that if they didn't re-elect Behrens, crime would return to Hobson Glen.'

'Return?' Clemson repeated. 'It was never here in the first place. This town has the one of the lowest crime rates in the state, and I'm not just saying that because I'm sheriff. It's true.'

'I know it's true,' Edwin agreed. 'But try telling that to voters watching you and Tish out there solving murders.'

'Wait one minute. All of those murders were committed by locals,' Tish argued. 'It's not like some criminal gang came swooping into town randomly killing the residents of Hobson Glen.'

Wilson shook his head. 'Doesn't matter. Behrens has made a large section of voters afraid of what goes on outside Hobson Glen's borders. His approach was, "If murders are happening here, can you imagine what's going on elsewhere? At least, here, you have me to keep the criminals at bay." He was planning to work the same angle to get the Hobson Meadows development to pass. Tell everyone that the land would be developed anyway, so it's better if it's developed by someone who's looking after the town's best interest. That's what he was getting at after that controversial planning commission meeting. So long as you keep everyone feeling happy and safe in their own little world, they'll let you do anything.'

'Do you believe Behrens should have faced disciplinary action from the council for his efforts to deceive the residents of Hobson Glen regarding the development?' Reade asked.

'Of course, but I knew it would never happen. Behrens kept the council under his party's control – Sennette would never have jeopardized that. I did, however, think once news broke of his comments, that the people of Hobson Glen would retaliate. I had hoped that they'd kick Behrens and his plans for Hobson Meadows to the curb.'

The waitress returned with Tish's decaf, Reade's sandwich and water, and a regular coffee, French onion soup, and a slice of apple pie for Wilson. 'It's not your or Celestine's cooking, but until your café reopens, Tish, it has to do,' Wilson apologized once the waitress had left.

'Catch-as-catch-can,' Tish quipped.

'Definitely. My, um, wife, also has me on a diet, so if we can . . .'

'Keep this between us? Yeah, I think we can do that,' she assured. If Tish had ratted out even half the people who ate at her café for violating dietary restrictions, her business would never have gotten off the ground.

'Thanks, Tish. Anyway, when Sennette called Pruett's and my account of the incident "partisan politics" and then proceeded to bury the news item, I was shocked. I mean, to allow the man to essentially call their voting base "sheep" was a new low, even for him.'

'But Sennette always voted with Behrens,' Tish countered.

'He did, even though he didn't agree with him. Sennette was shrewd. He kept in good standing with Behrens for the day when Behrens became mayor. Then he'd move up the food chain by becoming deputy mayor and eventually mayor. But Sennette didn't like Behrens – not one bit. That's why I was so surprised when Sennette reacted the way he did. It was the perfect opportunity to leave Behrens to twist in the wind, but instead he doubled down in his support. It was a bizarre reaction to a situation that could have given him the upper hand. The only person who wound up being punished was the one who deserved it the least – Faye Wheeler. I tried to pull some strings to get her a job to supplement her retirement income, but her mother's illness precludes Faye traveling very far out of town.'

'So you were against Ms Wheeler's forced retirement,' Reade presumed after ingesting his first bite of sandwich.

'Absolutely. She had done a service to the community by leaving that mic on.'

'Then you believe she left the microphone on intentionally?'

'Definitely. I had seen Faye prior to the meeting and she wasn't her usual upbeat self. There was something weighing on her mind – something important. I recall I even asked her about it. I asked whether her mother and son were OK because that's how heavy her mood was. Looking back, it's clear she was struggling with her decision to expose Behrens for the fraud he really was. Sadly, all her worry was for nothing – exposing Behrens didn't make much of a difference.'

'I know you and your wife were with us at the time of the shooting and then you both hid under the table with Tish after the shooting occurred, but did you notice anything odd the day of the shooting?'

'No, I've been racking my brain, trying to remember if someone came into the offices during the time I was there – someone who may have had a complaint about Behrens, but apart from the usual grievances about parking tickets and the like, I came up empty, except . . .'

Reade raised an eyebrow. 'Except?'

'Bill Bull. He was a builder in this area years back.'

'I've seen that name cross my desk recently,' Reade recalled.

'I'm sure you have, Sheriff. You shouldn't have, though. Bull was a great builder. He did reasonably well for himself, too. Built himself a nice house on the outskirts of town. Even ran for town council. Lost to none other than Royce Behrens – wherein begins our story. Bull couldn't let the loss go. He accused Behrens of cheating and misrepresentation and a myriad of other offenses, which, in hindsight, sound completely plausible. But, back then, Bull's complaints were dismissed out of hand as simple jealousy and poor conduct.

'Then the recession hit,' Wilson continued. 'Bull's business slowed down to a crawl. No new homes were being built and any existing homeowners were holding on to their hard-earned cash best they could. As his business dwindled, his claims against Behrens amplified. All his problems, he thought, could be traced back to Behrens and his political loss. Bull's wife eventually left with the kids – she simply couldn't reason with him any longer – and his behavior worsened. He tried to sell his house, but no one was buying large properties, so he rented a small shop on Main Street where he also lived. When Bull received a fine for breaking code by parking his construction vehicles outside his shop, thus closing off the shoulder of the road, he refused to pay and accused the council of harassment on the grounds that he was a black man. Things finally came to a head—'

Reade completed the story, 'When Bull threatened to shoot Behrens in Town Hall and then kill his family in their home, the sheriff's office arrested Bull and brought him in. He was sent to prison for fifteen years for stalking, carrying an illegal firearm, drug possession, violating a court order of protection, and threatening a public official and his family.'

'You read the case file,' Wilson said, impressed.

'I read it and remember it. I was relatively new to the office back then, so the Bull indictment was one of the first big cases I'd encountered.'

'Well, then you'll also know that he was recently released.'

'He was. I received the paperwork from the State Office of Corrections a few weeks ago. Bull is staying with his sister in Lynchburg – he was remanded to her custody while he finishes out his parole.'

'That might be so,' Wilson allowed, 'but rumor has it that he was seen over in Ashton Courthouse just last week.'

'Clayton, I need you to trace the whereabouts of one William Bull, age fifty-two. Bull was recently released from Pocahontas Correctional Facility over in Tazewell County,' Reade directed into his phone after they'd finished their interview and their lunch. 'We made the convicting arrest. Yes . . . yeah . . . no, just call me when you track him down. Thanks, Clayton.'

'Do you really think Bull is our killer?' Tish asked as she drove the SUV to Gailey and Sheppard Development Company in Richmond.

'If he was in the area at the time of the shooting, he's a credible suspect. At the time of his incarceration, Bull was completely fixated on Behrens – he was absolutely convinced that Behrens, and Behrens alone, was the cause of all the problems in his life. Part of Bull's sentence included intensive therapy sessions. I'd like to think that those sessions worked and that the Prison Board received more than one medical opinion regarding Bull's mental state before sending him back out into the world. Funny thing about Bull is he blamed Behrens for interfering with his bids for town construction work, but a little nosing around revealed that Bull never entered a bid for the jobs he claimed were withheld from him.'

'So Bull fabricated the whole story?'

'Not quite. Bull actually believed he had submitted those bids and that someone had purposely removed them from consideration. Bull genuinely believed that he was the victim of persecution.'

'Meaning?'

'Meaning that if Bull was, in fact, fully rehabilitated at the time of his release, then . . .'

'Then he no longer had a motive for killing Behrens,' Tish concluded.

'You got it. We're going to have to check everything – his whereabouts, alibi, treatment – thoroughly. I mean more thoroughly than usual. When we arrested Bull, he had an entire arsenal in his house, so he's proficient with firearms. However, all his guns were confiscated during his arrest. Now that he's out of prison, his options are open. Firearms are regulated on a state level, but every city, town and municipality have their individual laws and loopholes. Lynchburg is particularly lenient, so he may have found it easier to purchase an AR-15 there. There's also the possibility that his sister or her husband purchased the gun for him.'

'But if he didn't have a motive . . .'

'That won't matter to the DA and other people in this town. They'll want this to be Bull. That's why we have to make sure we look at every possible angle. The crazy guy who threatened Behrens all those years ago returning to finish the job offers everyone involved with it a tidy narrative. All the loose ends tied into a neat little bundle – locals are assured that there is no random killer and the town is safe again, the guy everyone loved to hate is back in jail, Behrens looks like a martyr so his party's control over the council is secure, and the council never has to answer the difficult questions about the Hobson Meadows development and the other legislation they've passed.'

'So you *don't* think it's Bull?' Tish questioned.

Reade drew a deep breath and ran a hand through his spiky

hair. 'I don't know what to believe, Tish. All I can say is that I don't want anyone pinning Behrens's death on some guy who might be trying to get his life back together, and I think that's precisely the type of people we're dealing with here. I admit, it would be nice to wrap up this case and enjoy Thanksgiving and the holidays – our first holiday season together – but my job is to protect and serve *everyone* in this town. Something Behrens and a few of the other elected officials we've interviewed seem to have forgotten.'

'Well, in Behrens's case, it might have done him in.'

'What do you mean?'

'I mean that someone must have gotten tired of Behrens's lies. The only problem is that the hot mic news opens the field of suspects, doesn't it? What if that news story about the planning commission meeting wasn't buried quite as deeply as Tripp Sennette believed? What if one of the townspeople saw it – a follower of Behrens, perhaps – and felt betrayed? Everyone knew Behrens was going to be at Colonial Springs yesterday. And although his jog with Schuyler wasn't publicized, I'm sure someone in town knew about it. We know how that goes. Also, the Hobson Meadows development is huge. It must have made *someone* angry, don't you think?'

'We're in the right place, if it did,' Reade remarked as they pulled into the development company parking lot. 'Because I'm sure Gavin Sheppard would have heard about it.'

THIRTEEN

'Forty-four individual complaints,' Gavin Sheppard proclaimed as he plopped a manila folder onto his desk. He was tall, slender, thirty-ish – far younger than Tish had anticipated for a partner in a development business that occupied a block-long building in the center of the city – and dressed in blue pinstripe with dress shirt and no tie. The office was quiet, which wasn't suprising for nearly two o'clock on a Saturday afternoon – but the lack of personal items on any of the desks suggested that the silence wasn't temporary. 'That's not a lot of complaints for a project this size, but then again, it's early in the process.'

'You mean the closer the project gets to breaking ground, the more complaints you'll receive?' Tish questioned.

'Yes, I mean, that's what supposedly happened on other projects. I can remember my father once saying that he could wallpaper his entire office with the complaints he received for a project,' Sheppard recalled with a boyish grin.

So the Sheppard on the sign was Mr Sheppard Senior. 'Did you anticipate as many as that for the Hobson Meadows project?'

'Uh, what? Um, no. I mean, Councilman Behrens was in charge of managing expectations, so that we didn't get too many complaints.' He clicked his tongue. 'Hard to believe he's gone. I talked to him just the other day. We were going to do great things together, you know?'

'Such as?' Reade prompted.

'Hobson Meadows was the model for a whole chain of fine living communities across Virginia. If it worked out, we'd move to areas outside Charlottesville, Roanoke and Chesapeake.'

'Sounds like there was a great deal of money on the line.'

'Yes.' Sheppard quickly thought better of his answer. 'Not yet, though. Like I said, we were still in the planning stages. More money was being invested than being earned.'

'But the potential was there. Am I correct?'

'Yes, I, um, I suppose so.' The young man shifted nervously in his seat. 'But, I mean, we had a ways to go before we could cash in. A looong way,' he said with a self-conscious laugh.

'Mmm. Going back to those complaints, were any of them in any way threatening?'

'No. Not at all. You can read them for yourself.' Sheppard gestured to the folder on his desk. 'Take them with you. I have copies.'

'Thanks. You said that Behrens "managed expectations." How exactly did he do that?'

'Exactly? I don't really know. Politics aren't really my thing. I just let Behrens do what he did best. He was deputy mayor. I'm a real-estate guy. He had his job, I had mine.'

Reade did a double take. Tripp Sennette had used the same exact phrase just that morning.

'So you have absolutely no idea how Behrens was going to ensure Hobson Meadows passed council scrutiny and a public vote?'

'Nope. But we hadn't even put the plans before the town, so how *could* I know?'

'Yet you trusted Behrens to get the all clear.'

'Yeah, the guy was a magician. He knew what his people wanted. How long was he on the council – fifteen years or something?'

'Eighteen. So that planning commission meeting back in June – I'm guessing that Behrens didn't strike up that post-meeting conversation with you on his own, did he?'

'Which meeting was that?' a disinterested Sheppard inquired while scrolling through his phone.

'June twenty-ninth. The meeting, or post-meeting discussion, that landed you both on the Channel Ten nightly news. The microphone was left on and captured your conversation. Funny that you should refer to Behrens as a magician since he referred to using sleight of hand to dupe Hobson Glen voters.'

Sheppard threw his hands in the air. 'Hey, like I said, he did his job and I did mine. I have no idea what you're talking about.'

'Don't you? He mentioned distracting voters by showing them a shiny red ball so that they, quote, "don't care what goes on outside their own walls," unquote. Sound familiar?'

'A little. I had no idea what it meant then and I still have no idea what it means.'

'I think it means that you were looking for reassurance.

Reassurance that he could get the development plan through all the legal hurdles. You asked for that reassurance.'

'What? You're out of your mind . . .'

'Am I? I don't think so. Behrens had a habit of bragging, it's true. But why brag to you after you'd already formed a partnership? Why, after all these months of planning, should he feel the need to sell himself and his expertise to you again? Could it have been that you were having doubts about his abilities?'

'You have absolutely no idea what you're talking about,' Sheppard dismissed with a scowl. 'Behrens was always talking like that, but he never really said anything. That whole conversation was completely blown out of proportion by those other two councilmen and the media.'

'Really? Behrens made sure that a Town Hall employee lost her job over that exchange and then demanded that she sign a non-disclosure agreement. That sure doesn't sound like Behrens simply running off at the mouth.'

'I'm very sorry that the Town Hall secretary lost her job, but if someone in that position forgets to switch off the microphone at the end of a meeting, then I'm afraid there's no other choice than to fire that person.'

'And the non-disclosure?'

Sheppard shrugged, but his feigned nonchalance was unconvincing. 'Not surprising. She must have seen and overheard quite a bit while at Town Hall.'

'Or perhaps Behrens was nervous that the town and the media might find out just how much he was earning from your deal.'

'Behrens was an elected official. He was prohibited by law from accepting any payment for his help in guiding the Hobson Meadows development through the approval phase. You're an elected official, too, aren't you, Sheriff? You should know better than to ask that,' the young man replied.

'And you should know that just because something's prohibited, doesn't mean it doesn't happen,' Tish answered. 'You should also know that Royce Behrens never did anything unless it somehow profited him.'

Sheppard shook his head. 'Never happened. Behrens undertook this project for the good of Hobson Glen.'

'Doubling down?' Reade noted with a smirk. 'I should probably tell you that I've already retrieved all the calls, text messages and emails from Behrens's phone. If you don't help me, I'll find out for myself. And bring you in for obstruction.'

Sheppard sighed wearily. 'Ugh . . . OK, OK. Before I say anything, I want it to be noted that I didn't offer Behrens anything, so don't come at me with bribery charges or anything. I didn't do anything illegal.'

'Duly noted. Continue,' the sheriff instructed as he typed into his tablet.

'I'd been pitching the idea of a luxury housing community to a bunch of towns in the area for eight or nine months when I finally met Royce Behrens. I'd given a presentation to one or two town councils – the rest wouldn't even give me an audience. I was getting nowhere. Councils would hang up the phone when I called. Behrens did too, the first time, but I kept calling.

'One day,' Sheppard continued, 'Behrens called me back. He saw potential in the plan and wanted to learn more. He had friends who might be interested in investing and he had the perfect location in mind. He said he admired my tenacity and bravery for calling him back. Truth is I had nothing to lose. I inherited this business when my father died and was stupid enough to keep it and try to run it myself instead of selling it first chance I got. I thought I'd be able to run the place myself, but I'm not as good a salesman as he was. I'm not as good an anything as he was. It's been, you know, hard,' he cleared his throat, 'to face the fact that I'm running my father's company into the ground. The Gailey on the sign out there? He left the minute I took over. I had to buy him out. I can't afford to change the name of the business or the sign. Yeah, Behrens was like an answer to a prayer – if I actually, you know, prayed.

'I found out fast that I should have prayed – and hard. Behrens gave me the hard sell, emphasizing what he could bring to the table. He promised one hundred percent buy-in from the council and from the town. He told me that building permits would be no problem because he knew some people at the state and county level who would work things out for us. I was stoked. Completely and utterly buzzed. I was finally going to be able to save this company and maybe even stash some money away for myself.

'I was feeling really good about the whole project, about life – about everything, basically. That's when Behrens hit me up with his terms of the arrangement – ten percent of all profits from the sale of the units. You gotta understand, as a developer, I only get between five and ten percent. So what Behrens was asking for was really out there. Like, I laughed in his face when he demanded it, it was so ridiculous.'

'What changed your mind?' Tish asked.

'The realization that split profits were better than no profits at all. Behrens had experience and a whole network of connections who could make the Hobson Meadows development a reality. All I had were plans and a dwindling bank account, so I finally went along with the deal.'

'Did you happen to mention to him that it was illegal for him to earn money from the project?'

'I did. He gave me some story about the money being deposited to a trust or something, so that technically he wasn't receiving it. Made me think this wasn't the first time he'd done this kind of thing. You know, receive money for some sort of favor.'

'Tell me about the night of the planning commission,' Reade prompted.

Sheppard shrugged. 'I made a presentation outlining the entire project, including the timeline of the groundbreaking and construction. It was pretty basic stuff.'

'How were your plans received?'

'It went well. Everyone seemed to like what I put forth.'

'Everyone?' Tish questioned.

The young man sighed again. 'OK, not everyone. Two of the councilmen were dead-set against the plans. Like to the point of being aggressive. They kept asking me about my qualifications and whether I'd ever completed a project like Hobson Meadows before. There was a real "the young guy doesn't know what he's doing" kind of vibe. They also wanted to know how the development would affect property taxes five years from now. How should I know? I can't afford a tax analyst and Behrens wasn't about to provide one. He tried to intervene on my behalf, but it was the same old talk. Everyone had heard it all before.'

'And after the meeting?'

'After the meeting, I asked Behrens what the hell was going on. He'd promised me one hundred percent buy-in from the council, and yet there I was defending myself against two angry council members who were obviously itching for a fight. If those councilmen got talking to the townspeople, we were looking at a major battle getting our plans passed.'

'And yet very few people remember hearing about that meeting,' Reade stated.

'Yeah, but I'll never forget it. I remember coming home that night. I was already bummed about how the meeting had gone down when I started getting calls from my friends who'd seen the story. I completely freaked and called Behrens. Behrens turned around and pressured Sennette and the mayor to keep the news story from spreading. They got right on it – did a good job too. That's why the story only ran one night and disappeared. But the damage with those two councilmen was already done. They weren't about to let us move ahead with our plans. One of them – Pruett's his name – contacted the EPA. The other contracted a consulting firm to project where the town's finances will be after the development is constructed and all units sold. They're looking for any loophole. That's why I've been glad Tripp Sennette has been around to help.'

'Sennette?' Tish repeated.

'Yeah, he called this morning. We're going ahead with Hobson Meadows and he's going to help. As much as I appreciated Behrens calling me, I didn't realize until the planning commission meeting how much of a liability he was. Sennette is well-respected – a real politician. He made me see that most of the problems with the council were because of Behrens's personality. The guy talked about himself all the time. No one liked him because of it. Sennette is quieter. He flies under the radar.'

'So you two are partners now?' Reade paraphrased.

'Now that Behrens is gone, yeah. I mean, he helped so much after that meeting hit the news, and he's been around, so he knows a lot of the same people Behrens did. It seemed like a good idea.'

'And the terms of Sennette's partnership?'

'Oh, I, um, I didn't offer him anything. He's an elected official, just like Behrens.'

'Remember I can subpoena all your text, email and phone communications,' Reade cautioned.

'Ergh, OK. Sennette asked for six percent of the profits and that money doesn't even go to him. He wants it deposited into some charitable trust. Six percent is waaaay more in line with what a developer should expect – not Behrens's crazy ten percent request.'

'And when did Sennette present you with this information?'

'Wh-what do you mean?'

'Just answer the question.'

'He first mentioned a possible partnership a few days after the planning commission meeting. It was said during the course of conversation – something to the effect that had he known about my plans earlier, he would have helped me and maybe I wouldn't have had to work with Behrens. It stuck with me, you know? I thought about it for a little while and that's when I realized that the problems with the project were mainly because of Behrens and his behavior and reputation. The next time I saw Sennette I told him about my thoughts and that's when he told me he would have taken a far smaller cut than Behrens had.'

'When was this?'

'Mid- to late September. But we didn't actually put a number on it until today. Until now it's just been talk and hypotheticals.'

'Where were you yesterday around noon?'

'Where I always am since getting rid of my apartment and sleeping in one of the unused offices – here.'

'Did anyone see you?'

'No. I had to lay off my staff back in July.'

'And you wouldn't happen to own any firearms, would you?'

'I don't own much of anything, anymore, Sheriff. That includes firearms.'

FOURTEEN

'Royce Behrens was my client, yes,' Lucy Van Gorder said as she motioned for Tish and Reade to take a seat in the two cushioned wing chairs facing her desk.

It was the pair's seventh, and hopefully last, interview of the day. Indeed, a trip to see Lucy Van Gorder hadn't even been on their original schedule until Judson Darley mentioned the lawyer as being significant to the case. And so, when Ms Van Gorder offered to meet with them at three o'clock they readily agreed, even though, with their witnesses all living in such close proximity to each other, they'd nary a moment between interviews to gather their thoughts or discuss their findings.

Winding up this interview and then engaging in a non-investigatory activity, such as grocery shopping, sounded like the perfect way to regain their balance and their perspectives on the case.

'How long was Behrens your client?' Reade asked.

'Sixteen months.' The answer was swift and oddly specific.

'How did you become acquainted with Councilman Behrens?' Tish inquired.

Van Gorder sat behind her desk and tucked her long copper-colored hair behind one ear. 'At a conference. I was delivering a speech about the effect of distance between partners in venture capital investments and Royce was in the audience. He arranged to meet with me after the speech – he wanted to hear more. I had never met someone quite as excited about corporate law as Royce was. It was an interesting discussion, one which culminated in his offering to hire me.'

'Obviously he was successful,' Tish noted.

Lucy's face softened. 'Oh no. Not right away. I found him far too abrasive. Too forward. And he talked too much for my liking.'

'What did he talk about?' Reade asked.

Van Gorder smiled. 'Attorney client privilege,' she replied curtly.

'Ah, of course. What made you change your mind about accepting Councilman Behrens as a client?'

'He had a brilliant political mind and a keen business sense. He also appreciated my knowledge and expertise.'

An exceptionally lovely woman in her late thirties, Lucy Van Gorder indubitably encountered potential clients who wished to hire her based on her looks alone.

'Did Behrens discuss the Hobson Meadows project with you?' Reade proceeded.

'Yes, I represented him during the negotiations.'

'So he discussed all the plans with you?'

'Of course,' she replied, a slight laugh in her voice.

'If a client communicates with a lawyer for the purpose of committing an act of fraud, attorney–client privilege no longer applies. Likewise, the Commonwealth of Virginia renders attorney–client privilege null and void in instances where information learned from a client may prevent money lost due to a crime or fraud.'

'You definitely know the law, Sheriff Reade,' she said admiringly.

'I'm elected by the people of Henrico County to enforce that law, Ms Van Gorder,' he explained.

'Kudos. In my experience, most elected officials are either ignorant of the law or choose to ignore it completely. However, you're wrong about the fraud allegations.'

'Really? Then why was Faye Wheeler, an employee at Hobson Glen Town Hall, forced to sign a non-disclosure agreement?'

'I have absolutely no knowledge of a non-disclosure agreement, Sheriff. The town council and Councilman Sennette each had their own attorneys – one of them must have drawn up the papers.'

'The copy Ms Wheeler showed us had his signature on it. Are you saying he didn't have you review it?'

The corners of Van Gorder's mouth twitched. 'Apparently not.'

'But you were aware that Royce Behrens sought to profit from the Hobson Meadows development, despite it being in violation of his oath of office as deputy mayor, weren't you?'

'I advised against it,' Van Gorder explained. 'Royce Behrens was the type of elected official who thought that rules didn't apply to him.'

'Isn't that attorney–client privilege?' Tish challenged.

'No, more like common knowledge. Besides, it can't get him into trouble now, can it?'

'No, I suppose it can't. Did you spend a lot of time getting Royce out of trouble?'

Van Gorder inhaled deeply. 'No, I foolishly spent my time trying to prevent Royce from getting into trouble in the first place. I wrongly believed that I held some sort of influence over him. I honestly thought that with a few sage words, I could modify his behavior and make him both intelligent *and* kind, but I was deluded.'

'That's a fairly strong word,' Tish noted.

'It's the only one that accurately describes my frame of mind.'

'Rumor has it that your relationship with Royce Behrens was more than that of mere attorney and client.'

Van Gorder gave a sardonic laugh. 'Funny. I can recall a time when it was the older white women who would start a rumor in these parts. Their husbands would then swear that the rumor wasn't true. Now it's the older white men who start the gossip and their wives who carry it to oblivion and back. It's still women who are mostly being gossiped about, of course. A married man has an affair and the mistress is the hussy. Welcome to the "new" south!'

'I'm a transplant from New York, so I can't say much about the new and old south, but I imagine rumors and their creators are the same everywhere.'

'You're right, of course, but it doesn't help when you're the one in the eye of the hurricane and those rumors are meant to discredit you.'

'I'm sure it's incredibly difficult,' Tish sympathized. Her very public relationship and subsequent breakup with Schuyler Thompson had been the subject of town speculation and gossip for months, and now her relationship with Clemson – both romantic and crime-solving – had put her in the spotlight again. At least the notoriety was good for business. 'I do have to ask, however—'

'Did I have an affair with Royce?' The lawyer anticipated Tish's question. 'Yes. Yes, I did. It wasn't cheap. It wasn't tawdry. I genuinely loved him and, no, I don't think of myself as a home-wrecker. I believed that we had . . . *something*. He was one of the few men I've met who actually valued me for my mind. What I didn't recognize was that he was using me. He was using me physically, of course, but in addition to that, during our pillow talk, every clandestine meeting that wasn't billed he'd ask me questions – questions about the best way to approach the Hobson Meadows deal. Questions about the legality of specific actions. He was picking my brain for free legal advice while promising me the moon and the stars. It's one of the oldest scams in the book, isn't it? "My wife doesn't understand me. I'll be leaving her soon and then we'll be together." A tale as old as time, isn't it? And yet I believed the ending to our story would be different. It's the very definition of stupidity – knowing in advance how a situation will turn out but believing you can change it anyway.'

'I wouldn't call it stupidity. Love makes us believe in the impossible and, when it's real, love can truly overcome obstacles. When it's wrong – well, we've all had those relationships that made us wonder if we should have known better.'

'I recognize that my situation isn't unique and yet . . .'

'And yet, as an educated, successful woman, you berate yourself for not noticing the signs?' Tish guessed.

Lucy's eyes grew misty. 'Royce Behrens was a player and I allowed myself to be played. I allowed myself to get sucked into his world. I bought into the fantasy he had created – successful businessman, beloved politician, beleaguered husband, doting father. But he was none of those things. Everything about him – everything he told me – was a lie.'

'How did you discover he was leading you on?' Reade asked.

'At the beginning of autumn, I was beginning to sense that Royce was being dishonest about his marriage. He and I didn't see each other as often as we had earlier in the year, and when we did see each other, he was distant, preoccupied. I asked him about it and he claimed he was busy with the development project and work, but there was something in how he said it that didn't ring true. The day before yesterday, I acted on my suspicions. I suggested that with the holidays coming, perhaps he and I could steal a weekend away somewhere before the family obligations and celebrations began. We had often talked about getting away to a secret retreat – just the two of us,' Lucy explained. 'He nixed the idea without a second thought. He said that Amanda needed his help with the boys at Christmastime and that between those demands and those at work, he wasn't sure he'd be able to see me at all over the holidays, let alone make time for a getaway. It was the first time Royce ever mentioned doing anything with his wife, let alone parenting with her.'

'How did you feel about his reaction?'

'Nauseous, faint, furious and stupid – sometimes all at once.'

'Would it be fair to say you hated Royce Behrens for it?'

'Not as much as I hated myself for falling for him, but yes. I can't lie. I hated him at that moment.'

'And where were you yesterday around noon?'

'I had an appointment. I can't say where or with whom.'

'Do you happen to own any firearms?'

'I do,' she replied. 'I own multiple firearms, all legal and registered with the state. I might as well tell you both now, since you'll see it when you check my background – I was a member of the Virginia State High School Clay Target League. I received a five-thousand-dollar scholarship from them to attend college. I'm what people might call a crack shot.'

'At least Lucy Van Gorder came clean with us. It felt as if we were towing a truck uphill trying to get information out of Gavin Sheppard,' Tish remarked as they pulled into the parking lot of the Richmond Riverfront Market.

'Van Gorder's smart. She told us what she did because she knew we'd eventually find it out on our own. By telling us the truth, Van Gorder controls the narrative. In this case, that she's the fragile woman wronged, rather than the angry woman scorned.'

'Good point. You'd think Tripp Sennette would have learned that trick by now. Yet all he did was delay, dodge and deflect.'

They exited the SUV and selected a shopping cart from a nearby corral.

'Because it's all a power play to Sennette,' Reade stated as he pushed the cart to the market entrance and piled their reusable shopping bags into the top tier. 'Behrens's death opens the door to him becoming deputy mayor.'

'And Gavin Sheppard's new partner,' Tish added, extracting a shopping list from her handbag.

'Yeah, that was an interesting revelation. I didn't see Mister Conservative Red Necktie jumping into the real-estate development game, but I guess the money was too good to pass up.'

'Remember, Sheppard benefited from a partnership with Sennette as well. Sennette was less incendiary than Behrens *and* better connected.'

'Odds are Sennette didn't make promises he couldn't deliver, either,' Reade noted.

'Sheppard denies owning firearms, but he also has no alibi for the time of the crime. I'd say he's still a prime suspect, wouldn't you?'

'I would.'

'Sennette, however, is in the clear. He fired the starter's pistol and was at the trailhead with the rest of us while the shooting took place.'

'I wouldn't say he's entirely in the clear. As far as I can tell, no one recalls seeing Sennette after he fired the pistol. He allegedly hid by himself and out of view of anyone else present in the clearing. Given what Clayton showed us about secret trails at the Springs, and the fact that Behrens and Thompson set off at a leisurely jog, Sennette easily could have ducked into the bushes, shadowed Behrens and Thompson along one of the hidden trails, shot Behrens and doubled back to the clearing.'

'And the gun? Where was it while he shot the starter's pistol and again when he returned from the shooting?'

'I admit, I haven't gotten that far,' Reade confessed with a sheepish grin.

'Mmm,' she grunted in reply, and led the way through the automatic doors of the market. 'You know who else doesn't have an alibi? Lucy Van Gorder. She had a meeting yesterday, but she can't tell us anything more about it. Unless that meeting was with the FBI, that's not much of an alibi at all.'

'I noticed that too. All she needed to say is that she had a client meeting. Clayton and I would have confirmed the meeting took place and the topic would have been closed. By being so ambiguous, she drew more attention to the meeting than actually necessary.'

'Maybe because it *was* necessary,' Tish reasoned.

'You think she was trying to tell us something?'

'I don't know. If she was telling us something, I can't imagine what it might have been.'

'She also seemed incredibly eager to tell us about her marksmanship skills,' Reade said, pulling the shopping cart to a halt by the Brussels sprouts.

'Yes, it was almost as if she were boasting.' Tish selected

approximately one half-pound of sprouts and placed them into a mesh bag. 'I wonder if Amanda Behrens knew about her husband's affair with Lucy.'

'Annabelle seemed to know all about his conquests, so I'd assume Amanda knew too.'

'Not necessarily. Annabelle holds her daughter-in-law in high esteem. She may have covered up her son's transgressions in an attempt to shield her – Amanda is a very anxious individual – or to keep her in the family.'

'I have Clayton pulling Amanda's financial records. Since she has a solid alibi for the time of the murder, we need to rule out that she contracted someone else to do it.'

'Amanda has an alibi? Did I miss something?'

'Oh, sorry. Clayton texted a short time ago and confirmed that Amanda was in her car in the parking lot at the rec park at the time of the shooting. She dropped Chase there and was waiting, reading a book, while he ran and trained. Witnesses saw her pull in at eleven thirty, and she was still there when the Turkey Trot started at noon.'

'Well, at least we can cross someone off the list. That still leaves Darley and Pruett,' Tish continued, as if the grocery list in her hand was, instead, a list of suspects. 'They don't have alibis either.'

'Pruett intrigues me.' They strolled over to a counter of onions, where Reade chose two sweet Vidalias and placed them into the cart. 'Just as Lucy Van Gorder was proud of being a crack shot, Pruett was equally adamant that he didn't own a gun.'

'To be fair, gun ownership doesn't really match his lifestyle.' She led them to the celery, where she snatched a lush green head and added it to their shopping.

'Wasn't it you who once chastised Clayton for assuming that a vegan might be less likely to commit a homicide than a non-vegan?' he reminded her.

'It was, but if you recall, Clayton's exact theory was that the vegan couldn't have committed a stabbing because they wouldn't have owned a butcher's knife. Obviously Clayton has never tried to cube a butternut squash,' she said, leading Reade to the bakery department. 'In this case, Leonard Pruett's veganism doesn't even come into play. I'm simply not sure he had a strong enough motive to want Royce Behrens dead.'

'I disagree. If it wound up that Hobson Meadows encroached on local flora and fauna, he'd be furious.'

'Hmm,' she replied, while studying a sturdy loaf of country white bread to use for stuffing, 'perhaps, but I can't imagine Pruett firing an AR-15. A handgun, maybe, but a weapon that turns people into Swiss cheese? I just can't see it. Judson Darley, on the other hand . . .' She tossed the bread into the cart.

'Darley? He did seem to hate Behrens for jumping into the deputy mayor position.'

'More than that, he had a serious axe to grind with Behrens over his treatment of Faye Wheeler and Ms Annabelle.'

'Annabelle?'

'Yes. Darley knew an awful lot of intimate details about her relationship with Royce. Didn't you notice?' She led him to the canned goods, where she collected a tin of organic pureed pumpkin before moving on to the dairy section to retrieve milk, heavy cream and a dozen large eggs.

'No, I didn't. But now that you mention it, he did mention Royce turning physically violent, didn't he?'

'On more than one occasion. Now, I don't imagine Annabelle spread that around town herself, do you?'

'Probably not. But what does it mean?'

'Don't know, but right now we have other things to hunt than a killer.' She leaned over and gave him a kiss on the cheek before making her way toward the butcher counter.

'Agreed. Buying a turkey for our first Thanksgiving together is a special occasion. One that, a year ago, I wouldn't have believed we'd be sharing,' he said.

'Me neither. Last Christmas I watched as you drove out of my café and was convinced I'd lost you forever. Having you here, in my life, is something I'm thankful for every single day.'

'Same. I promise to never take it for granted, either.' He wrapped an arm around her waist. 'So which of these birds is coming home with us?'

'There's a lovely fresh turkey breast.' She pointed to the refrigerated case in front of the counter. 'Eight pounds will give us plenty of meat for dinner, leftovers, soup, and to send over to Enid Kemper on Thanksgiving Day. I'd invite her over, but I know she'd just say no.'

'And enough in case Mary Jo and Kayla find that Gregory has other plans.'

She smiled. 'You thought about that too?'

He nodded.

'You don't mind if they come over? I mean, this was supposed to be a cozy dinner for two.'

'I'm more than fine with them joining us, especially if their plans fall through. So long as we're together.'

'Good. The eight-pounder it is.' She picked up the tightly wrapped roast and placed it in the cart, but not before a set of beautiful Cornish game hens caught her eye. 'Ooh!'

'We have a chest freezer in the garage,' Reade said, following her line of sight. 'Get them and we'll put them away for Christmas Eve. Or New Year's Eve. Or Valentine's Day. Or whenever we're alone and want a special meal.'

She joyfully rescued the pair of poussins from the cold storage, already dreaming of a romantic, candlelit Middle Eastern-themed meal. As she did so, Reade's phone rang.

He answered with a frown that only deepened as the caller made the reason for their communication clear. 'That was Clayton,' he announced after he had disconnected. 'He has a lead on that winter white jacket. It belongs to Connie Ramirez, our gun control activist. He's bringing her in for questioning now.'

FIFTEEN

As the sun began its slow descent in the western sky, Tish and Reade deposited their holiday haul at the house, subsequently shooed Tuna and Marlowe from their forbidden lounging spots on the bed, fed both cats their supper, and then met Clayton at the sheriff's office, where the young officer had begun preliminary questioning of Connie Ramirez.

Reade joined him in the interrogation room, while Tish observed from behind the two-way mirror.

'Look, I was there, but I didn't kill the guy,' Ramirez maintained.

'Then what were you doing at the Turkey Trot?' Reade asked as he took the seat beside Clayton.

'I was there to make a statement. Gun violence is at an all-time high in this country, yet the Hobson Glen Town Council decided to stage a shooting contest. It's irresponsible at best. The town council was either ignorant to the violence transpiring nationwide or they were condoning it.'

'And how did you plan to make this statement of yours? With a firearm, perhaps?'

'No. I'm fully committed to the cause of stricter gun laws. I would never use one as a prop. I had hoped to splash the mayor and deputy mayor with blood. You know, to represent the blood of gun violence victims that they now had on their hands for bringing a pro-gun event to Henrico County.'

Reade raised an eyebrow. 'Blood?'

'Yes. I mean, no. It wasn't *real* blood. I called around Richmond looking for pig's blood or goat's blood or some other kind of blood, and then I figured out I might end up on a watch list somewhere, so I went to Sherwin-Williams and bought paint. Had it custom mixed and everything. It really looked like blood.'

'So you were at the Turkey Trot to cover Mayor Thompson and Deputy Mayor Behrens with paint,' Reade summarized.

'Not cover, but splash. I loaded the paint into a backpack and parked my car at the overflow parking lot right after it opened. I took the trail through the woods that connects with Colonial Springs. When I arrived, I waited behind a wide oak on the trail. It was a long wait, but worth it, I thought, to surprise Schuyler and Behrens as they jogged past me. They would have looked like they'd been shot . . .' Ramirez's voice trailed off as she realized the significance of her words.

'Behrens *was* shot, Ms Ramirez.'

'I know. I saw it happen.' Her face went ashen and her brown eyes welled with tears. 'I was excited to hear the starter's pistol go off. I removed the lid on my jar of paint and waited for Thompson and Behrens to appear on the trail.'

'And where were you positioned?'

'Several feet farther up the trail, to the right of the mayor and deputy mayor.'

'What happened next?

'I was so frightened and anxious, I dropped the paint lid. I bent down to pick it up, but then stopped. The movement rustled the undergrowth and made a noise so loud, I knew someone must have heard it. I looked up to see Mayor Thompson looking in my direction. I thought it was all over. I thought he'd call you guys and have me escorted from the Springs. But then, there was the shot—'

Ramirez's tears came hard and fast as she continued her story through her sobs. 'Behrens – Behrens was in front. I saw him fall. And I saw the blood. So much blood. It was everywhere.'

Reade pushed a box of tissues across the table and directed Clayton to retrieve a glass of water for their suspect. 'Did you see the shooter?'

She shook her head. 'No. It was all a blur. I don't remember much after that except running. I ran all the way back to the parking lot, got into my car, and drove straight home. I never stopped. Somewhere along the way, while running, I tore my jacket. I don't know where. I didn't even notice the rip in it until late last night when I hung the jacket in my closet. Then this morning, I found out you were looking for someone with a jacket like mine—'

This last statement spurred a new spate of tears. Thankfully, Clayton had returned with a cold glass of water. Ramirez drank it down and then blew her nose.

'Thank you. I'm sorry for – for being so emotional,' she

apologized as she smoothed her curly dark shoulder-length hair into a ponytail, using an elastic band she had been wearing as a bracelet.

'Watching a man die is an emotional event,' Reade noted.

'Yeah, I watched my older brother die. He was fifteen years old – a victim of gun violence. That was almost ten years ago.'

'Were you perhaps seeking an eye for an eye?'

Ramirez's face grew red, this time out of rage. 'I could never shoot anyone. I know what someone dying like that does to a family. It tears them apart with grief and anger. My mom blamed my dad for what happened to my brother, and my dad blamed my mom. They split up and I bounced between houses before leaving for good at sixteen because of the guilt I felt for being the kid who lived. I don't wish that on anyone, Sheriff. That's why I do what I do. That's why I protest for stricter gun laws – so other people don't have to live through what we lived through.'

Reade looked at Ramirez for a good while before speaking again. He could detect no sign of deception or malice in her face. 'Going back to your jacket –it's on its way to the lab to check for blood and other fibers. What were you wearing beneath it?'

Ramirez appeared puzzled by the question. 'Huh? Um, a chunky crocheted sweater – green. A pair of jeans, um, torn at the knees and turned up at the cuffs. And a pair of black boots – the lace-up kind.'

'Were you wearing a T-shirt under that sweater? And, yes, it's pertinent to the case.'

'No, the sweater is pretty bulky. I never layer it with anything else.'

'Do you remember anything else from that day? Anything at all?'

'Actually . . . no. No, it sounds crazy.'

'Go on,' the sheriff urged.

'The reason I dropped the paint lid, and the reason I was so anxious and scared is because I thought I heard someone else in the woods.'

'You mean someone other than Behrens, Thompson and the shooter?'

She nodded. 'I heard a sound like grass or twigs crunching and snapping underfoot, coming from the bunch of trees to my left. I thought – I hoped – that it was an animal, like a deer or a fox or something. I don't think it was or it would have run away as the deputy mayor and mayor approached. Again, I know it sounds crazy, but I think it was a human being. I don't know why they were there or what they were doing, but I'm glad they let me get away.'

'Her statement meshes completely with Schuyler's,' Tish stated as she stepped into the interrogation room after Clayton had escorted Connie Ramirez to the front desk to sign her statement. 'Right down to hearing someone or something moving in the undergrowth to her left. She's innocent.'

'Of murder. Once Schuyler finds out why she was at the Springs, he'll want to press charges.'

'But Connie never actually threw the paint.'

'Doesn't matter. Attempted assault of an elected official? Schuyler and Sennette will take it and run. They'll make an example out of Connie and use her as the poster child as to why we need all the useless crime laws they want to pass.'

'Just what a woman in her early twenties needs – a criminal record,' Tish said drily as she folded her arms across her chest and leaned back against the interrogation table. 'As if she hasn't already been through enough.'

'There's not much I can do. If Schuyler presses charges, I'll have to bring her in. Only one of the five judges in this county won't see Ramirez's activity as a protestor as a mark against her character. I can do my best to recommend that he hears her case, but I'm pretty sure Schuyler and Sennette will pull whatever strings necessary to ensure the case goes before a judge who's more sympathetic to their side.'

'They really have this town at their mercy, don't they?'

'Yeah, but don't give up yet. When we find Behrens's killer, that will become the focus, and the outrage and interest in Connie will probably fall by the wayside.'

She pursed her lips together. 'I hope so.'

'Mm, let's go home, have some dinner, and review our interviews and case files.'

'Sounds good to me. I've had it for one day.'

'Same.' He led Tish out of the interrogation room and toward the front desk where Clayton was finishing some paperwork. 'Hey,

Clayton. Good work today. Why don't you pack it in for the evening? We'll start fresh in the morning.'

Before Clayton could reply, one of the front desk phones rang. He answered it. 'Henrico County Sheriff's Office. This is Officer Clayton. Yes . . . where? Jeez. We'll get some cars out there right away. It's Bill Bull, sir,' Clayton reported when he'd hung up the phone. 'He's checked into the Abbingdon Green Bed and Breakfast.'

'Well, get a car over there to question him,' Reade directed.

'No, sir. It's more than that. There's an angry mob outside the building, demanding Bull turn himself in for Behrens's murder.'

SIXTEEN

Tish and Reade arrived at Abbingdon Green Bed and Breakfast at six p.m. to find a crowd of approximately seventy-five people congregated outside the inn's front porch. Some bore torches, others flashlights, and still others carried makeshift signs which read, *Surrender Bull* or some variation thereof.

'Wait in the car,' Reade instructed.

'I didn't come with you just to sit in the car, Clemson. I need to check on Glory.' Seventy-two-year-old Glory Bishop was the B&B's proprietor.

'The mob hasn't breached the front door.'

'I know, but she must be terrified. I need to see her and make sure she's OK.'

Reade capitulated. 'Let me get the crowd under control first. When I give you the sign, go in through the kitchen door.'

Tish nodded. Clayton and a handful of uniformed officers and their squad cars stayed at the bottom of the hill in order to block the B&B entrance and keep nosy neighbors and potential new protestors at bay. Meanwhile, Reade and a team of officers in body armor had driven up the driveway and blocked the parking lot to the rear of the building. It didn't matter to the members of the mob – they had pulled their vehicles directly onto Abbingdon Green's beautifully manicured lawns. A few of the individuals assembled stood on the front hoods and flatbeds of those vehicles.

Reade stepped out of the SUV and, through a bullhorn, advised the parties assembled there to return to their homes. The crowd booed and hissed, with a few hecklers – clearly the ringleaders of the group – going so far as to call him colorful names.

Reade was unfazed, but the situation made Tish nervous. As much as she wanted to check on Glory Bishop, part of her wanted to wait and make sure that Reade, Clayton and the other officers were safe. Reade stepped forward and spoke in a calm, measured voice in order to diffuse the situation. The crowd assembled there watched with rapt attention, prompting Reade to gesture, with a backhand motion, for Tish to leave the vehicle.

Switching off the inside light, Tish snuck out of the passenger side door, softly closed it, and crept along the driveway – taking care to remain in the shadows and away from any exterior lights – to the door she last used to load out glassware, silverware and serving vessels, after catering a wedding that August. Tish drew a deep breath and gave the handle a turn. She was both relieved and nervous to find it unlocked.

'Glory?' Tish called, tentatively at first, and then more frantically. 'Glory. Glory!'

'I'm in here,' came the familiar lilt of Glory's Virginia accent from the guests' sitting area. Glory herself resided in the property's carriage house that had been converted into a bright and spacious two-bedroom cottage.

Tish rushed to the sitting room on tenterhooks. 'Glory, are you OK?'

As anticipated, the innkeeper was not alone. What was not anticipated was that she was wielding an antique shotgun. 'I'm fine, honey. It's those folks outside who've lost their minds. This is Mr William Bull, by the way,' she gestured to the dark-skinned man seated beside her on the antique Victorian settee. The lights in the room were switched off – most likely an attempt to conceal Glory, Bull and the firearm from the mob of people gathered less than fifty feet from the sitting room's bay window.

The gentleman immediately stood to shake hands. Although such conventions didn't seem quite appropriate to the situation, Tish tentatively accepted. 'Hello, um, yes, I, um, I've heard quite a bit about you, Mr Bull.'

'You're not the only one. The minute I checked in, they all showed up. I have no idea how anyone knew I was coming here. If I did I wouldn't have stepped near the place. I never meant to bring all this on Glory. I was a member of her father's church before he passed and I called here as a friend, but I can see I no longer have that luxury.'

'Don't be a fool, Bill,' Glory chastised. 'You're always welcome here. It's those bigots on my front lawn who are the problem. Terrorizing an old woman is bad enough, but doing it in her own home – the property her family has owned for over a century and a half is beyond the pale. People have no manners or decency these days.'

Organizing a mob to intimidate a possibly innocent man wasn't a matter of etiquette, but Tish was more intent on addressing the elephant in the room. 'Uh, Glory, what are you doing with that rifle?'

The older woman glanced down at the weapon in her hands as if she had forgotten she was holding it. 'What, this?'

'Yeah, that. Does it even fire?'

'I haven't the faintest idea. I took it off the wall in the upstairs hallway. It belonged to my great-great grandfather, but it's not as if I ever learned how to shoot it. I just thought it might frighten off some of those ruffians out there.'

'Frighten them off? It's more likely to incite them to riot if they catch a glimpse of it.'

'That's what I tried to tell her,' Bull said. 'The less she says and does, the better off we'll all be.'

'With all due respect, I'm not about to let those people take over my B and B without a fight!'

'I've already told you, they're not after your B and B, Glory. They're after me. I'm sorry I came here. I had no idea anyone knew I was coming. No idea at all. Then suddenly, after my arrival, I see that it's all over Twitter.'

'Twitter?' Tish asked.

'Yeah, Tripp Sennette Tweeted my location. How he knew . . . I guess he has spies or surveillance people working for him.'

'Did Sennette tell people to come here to the bed and breakfast?'

'Not directly, but he didn't have to. He told people not to allow the murder of their deputy mayor to go unavenged. I got a screenshot of it on my phone.' Bull held the device aloft for Tish to see.

'Good. You need to show it to Sheriff Reade when he talks to you later.'

'The sheriff? He won't believe anything I say. The last sheriff didn't. He'll want to arrest me for Royce Behrens's murder. Only I didn't do it. I swear I didn't.'

'I think you'll find that Sheriff Reade is open to hearing your story,' Tish assured him. 'But for now we need to move you and Glory to a safe place.'

'We're fine right here. We have the lights off,' Glory argued.

'That doesn't matter. Someone could throw a rock at the window or try to break through the front door. The two of you need to get upstairs and to the back of the house – even if you stay in the main hallway, I'm sure your guests will understand.'

'Oh, I have no guests. I'm closed until Wednesday so we can give the place a good cleaning before the holidays.'

'Even better,' Tish proclaimed. 'Go to the room farthest from the front of the house and stay there until Clemson gives us the all clear.'

'It still seems as though I should stay here and fight,' Glory grumbled as she rose from the sofa.

'No, Glory,' Bill replied. 'I'd rather turn myself over to them than let anything happen to you or your home.'

'Neither one should be necessary,' Tish said with certainty, despite the growing sound of unrest from the crowd outdoors. 'Now hurry up and get upstairs.'

No sooner had Glory and Bull ascended the stairs when something akin to a battle cry erupted from the front lawn. Tish glanced out the window nervously. Reade and the police had managed to keep the majority of the crowd under control; however, over a dozen members had broken free and were charging toward Abbingdon Green's front porch.

Tish dashed as fast as she could to the front door. An innkeeper for the past forty years, Glory, who had inexplicably decided to arm herself with a two-hundred-year-old firearm, had also, through force of habit, managed to leave the main entrance unlocked. With trembling fingers, Tish turned the cylinder in the door handle until she heard the latch click. Recognizing that a single lock wasn't sufficient in preventing a dozen men from kicking the door in, she then scanned the nearby coat rack and window ledge for a key with which to secure the door's deadbolt.

Finding a small keychain dangling from a nail near the doorjamb, she tried all five keys in the lock, but none of them appeared to fit the lock in question. As the angry men – at least it sounded like men – on the porch shouted Bull's name and began to bang aggressively on the door, Tish sought other means of securing the passageway. Scanning the foyer, she spied a high-backed blanket chest that guests sat upon while donning their boots in the wintertime. Moving swiftly, she sprinted to the chest and, with all her strength, pushed the chest along the floorboards, toward the front door.

It was slow, backbreaking work, and Tish was uncertain if she'd be able to place the piece of furniture before the men successfully broke through the door. She was just about to give up and devise another plan, when the weight of the chest lightened considerably. She looked up to see Bill Bull at the other end of the chest, lifting upward and dragging it, with minimal effort, in the same direction as Tish.

She nodded toward him and the pair secured the chest in front of the doorway, just as the crowd's angry pounding gave way to angry kicks. 'Thanks, but you should be upstairs.'

'What, and leave you down here to fend for yourself? Uh uh. Those people are here for me. That makes this my party,' he insisted.

'Glory might follow you down here if you stay too long,' Tish warned.

'Nope. My daughter has it under strict orders to make sure Glory doesn't move a muscle.'

'Your daughter?'

'Yeah, you think I came all the way out here for a day trip? I hadn't seen my baby girl since I went to prison. Tamika was just a kid back then. Now she's training to be a nurse – and a great one at that. I snuck over here on the train to meet with her and catch up because she couldn't spare a whole day away from class. When we'd finished talking, I was going to take the late-night train back to my sister's place. The only person I trusted enough to host the meeting was Glory. She was the only one who stayed in touch while I was away.' He shook his head. 'Nice way of repaying her kindness, huh? With a bunch of thugs trying to break down her door.'

'This isn't your fault,' Tish called after Bull as he moved into the sitting room.

'Yes, it is. Those folks aren't out there because I've led a good life. They're looking to blame me for Behrens's death because I messed up in the past. I threatened him, an elected official, and was sent to jail.'

'Yes, and you've done your time.'

'The people out there don't care about that.' He continued down the hall and into the kitchen.

Tish intended to follow him, but before she could make her way out of the sitting room, there was a deafening crash. Something broke through the picture window and sailed past her head, sending shards of glass flying everywhere. Tish shielded her face and head with her hands and forearms and, although her instinct was to run to the safety of the kitchen, she found herself frozen to the spot where she stood.

The clamour was enough to draw both Glory and a young woman with dark, naturally curly hair and bright blue eyes from their upstairs hiding spot. 'Oh my goodness! What happened?' the innkeeper demanded.

'The cowards couldn't get through the door, so they smashed the window with a brick,' Bull explained, a note of contempt in his voice. 'Cowards,' he shouted at the perpetrators as police in riot gear apprehended them.

'Oh! Tish, honey, your head is bleeding,' Glory exclaimed as she wrapped an arm around the caterer's shoulders.

'I'll get my bag,' Tamika announced before bounding up the stairs.

'Come on, you two. It's not safe in here.' Bull waved both women into the kitchen and fixed Tish a glass of water before moving to the back door.

'I locked that on my way in,' Tish told him.

'Good. One of you be sure to lock it after I show myself out,' he directed.

'No!' Tish rushed forward to stop him.

'I've got to, Tish. Like I said, this is my party.'

'But that mob could kill you. What about Tamika? She's just getting to know you again.'

'She's the reason I'm going out there. Tamika grew up with her Pops in jail and hearing all the stories about the crazy things he did. It's high time she got used to her Pops doing the right thing.' Bull turned on one heel and proudly strode through the kitchen door and down the driveway.

Tamika had since returned with her medical bag. 'Pops? Wait! Pops. Pops!'

Tish, a trickle of blood still running down her forehead, hurried to Tamika's side and steadied her. 'You need to stay here with Glory,' she commanded as she grabbed her cell phone from her coat pocket and texted Reade: BULL IS COMING OUT.

'No! Pops – my father – they'll kill him!' the young woman shouted.

Tish was uncertain whether Reade had seen her message. There was only one way to find out. 'Not if I can help it,' she announced before heading out the back door after Bull.

'But your head,' Glory reminded.

'It will wait. This won't.' Tish shadowed Bull as he marched, chest and head held high, down the driveway and toward the front yard.

At the sight of him, the mob, now subdued by Reade's team, let out a mighty roar: 'Murderer! Lock him up! Send him back to jail! Animal!'

Reade had apparently received Tish's message, for he and Clayton met Bull halfway down the drive.

'I didn't kill Behrens,' Bull told the sheriff.

Reade nodded. 'I still need to take you in. By being here, you've violated the terms of your release.'

It was Bull's turn to nod. 'It's OK. Everyone would be safer that way.'

Reade gestured to Clayton to place Bull in handcuffs. He then looked up to see the gash on Tish's head. 'My God! Are you OK?'

'Yeah, just a cut. It must have come from a wayward piece of glass. It stings more than it actually hurts. I'll go back in the house and have Tamika look at it.'

Reade pulled out a handkerchief from his back pocket and dabbed at the wound. 'Tamika?'

'Yes, Bull's daughter. She's the reason he was here today. He hadn't seen her for years.'

Reade drew a deep breath. 'I hate bringing him in, but I have to. I have no choice.'

'I understand. It's probably better for him to be in custody right now – especially since Tripp Sennette called out the wolves.'

'Sennette?'

Tish explained about Sennette's provocative Tweet. 'Have Clayton check Bull's phone. He took a screenshot.'

'Will do.'

With the window-breakers having been taken into custody, and the remainder of the mob dispersed, Reade took some time to accompany Tish back into the house. They had taken just a few steps when a familiar voice called to them.

'Sheriff! Tish! Are you guys OK?' It was Maurice. He and his camera had been sent to Abbingdon Green by NPR to photograph and film the incident.

'Tish might need a stitch or two, but apart from that, we're fine,' Reade assured.

'Thank goodness. There's been enough grief and upset these past couple of days.'

'Yeah the shooting was a traumatic event for our town. The last thing any of us need is more violence, although it seems as if some folks disagree with that assessment,' the sheriff reflected as he watched the team direct the troublemakers in the mob into the back of the sheriff's office van.

'Crazy.' Maurice clicked his tongue. 'I, um, I hate asking you, Tish, considering everything you've been through, but . . .'

'Asking me what?'

'Have you heard from Julian at all today?'

'Not since he left our house this morning, no. Why?'

'I've been trying to call him and check in on how he's doing, but he doesn't answer.'

Tish's blue eyes narrowed. 'That doesn't sound like Jules. He's usually eager to hear from you. Is everything OK?'

'Julian and I broke up this afternoon,' Maurice blurted.

Tish was genuinely shocked by the news 'Broke up? But you and Jules seemed so happy together – so in love.'

'I do care for Julian. I really, truly do. Too much so and far too quickly. It's not healthy for Cassius, my jumping into another long-term, committed relationship so soon. The man who was supposed to be his daddy – who said he wanted to be a father – has been gone less than a year. What if my relationship with Julian doesn't work out? Cassius is growing attached to him and he'd be left without a dad again. It's not fair to him. He needs a dad who can give him his fullest attention, not a single father who's juggling work and trying to maintain a relationship.'

'I'm sorry to hear it, Maurice. I honestly believed that you and

Jules had what it takes to make things work – not just as a couple, but as a family.'

'I thought so, too. Or, at least, I hoped. In a different time and place, probably, but not now.'

'I'm not about to suggest that you change your mind, Maurice. However, is it possible that your decision was based upon the fact that Julian might have been killed yesterday? It seems a very sudden and serious decision to make so soon after a traumatic event, but then again, everyone does react differently in these situations.'

Maurice shuffled his feet and stared down at the ground.

'You needn't say anything right now,' Tish said. 'Just some food for thought. I'll give Jules a call and text you when I know he's OK.'

'Thanks, Tish. You've been a good friend – to all of us.'

She nodded her farewell and watched as Maurice went back to work filming eyewitness accounts to the march on Abbingdon Green.

'You think Maurice was frightened by the intensity of his feelings?' Reade asked.

'You're the guy who left town because you thought Schuyler Thompson was going to ask me to marry him,' Tish reminded him with a smile. 'You tell me.'

SEVENTEEN

Tish and Reade arrived home to find Jules and Biscuit waiting on the front stoop. In one hand, Jules held Biscuit's leash. In the other, the handle of a small roll-away suitcase.

'Oh, my goodness,' the weatherman exclaimed as he took note of the bandage on Tish's head. 'What happened to you?'

'Hazard of being a consultant for the sheriff's department,' she quipped. 'I'm fine. Just a couple of stitches.'

'Oh! I'm so grateful that you invited me over here – even with everything going on with the two of you and this case. I couldn't bear being alone again tonight.'

'We're glad you answered your phone,' Reade responded as he unlocked the front door and led the way inside. 'How are you doing?'

Jules shrugged. 'Not good. I mean, I'm not dying or ill and there are people who have it worse than I do so I shouldn't complain, but . . . yeah, not good.'

Reade placed Biscuit behind the office gate, just as he'd done the previous evening. 'We'll do our best to get you through the worst of it. In the meantime, I could eat a horse. How does Thai sound for dinner?'

'Perfect,' Jules and Tish replied in unison as they hung up their coats.

'Cool, the usual for everyone?'

'Yes, please,' Jules answered before setting off for the kitchen.

'Um, maybe a little extra,' Tish suggested, sotto voce. 'Jules is a stress-eater.'

Reade glanced up from his phone to see Jules inspecting the contents of the fruit bowl. 'Yeah, good call.'

'Oh, you may want to order an extra pad thai or something,' Jules recommended between bites of apple. 'Celestine might stop by.'

'Miss Celly?' Reade questioned.

'Didn't you hear? I thought MJ might have called you, Tish. Celestine had a falling out with her daughter. I'd probably better let her explain it to you, since I didn't quite get all the details – Maurice had just broken up with me, so I was crying, Celestine was crying. It was a mess.' Jules waved his hand and took another bite of apple.

'Poor Celestine. I'd better call her,' Tish determined, pulling her phone from her handbag,

'That won't be necessary,' Reade announced, extracting a bank card from his wallet to pay for the Thai food. 'She just pulled into the driveway.'

After several hugs, a good long cry, and a generous bowlful of chicken in coconut soup, Celestine felt well enough to explain her troubles. 'My daughter, Lacey, came by my house this mornin' to find that Daryl had stayed the night.'

'Oh,' the trio at the kitchen replied in startled unison.

'I don't mean he stayed the night in *that* way. Not now – not yet!'

'Sorry,' they murmured in reply.

'No need to apologize. Y'all make me feel like some hot young thing,' she said with a self-deprecating laugh. 'Anyways, I couldn't sleep last night. My mind just kept traveling back to the Springs. I couldn't call Lacey or my other kids at that hour – they all have jobs and kids of their own – and I didn't want to trouble you folks.'

'You could have,' Jules said. 'Tish and I were awake, too.'

'I didn't know, so I texted Daryl just to see if he was awake. He was. He said he'd been thinkin' of me and wonderin' how I was doin'. We texted back and forth for a little while and, next thing you know, he was at my door. We sat in the living room and talked and had some tea and cookies and toast. When I didn't feel like talkin', Daryl read to me. Poetry. Beautiful, soothing poetry. He rubbed my feet. He comforted me. It was . . . wonderful. He turned a nasty situation and made it a good one just by bein' there.' Celestine's eyes welled with tears – this time they were happy. 'I nodded off from time to time while he was readin' – the tone of his voice was so soft. He nodded off from time to time, too. He was in the recliner. I was on the sofa, but I knew he was nearby. Every time I woke up, he was right there makin' me feel safe. Before we knew it, it was mornin' and Lacey was comin' in the door.'

'And Lacey became angry over that?' an incredulous Tish asked.

'No, like y'all, she thought that Daryl had spent the night the *other* way. You see I was in my nightgown and it was obvious Daryl was wearin' the clothes he'd worn the previous day, so naturally she thought the worst. After her carryin' on for some time, I was finally able to explain, but it didn't make any difference. In Lacey's eyes, I was bein' unfaithful to her daddy.' Celestine threw her hands up in the air.

That Daryl Dufour might actually be Lacey's father – a product of a high school romance that had been in full swing when Lloyd Rufus had arrived in town and swept Celestine off her feet – was a secret Tish had sworn to keep concealed. 'Maybe if you give her some time to process?' the caterer suggested.

'Yeah, that's what Daryl and I thought, too. But when she called me in the afternoon she was in an even worse state than she was this mornin'. She told me, in no uncertain terms, that if I was still keepin' company with Daryl, I was no longer welcome in her home. She then told me that her brothers and sisters felt the same way and that they'd all decided I was no longer invited for Thanksgiving. Invited, as if I were a casual acquaintance and not a contributing member of the family. I was crushed.'

'Did you tell Lacey how much she'd hurt you?' Jules asked.

'No, I dug in and doubled down. I was so hurt and angry, I told her about my date with Daryl next Sunday.'

'Date?' her friends repeated, once again in unison.

'Not *that* kinda date,' Celestine clarified, and then backtracked. 'OK, maybe it is *that* kinda date, but it's not like a romantic evenin' in the city or some grand event. We're goin' to the tree lightin' ceremony in town square. I'm gonna pack some leftover pumpkin pie and a thermos of cocoa and we'll find a bench somewhere and enjoy. It's to relive a date we had as kids – only thing is, the ice-cream shop we went to after the tree lightin' is closed, so we improvised with the pie and cocoa.'

'Sweet,' Reade remarked.

'Yeah.' Celestine flashed a smile. 'Yeah, it is. I was so lookin' forward to it . . . still am, I guess, even though it's been tainted by all of this. We'll see how I feel about it later this week.' Tears returned to her eyes. 'You know, I loved my husband, Lloyd, with all my heart, but it could be awfully lonesome sometimes. Romance fades over time, especially when you're tryin' hard to take care of a family . . . I understand that, always did – but Lloyd and I were often livin' separate lives. He worked all the time and I raised the kids. If he wasn't workin' he was mowin' the lawn or goin' fishin' with his buddies. We didn't spend much time alone together. When the kids were teenagers, I found out he was havin' an affair with the woman who ran his office. We went through a rough patch, for sure, but I forgave him in the end – namely because I didn't want to break up our family, but it was hard. I'd forgiven him, but I hadn't forgotten. I never could forget. For a while, I worried he might do it again and maybe, the next time, leave me and the kids to be with her. It seems ridiculous now, the thought of him runnin' off like that, but at the time it was very real. Of course, I couldn't say nothin' to anyone. My family didn't like Lloyd as it was, after he knocked me up on our first date and all, so I never told them about his steppin' out. And I couldn't say anything to the children. You can't tell your kids that the father they adore isn't the man they think he is – that'd only turn them against him, and I couldn't do that – so I kept it all inside mostly, except for the few times I'd run into Daryl at the market or the library. I'd talk to him and tell him about my life and, despite my throwin' him over for Lloyd, he listened. He genuinely listened. I never told anyone, but he's the one who encouraged my bakin'. I threw myself into it and it was like a godsend – a new lease on life. Bakin' led to my job at the bakeshop and now with you, Tish. It's been the only thing in life that's been totally mine and it's all because of Daryl's encouragement. After the shootin' yesterday, it occurred to me that all my life – all the time I've known Daryl – it's been like that. Comfortable, easy, and like you said, Clem, sweet. I suddenly realized how short life is. Oh, I knew after Lloyd's death that I wasn't gettin' any younger, but yesterday made it clear. Ain't none of us are here forever. Isn't it better to enjoy our time while we're here? Daryl and I may not have a lot of time as it is, gettin' together again as late in life as we are, but why should we shorten it even more?'

'Well, I for one am in favor of anything that makes you happy,' Tish stated.

'Hear, hear,' Reade rejoined.

'Make that three votes in favor,' Jules added.

'Thanks, y'all. You've really helped this old gal tonight. Thing is I don't know how to move forward. I thought my kids, of all people, would be happy that I'd found companionship with someone who's been a friend of the family for years, but apparently I was wrong. Even once I'd explained everythin', Lacey was concerned about how Daryl bein' at my house looked to other people. At my age, I no longer care about other people's opinions, but I *do* care about my family. So do I tell Daryl I can't see him anymore and then call Lacey to apologize for my selfishness? Or do I stand firm and lose my kids and grandkids?'

'First of all,' Tish started, 'you're not selfish.'

'You are, by far, the least selfish person I know,' Jules added.

'Hey!' Tish replied in mock indignation.

'You're the second-least-selfish person, Tish.'

'I'm with Jules,' Reade chimed in. 'If it weren't for your caring, I may never have returned to town and Tish and I wouldn't have gotten together.'

'Clemson's right,' Tish agreed. 'Without you, my café would never have been a success.' Celestine began to argue but Tish stopped her. 'That's as much due to your caring as it is your baking. And then there's Mary Jo. Without you offering your home, she and Kayla wouldn't have had a place to stay when I was evicted. Celestine, you do so much for so many people – you babysit the grandkids, you bring food to your children and help them with their problems. You nurture everyone you meet. Wanting to be happy and loved isn't selfish.'

'For some people, maybe, but my primary job as a mama and a grandmamma is to make sure my family's happy. If they're not . . .'

'Look, I can't advise you what to do, Celestine. None of us can. You and your family both need to live with your decision. However, I am going to warn you against acting too hastily. Your children are still navigating life without their father – that's probably coloring their reaction to your relationship quite a bit. And you, well, your history with Lloyd is influencing yours. I don't think you should be cutting anyone out of your life right now.'

'But Lacey – my kids – they need me.'

'I know, but as a highly intelligent woman once told me, you can't help anyone if you're falling apart.'

Celestine chuckled. 'I don't think I used those words exactly.'

'No, yours were more colorful, but the message was the same. Put the oxygen mask on yourself first, then help others put on theirs. A happy mother is going to be far more capable at helping her own family find happiness.'

'Using my own words against me, huh?' she said affectionately.

'I'll use whatever works.'

'Thanks, Tish. And thanks, Clem, for having me here.'

'Of course, Ms Celly,' the sheriff replied. 'And don't worry. If things don't work out in time, you can spend Thanksgiving with us. We'd love to have you.'

'Do you have room for one more?' Jules ventured. 'I just can't bear to face my family and explain why I'm single again.'

'Of course.' It was Tish's turn to reply.

'Oh, good! The prospect of Tish's roast turkey has lifted my spirits a bit . . . and my appetite. Where did that leftover pad thai get to?' he asked, glancing around the kitchen table and counters.

'You ate it!' his companions shouted.

'Thanks for inviting Celestine for Thanksgiving dinner,' Tish said to Reade as they settled into bed. Celestine was comfortably ensconced in the guest bedroom across the hall and Jules and Biscuit had again taken up residence in the downstairs office.

'Of course. I could never leave Miss Celly alone on a holiday. Jules either, for that matter,' he explained.

'I'm glad you feel the same way I do about those things. Although I'm sorry that this means the end of our romantic solo holiday supper. I promise we'll do something quiet and intimate at Christmastime.'

'No, we won't.'

Tish was stunned by Reade's apparent negativity. 'What?'

'I know you. Once Thanksgiving is over and the holidays are in full swing, you'll be busy planning specials at the café and decorating both there and here at home, and you'll be inviting our friends around to share in the food and the festivities and, naturally, the presents. You're in your element when you're cooking and entertaining . . . and I, for one, love it.'

'And I love you.' She nestled beneath the covers and leaned over to bestow him with a kiss. 'You're right, you know. I'm really looking forward to having people here for the holidays. There was that potluck gathering at the café last year, but I'd just gotten out of the hospital and you weren't there, so it wasn't as festive as it might have been. This year, however, we have a lot to celebrate.'

'We do. I'm looking forward to all of it. This house has been quiet for far too long – since I've moved in, it's basically been just me and Marlowe. It could do with some noise and rowdiness. After Christmas, however, I'll definitely be in the mood for some alone time with you.' He snuggled beside her.

'I'll ink you into my calendar – happily.'

'Good. How are you feeling tonight?'

'Tired, but otherwise OK.'

'I know the shooting kept you awake last night. Is there anything I can do to help?'

'No, I'm in a much better headspace than I was this time last night. I still wouldn't recommend sneaking up behind me and shouting "Boo!" but I'm far less jumpy.'

'I'm glad. Anything in particular help to soothe your nerves?'

'Yes, you as a matter of fact. This evening, during dinner, I got to thinking how lucky I am that we're together and we're both safe and healthy after everything that's transpired in the last forty-eight hours.'

'True. Either one of us could have been injured . . . or worse. It will be a very meaningful Thanksgiving for me.'

'And for me. Having you – someone who loves me for who I am and who will stand by my side no matter what – has made such a tremendous difference in my life. Sitting at the table tonight, I realized that I went through everything Celestine and Jules did at the Springs yesterday but, unlike them, I have you to lean on. Now that he and Maurice have broken up, Jules is alone again and, although Celestine has Daryl, she's being forced to choose between him and her family. It's not fair, is it, her having to choose? I'm not about to say that to anyone other than you, but it isn't fair to her at all.'

'No, it isn't. I can understand her family being concerned that maybe she's moving a little too fast, but she's known Daryl most of her life. The family knows him, too. They should realize that he'd never do anything to hurt her.'

'I couldn't agree more with your assessment.'

'And are you OK after what happened at Glory's?' he asked.

'Yeah, my head doesn't bother me much at all. I just hope it heals without leaving much of a scar.'

'I wasn't talking about your head, although I'm glad to hear it isn't causing too much discomfort.'

'I'm OK, Clemson. Really. I was shaken up when it first happened. Then, when Bull decided to go outside, all I could think of was alerting you to the situation before anyone got hurt. Now that it's over and I've had some time to think, I'm angry. Tripp Sennette fueled what happened this afternoon just as surely as if he'd lit a match in a dry forest.'

'I know. I'm angry too – even angrier that you got hurt during this whole mess. What happened today should never have happened. I was working with the Lynchburg authorities to bring Bull in for questioning. How he was able to board a train without the authorities knowing, while Tripp Sennette was able to detail Bull's destination on Twitter, is beyond me. Did Sennette work with the Lynchburg police? Did he hire a private investigator?'

'I asked myself the same questions. The only thing I can say with any certainty is that William Bull didn't kill Royce Behrens. If he'd been seen anywhere near Hobson Glen that day, the mob that was outside Abbingdon Green would have formed at Colonial Springs.'

'Precisely what I was thinking. The irony is that Sennette prompted violence against Bull for his role in Behrens's death, but in the end, Sennette only strengthened Bull's alibi.'

'Not that the angry mob who showed up this afternoon will believe his alibi – no matter how strong it is.'

'Mmm,' Reade answered meditatively.

'I know that sound,' Tish joked.

'Yeah, umm, you know I love having you with me on these cases—'

'Why do I sense a "but" coming?'

'Because it is. After I meet with Clayton in the morning, I need to speak with Sennette and possibly the DA. I think it might be best if you're not with me.'

'What? Why?'

"Because if Sennette isn't completely happy with what I have to say to him – and I suspect he won't be – he's probably going to try to make trouble. For me, that means coming after my job. For you, that could be in the form of trying to shut down your café, levying taxes on your property or business – who knows? If he's willing to place citizens in harm's way in order to frame an innocent man of murder, who knows what he's capable of?'

'Do you think he might have killed Behrens?'

'I wouldn't put it past him.'

'Again, what about the AR-15?' Tish questioned. 'What happened to it?'

Reade shook his head. 'That's the only flaw in my theory. He could have stashed it in the woods somewhere to collect later.'

'Except your people have scoured every inch of that trail and have turned up nothing. I'd be as happy as you are to pin this all on Sennette, but we can't fit the evidence to the narrative—'

'We need to fit the narrative to the evidence. I'm kinda regretting the day I ever told you that,' he said jokingly.

'Well, it's true. I will say, however, if Sennette *did* kill Behrens, he didn't pull the trigger himself. He's not the type to get his hands dirty, so if you didn't find the weapon, that doesn't exactly exonerate him – at least not in my mind.'

'That's why I have Clayton checking bank statements for both him and Amanda. Either of them could have afforded to hire a shooter.'

'The grieving widow, huh?'

'Yeah, Clayton got a hold of Behrens's will. Amanda inherited everything but the house.'

'Really? Who did Royce leave the house to?'

'No one; it wasn't his to give away. The residence belongs to Royce's mother, Annabelle. Her house, Lobelia Hall, was passed down to her by her father. Royce's house was given to her by her mother. When Annabelle passes, she gets to decide who inherits it.'

'Hmm. The inheritance alone might be worth killing for, especially when you add Behrens's infidelity to the mix.'

'Yep. We'll see if there's been any unusual activity in her bank account, in case she hired someone else to do the job.'

'Makes sense. Since we're looking at relatives, what about Tamika?'

'Tamika?'

'Yeah, she's been without her father for years and now that he's finally out of jail, she's still having difficulty seeing him because he's remanded to his sister's place in Lynchburg. She could have held a grudge against Behrens. And you have to admit the timing of the shooting is intriguing, coming just two weeks after Bull's release.'

'What would I do without you?' he asked with a smile.

'You're about to find out tomorrow – for the morning, at least.'

'I'm sorry, Tish but—'

'It's OK, honey. Having some time at the café tomorrow actually works out well. There are a few special deliveries I'm expecting and the new menus should be ready to pick up from the printer – they've adopted a new locker system where you can pick up items even on the weekend. I'll bring Celestine down there with me to help get things organized. Some work might be a good distraction for her.'

'Might be good for you, too.'

'Yeah, it probably will be. Oh, maybe I'll stop by the market tomorrow morning, too.'

'Good idea. It sounds like we're going to need another turkey.'

'Sweetie, you saw how Jules was eating tonight. We're going to need another *everything*.'

EIGHTEEN

'I didn't kill Royce Behrens,' William Bull asserted from the bunk inside the sheriff's office holding cell in which he'd spent the night.

'I know,' Reade replied, perched in a chair nearby. 'We called your sister. Witnesses in Lynchburg confirm that you and she were at your local grocery store at the time of the shooting.'

Bull's face registered relief. 'Then you're not pressing charges?'

'Not for that, no.' He handed the prisoner a wax paper parcel containing an egg and cheese sandwich on a Kaiser roll. 'Hungry?'

Bill accepted the package eagerly. 'Thanks.'

'Tish made it for you before I left this morning. Until her café opens, there are no breakfast places in town, so she decided to provide the catering.'

'Tell Tish I said thanks,' Bill said before unwrapping the sandwich and taking a bite.

'Want some coffee or tea?' Reade offered.

'Nah, one of your guys brought me a bottle of water. I'm good.'

'So, to answer your earlier question, I'm charging you with violating the terms of your release, but given your circumstances – that you were here visiting your daughter and never approached the Behrens family or anyone in Town Hall – I've recommended that you be put on probation. I know it's a step backward from total freedom, but it's the best I can do.'

'I can definitely live with probation. I could even live with another year in prison if I absolutely had to, but I can't lose contact with Tamika again. Not now that I've finally found her again.'

'I'll help you in any way I can,' Reade promised.

'Thank you. I gotta say I'm surprised.'

'Because I'm a cop?'

'Yeah. The last sheriff made it seem like putting me away was the highlight of his career. I know I had my problems back then and I make no excuses for my behavior. I was a wreck, but the last sheriff, he acted like I was a serial killer. It's a stupid complaint for someone with my history, I guess, but it's the truth.'

'I have no reason to have any issues with you. You did your time and you did so without incident.'

'Because I wanted to see my kids. My son is younger and doesn't remember much about me, apart from what his mother's told him, but I hoped that Tamika still remembered and still cared. I'm so happy she did.' Bull's ebullient smile broke only to take a bite of sandwich.

That Bull served fifteen years in prison when he should only have served ten, maximum, for the crimes he committed, bothered Reade. He couldn't get those years back for him, but perhaps there was still a chance for justice. 'I need to ask you about the bids you submitted to the town back around the time your troubles started.'

'I didn't submit any bids, Sheriff. I was strung out on booze and pills back then. Like I told the board before I was released, I thought I'd submitted those bids, but I was mistaken,' Bull swiftly corrected the law enforcement officer, his right eye fixed on the camera in the corner of the cell the entire time.

Reade had watched hundreds of hours of footage taken from that camera during his time as sheriff – he knew precisely the area and range its lens was capable of capturing, as well as the device's audio limitations. Pulling his chair closer to Bull's bunk and angling it, Reade sat down and positioned himself so that his back was to the camera and his head blocked the view of the inmate's face.

Bull watched him in disbelief. 'Sheriff, you're not—'

'I'd have someone switch the damned thing off, but there might be questions.'

Bull shook his head. 'I have nothing to tell you.'

'Nothing?'

'Look.' Bull's voice dropped to a whisper. 'You have no idea what I had to do to get out of jail, OK? No idea.'

'No, I don't. I also have no idea what you went through while you were there. You cleaned up and got sober, sure, but it must have hurt to be away from your kids. Away from home.'

Bill pursed his lips together. It was clear Reade's words had hit home. 'Part of my treatment was to stop blaming others for my actions. I had to accept responsibility for everything I'd done.'

'Even those things you didn't do?'

'For those, I had to let go of my anger. It was part of my rehabilitation. When I went in front of the parole board, I had to be cool, like none of it mattered anymore and, honestly, it doesn't. All that matters is that I'm free and can see Tamika and, eventually, maybe my son will come around.'

Reade raised an eyebrow.

'What I'm going to tell you,' Bull went on to explain, 'I'm only going to say once, you hear?'

'I do.'

'I'm saying it once but I don't want to hear it repeated. I don't want anyone to say that I lied to get out of jail. And I – I don't want to let it into my heart again, you understand? I can't.' Bull was whispering, but his tone was resolute.

'I understand,' Reade said solemnly.

'Halfway through my treatment, I started wondering about those bids. I remembered working on them, you know? I remembered, clear as day, spending hours working the numbers and trying to get them to be competitive. Drunk or high, I wouldn't have done all that work and not submitted it. Not when my business was drying up and my kids could go hungry. I am many things, Sheriff, but I would never not take care of my kids. I'd never let them want for anything if I could help it. I mentioned something to my sister during one of her visits. She went home and started looking through the boxes of stuff she and my brother-in-law had taken from my place. It took a while, maybe a couple of months, but she found them. She found my plans. All of them had fax cover sheets and proof of transmission.'

'You sent them to Royce Behrens?'

Bull shook his head. 'Nope. I thought I had, because Behrens was on the planning commission, but like I said, my head wasn't screwed on straight back in those days. No, the bids were sent to the *head* of the planning commission. They were sent to Tripp Sennette.'

'Sennette's laptop and phone have been wiped clean of emails and text messages. Their memory caches have been emptied as well, so we can't even see what websites he might have visited recently. Same goes for all the computers in Town Hall,' Clayton informed Reade, who, prompted by the chime of a text message, picked up his phone to find photos of faxed construction bids sent to him by Bull's sister.

'Of course,' the sheriff distractedly replied, scrolling through and noting the fax transmission times and dates.

'Sir?'

'I'm pretty sure we just figured why the town offices were shut down after Behrens's death.' Putting his phone down, he picked up the French press from the break-room stove and poured two mugs of coffee.

'You think Sennette is responsible?'

'I do.' Reade passed a mug to Clayton. 'There's a good deal of information Sennette is hiding. I also think that to scrub all those computers clean would have required time – either for Sennette to do it himself or, more likely, for him to bring in a tech to do it for him.'

'Behrens's death occurred on a Friday, too. That would have given him all afternoon and the weekend, unless someone tried to log in remotely.'

'That's the beauty of closing the office due to mourning. Anyone doing work over the weekend is going to feel as if they're being disrespectful.'

'Well, anyone except Mayor Thompson,' Clayton noted.

'Yeah, that raises an excellent question. Was Schuyler aware of the reason behind the shutdown? As mayor, he might – or should – have been notified.'

'I'll do my best to find out who knew what and when. As for the data, our tech team is confident that they can retrieve it all in a day or two. The good news is we don't have to wait that long.'

Reade poured some milk in his coffee and led the way back to his office. 'You've got something for me?'

'I do. Whereas Sennette was very careful to clean up his digital trail, Gavin Sheppard was . . . not. He and Sennette began talking about Hobson Meadows at the beginning of the year. It all started with an email from Sennette this past February, asking Sheppard if he could get in on the development deal. Sheppard informed him that he was already partners with Royce Behrens. Over the next few months, Sennette tried to convince Sheppard to ditch Behrens and partner with him instead. In some emails, Sennette appealed to Sheppard using logic – he had lifelong contacts with builders and could navigate, or in some cases circumvent, the whole permit system.'

'Circumvent? That's quite an interesting selling point,' Reade remarked as he thought back to Sennette's time on the planning commission and wondered just how long he'd been 'circumventing' building codes and regulations.

'At other times, Sennette said to Sheppard what he would never have said in public,' Clayton continued. 'That Behrens was a loser, a "mama's boy," and a liar. By springtime, Sheppard was echoing Sennette's sentiments. He was tired of Behrens and his constant over-promise and under-deliver strategy, and he actually told Sennette of his weariness. Soon afterward – late May or early June – the pair had an in-person meeting where Sennette pitched a potential deal. There was no mention of the details of the deal, but I do have evidence that Sennette's foundation was paying the lease on the building Sheppard used for his business.'

'A building in which Sheppard has also been living as of late. Nice work, Clayton.'

'Thank you, sir.'

'So, how much were these lease payments and when did they start?'

'Six thousand dollars every month, starting July first.'

'Right after the planning commission meeting,' the sheriff mused aloud. 'So, with Behrens, Sheppard had to wait until units sold to get his payday, but with Sennette, not only did he get a less volatile, less greedy partner with better connections – although about the same amount of scruples – but he also got the added security of knowing that he wouldn't be evicted before that payday arrived.'

'I know which partner I'd choose,' Clayton said while sipping his coffee. 'Although there might have been an additional catch to their agreement.'

'A catch?'

'Yeah, there was an additional ten-thousand-dollar deposit in Sheppard's account from Sennette's foundation the day before the murder.'

'You're thinking Sennette might have paid Sheppard to get Behrens out of the way?' Reade questioned.

'That's how I figured it. There was no way Behrens was going to step aside and let Sheppard take Sennette on as a partner, and both men benefit from his death. If Sheppard was hungry enough—'

'And Sheppard was – and is – literally hungry . . .'

'Then he might have murdered Behrens for a price.'

'Ten thousand isn't enough to risk life imprisonment with no parole. And why would Sennette pay Sheppard prior to the murder? Why not wait until he finished the deed?'

'Maybe it was a down payment,' Clayton suggested. 'Something to help Sheppard overcome his cold feet. Or maybe it was to help Sheppard buy the gun and ammo.'

Reade remained skeptical. 'I suppose it's possible. Both of them benefited massively from Behrens's death, but Sennette even more than Sheppard since he's now eligible for the deputy mayor position. But if so, what happened to the second and more significant portion of the payment?'

'I don't know. You've got me there.' He shrugged. 'All I know is that Sennette's a politician. He's arrogant and has gone out of his way to try to cover his tracks. If Sennette is responsible for Behrens's death, there's no chance he'd have pulled the trigger himself. He'd have someone else do the dirty work for him.'

Reade drank back the last of his coffee. 'Yeah, Tish and I came to the exact same conclusion last night.'

'By the way, where is Tish this morning? Is she OK?'

'Yeah, she's been shaken up by events these past two days and she has a few stitches in her head, but otherwise she's fine. She has some work to do over at the café and, quite honestly, I didn't want to subject her to Sennette when I confront him today. The guy wields a little too much power for a councilman.'

'Yeah, anyone who can rile up a mob the way he did is dangerous. And he seems determined to frame Bull for Behrens's murder.'

'He certainly wants Bull out of the way,' Reade agreed. 'I can't figure out if it's just to cover up for his past transgressions, or if he also wants to deflect from his own guilt.'

'Past transgressions?' Clayton questioned.

'Yeah, I'll explain it to you when the case is over.'

'OK. Now that I know there are past transgressions involved too, I'll say he's also covering up for the fact that he either directly or indirectly murdered Behrens. Like you said, Sennette had two reasons for wanting Behrens dead. Framing Bull also demonstrates what we just discussed – Sennette lets other people do his dirty work. In this case, he stirs up a mob to take Bull out for him.'

'True enough, but the Sennette-Sheppard murder theory still doesn't feel quite right to me. It's one thing for Sennette to pay for Sheppard's rent out of his foundation, but to pay him for a killing from that same account is another matter entirely. Sennette can lie his way out of using his political office to facilitate a real-estate deal – Behrens did it all the time and no one batted an eye – but he can't lie his way out of financing a murder. No, leaving a money trail that connects him to a contract killing is both messy and stupid, and Sennette doesn't strike me as either. That Tweet he sent yesterday afternoon was very carefully worded to incite violence while avoiding any mention of it altogether. Sennette is a man who takes his time and thinks things through. That's how he's managed to stay out of the limelight all these years.'

'Are you saying you don't believe Tripp Sennette killed Royce Behrens?' Clayton challenged.

'I believe Tripp Sennette is capable of just about anything if it involves money or power. He and Royce Behrens were at the heart of everything that's corrupt in this town, but so far the evidence doesn't substantiate our theories. That doesn't mean I'm not going to come down hard on him for the stunt he pulled yesterday, or for what he's done in the past. The guy should be kicked out of office but, if we don't have the evidence to go after him for murder . . .' Reade's voice trailed off. 'Clayton, can you check out all the builders Sennette has had connections with?'

'Yeah, sure. Anything in particular I'm looking for?'

'I want to see how many of them did work on town projects.'

'OK . . .' the officer sang.

Reade had hoped to keep Clayton in the dark about his conversation with Bull, but he realized that, without being specific, he needed to keep him somewhat in the loop. 'I have reason to suspect that it was Sennette and not Behrens who tossed Bull's bid documents.'

'You mean he tossed them in favor of his usual guys,' Clayton completed the thought.

'The usual guys who circumvented local laws and building codes so that the jobs came in under budget.'

'Leaving the contractors and Sennette to pocket the rest of the cash.'

'Tripp Sennette has been on the planning commission of this town since before I arrived. He'd know how to make bids disappear.'

'It also provides another reason for Sennette to wipe the Town Hall computers clean,' Clayton reasoned. 'And you're still not convinced that he's Behrens's killer?'

'No, not thoroughly.' Reade was still reluctant. 'If Sennette's been defrauding the town of construction permit fees and who-knows-what-else, he's not going to make the mistake of paying someone to kill Behrens with a bank account that can be tied to him.'

'You're right, but it's frustrating,' Clayton lamented. 'I'm sure Sennette is our guy.'

'Police work can be frustrating,' Reade commiserated. 'The important thing is to stay focused, but not so focused on what we believe to be the truth that we miss other possibilities. That said, what else did you happen to find?'

'Amanda Behrens's financials checked out clean. She and her husband shared a checking and savings as well as a few investment and credit card accounts. Converse to Royce Behrens, who had three individual bank accounts, Amanda has nothing in her own name – no credit cards, no savings account, not even the utilities are in her name – and all the expenditures she's made have been for groceries, sporting goods and clothes for the kids. About what you'd expect from a mom.'

'A mom in 1957, maybe. Are you positive she had no credit cards or accounts of her own?'

'Not a single one.'

'Odd. What about hair appointment charges? Nail salons? Clothing for herself?'

'No nail salon charges, but there are the occasional hair salon or clothing charge. Nothing on a regular basis and nothing expensive either – just the basics. She bought tons of stuff for the boys, though.'

'Annabelle did say that her daughter-in-law's attention went mostly toward the children.'

'Yeah, unlike her husband, whose attention was elsewhere – in this case, Lucy Van Gorder.'

'You found something?'

'Van Gorder made a cash deposit of twenty thousand dollars into her personal checking account the day before Royce's murder. In five years of bank statements, there was never an instance where she made a cash deposit that large into her personal account. Into her business account? Sure, but she was meticulous in listing each the case name and payee for every transaction. She paid herself a biweekly salary, and only in rare circumstances did she make a transfer from her business account to her personal account. Again, when she did so, she listed the reason for the transfer.'

'Twenty thousand dollars that's unaccounted for,' Reade thought aloud. 'That's closer to what a paid gunman would receive as a deposit. And Van Gorder bragged that she was a crack shot.'

'Uh, yeah but no. On the day of the murder, Van Gorder made an eight-hundred-dollar debit payment to a women's health clinic in Richmond. I followed up with the health clinic. They refused to tell me the nature of her visit, but confirmed that she was there from eleven o'clock in the morning until five o'clock in the evening.'

Reade frowned. 'Six hours. You don't have to be a doctor to figure out what happened there, do you?'

'No, sir. I tried to track down who gave Van Gorder the money, but I've come up empty.'

'Well, we can both make an educated guess, can't we?'

'I've already pulled Behrens's financial records and started looking through them. So far, no trace of a twenty-thousand-dollar withdrawal.'

'If he made the payment, it will show up somewhere. Hey, Lucy Van Gorder earns a fairly sizeable income, doesn't she?'

'About half a million a year,' Clayton replied before polishing off his cup of coffee.'

'Tossed aside by the lover who got her pregnant, she has a strong motive – and she easily could have afforded to hire a killer as well.'

'Except that I haven't seen any weird withdrawals or payments in any of her accounts.'

'Well, keep digging, Clayton. We'll find the answer somewhere.'

The phone on Reade's desk rang. The sheriff answered it and, after several seconds, thanked the caller and hung up. 'It looks like you'll be going with me this morning after all.'

'Sir?'

'Another angry crowd has assembled. This time it's outside Town Hall.'

'I'm not sure why you're here with me when you should be out with Clem,' Celestine said to Tish as they unloaded boxes of supplies and loaded them onto the shelves of the café's storeroom. 'Y'all have a shooter to catch. It also hasn't escaped my attention that Clem is a whole lot better lookin' than I am.'

'There's a lot of work to be done before we open,' Tish explained. 'I can't expect you – or anyone else for that matter – to do it all alone while I'm off on a case. We have shelves and fridges to stock, curtains to hang, bathrooms to outfit, and menus to proof.'

'Oh, the menus are in? I can't wait to see 'em. I love the new items you've added. Those "Waiting for Go-dough" savory breakfast rolls with ham and smoked Gouda that we tested were such a clever riff on cinnamon rolls.'

'Yeah, well, when you top anything with herb butter, it's bound to taste good.'

'And the "Taming of the Stew" should be a huge hit this winter. I expect some of our seniors might request it for their Sunday lunch. I swear, I've never tasted lamb stew as good as that one.'

'It all came together by accident. I was experimenting at home to see if lamb shoulder – which many people think of as too gamy – would mellow out if cooked like the shank, so I threw in some leeks, onion, root vegetables, fennel, and plenty of red wine. The minute he tasted it, Clemson requested the leftovers for his lunch the next day.'

'Lucky man, gettin' to taste-test your recipes.' Celestine punctuated the sentence by breaking down an empty box with her foot.

'Meh, not all of them are successes. He's eaten through some pretty so-so dishes.' Tish picked up a carton of canned tomato products and placed it in front of Celestine to be unpacked while she unloaded a case of pasta.

'With a smile, no doubt.'

'Yeah he's good-natured about that stuff.'

'He must be missin' you today,' Celestine noted. 'Big case like this and him workin' without you?'

'On the contrary, Clemson didn't want me around when he confronted Sennette for stirring up trouble at Glory's yesterday.'

'I can understand him takin' that position. You've been through enough, thanks to Mayor Schuyler "too-big-for-his-britches" Thompson. You don't need another so-called "fine gentleman" of this town makin' trouble for you. Not now that you're settled and set to open your new café.'

'I suppose,' Tish allowed. 'I'm just afraid of what Sennette might do to Clemson.'

'You bein' there ain't gonna control that,' Celestine wisely advised her friend. 'Whatever that man's gonna do, he's gonna do. People like him don't stop for anybody.'

'You're right,' Tish agreed, breaking down the now-empty carton of pasta and preparing to unload a variety of cooking oils. 'Besides, Clemson knows what he's doing.'

'That he does. He'll figure out how to handle Sennette and his bullyin'. You worryin' about him won't help. It'll only make you jumpy, and there's been enough of that goin' around already.'

'Oh, I know. Did you get any sleep at all last night?'

'A little more than the night before. That bed in your spare room is awfully comfortable, but my brain kept getting' in the way. I finally drifted off sometime round three. I'll count that as a win. How about you?'

'It took me a little while to fall asleep, but once I did, I crashed.'

'Good. Say, I, uh, I'm goin' out around lunchtime – if you want me to pick up those menus from the lockbox, I'd be happy to do it,' Celestine offered.

'Yeah, if you don't mind, that would be great. I don't want it to interfere with any of your other errands,' Tish, moving the box of oils to the kitchen area, said.

'No errands to interrupt. I'm meetin' Daryl.'

'Oh, a little lunch date? How nice.'

'Yeah, it's not a date, really. I'm gonna tell him about Lacey and the family disownin' me. I was goin' to tell him this mornin' when I called him, but I couldn't tell him like that – not over the phone.'

'I'm sorry, Celestine. I really am.'

'I know, honey. Nothin' you can do about it. Just somethin' I have to figure out on my own.'

'You're not saying goodbye to Daryl, are you?'

'No, not yet. I'm gonna explain what happened and see if he has any suggestions.'

'I think that's a very smart move. The two of you need to face this together.'

'I don't know, Tish. I was also thinkin' of us takin' a little break until I can sort things out.' Celestine disassembled another box, a deep frown upon her face.

'Do you want to take a break from Daryl?'

'No. We've really been gettin' to know each other better these past few weeks. It's been a joy. A genuine joy. But,' she added with a sigh, 'family comes first.'

'I recommend that you not make any hasty decisions. Meet with Daryl and see what happens. Listen to him, let him comfort you, and then wait and see how you feel. You can always decide later that you want to break things off for a little while, but don't let it be a knee-jerk response to your family's disapproval. Take some time and be patient and gentle with yourself.'

'How'd you get so good at handin' out advice?' the baker asked with a warm smile.

'By listening to you.' Tish gave the woman a quick hug and then proceeded to arrange the cooking oils near the stove for easy access. When she looked up from her work, she noticed a boy doing wheelies in the parking lot on his bicycle. He was tall, thin, and tow-headed, and clad in black sweatpants and a black hoodie tied tightly over his head. Although the activity he was engaged in was a happy one, there was an air of impenetrable sadness about the young man, which matched the dark clouds that littered the sky on that late November Sunday. 'Celestine, who's that?'

'That's the Behrens's boy,' Celestine answered as she peered over Tish's shoulder out the window. 'The younger one.'

'Ladd?'

'Yep, that's the one. He looks more and more like his mama with each passin' day. Includin' that puckered brow of hers.'

'The poor boy just lost his father,' Tish reminded.

'Oh, I know, honey. That wasn't a criticism of Ladd. Not at all. I feel mighty sorry for the boy – always have. You know how the Royal Family has an heir and then a spare? Ladd's the spare. Charles – folks call him Chase for some reason – is the heir apparent in that family. Tall, dark, athletic – Charles is the son most likely to follow in his daddy's footsteps. And, if Ms Annabelle had her druthers, in his granddaddy's too. That's not to say Ms Annabelle doesn't love both her grandkids, but Chase is the one folks have their money on to carry on the family political tradition.'

'I know you talk to lots of people, but how do you know all this?'

'Royce and Amanda used to live on my street when they were first together – right up to the time when Ladd was first born.'

Celestine's lovely tree-lined but decidedly working-class neighborhood stood at odds with the Behrens's social standing within the community. 'On your street?'

'Yeah, you know the yellow dormered cape just before the stop sign? Well, it was blue back then, but that's the house. Royce bought it when he'd just been elected to the council. He used to live in the big old house up on High Ridge, the one left to Ms Annabelle by her mama, but she lost patience with all the lies he told during the campaign and his overall bad behavior after bein' elected – you know, drinkin', womanizin', comin' home all hours. She kicked him out of the family home and wouldn't give a red cent toward findin' a place to live. If Royce proved himself, she'd welcome him back into the fold – and her bank account. So, with the money he did have in his own name, he bought the cape down the street. It was a real fixer-upper, but he put in the investment. Turned out nice, too. Not flashy, but nice. Once the house was remodeled, he took the next big step in provin' he was a "man."'

'Marriage,' Tish guessed.

'Amanda Coker from the Northern Virginia Cokers. Amanda told me all about her family history one day when I was out mowin' the lawn and she was out walkin' the dog. It was like a Who's Who of the American Revolution, and she . . . she talked to me like I was the only friend she had in the world, which maybe I was at that point in time.'

'So she was lonely,' Tish summarized.

'I think so. She'd given up a lot to marry Royce Behrens. She'd graduated with a degree in science – can't remember which one – and wasn't much interested in marriage, by all accounts. I'm not sure if that was because she genuinely wasn't interested, or because she'd been considered a bit of an ugly ducklin' all her life. Amanda was born with some health issues – I can't recall what they were, but she was always thought of as bein' kinda frail. But then she suddenly fell for Royce. And she fell hard. It wasn't long after they'd met that she moved in with him. I remember seeing the light on in that little kitchen of theirs in the evenin's just before Royce would get home from work. It wasn't long before they were engaged to be married. Mama – Ms Annabelle – stopped by once, just after the engagement, to inspect things.'

'You mean she checked to make sure the relationship was legit or that Amanda was up to her standards?'

'Both. I think she was concerned because Amanda's family had the name, but no money. She eventually took a likin' to Amanda, but hoo boy, there were some knock-down, drag-out fights between her and Royce before the weddin' took place. And a good number after, when Royce wasn't exactly toein' the line.'

'By toeing the line, you mean Royce had strayed?'

'Oh yeah. Ms Annabelle didn't abide by infidelity. Her husband did enough of it to last her more than a few lifetimes. I remember one night after Amanda and Royce had had a fight, Ms Annabelle came pullin' into their driveway, tires screechin'. She gave Royce a real dressin' down. It was summertime and all our windows were open, and I could hear Ms Annabelle tellin' Royce that she'd brought him into this world and she was capable of takin' him out of it, too. That brought him down a notch or two. He must have made some sort of bargain with her though, because it wasn't long before he and Amanda put the house up for sale and moved back into the house at High Ridge. They've lived there ever since.'

'What sort of bargain?'

'I have no idea, but I could only guess that Royce had to promise to behave himself and be a better husband and father. Ms Annabelle wouldn't have abided by him messin' up like that and upsettin' Amanda again. She simply wouldn't have abided by it.'

Tish watched in silence as Ladd Behrens performed jumps over a series of parking stops before he was approached by the driver of a black Mercedes-Benz.

It was Amanda Behrens. In the passenger seat was Chase.

Amanda popped open the trunk of the car and gestured for Ladd to put his bike in there and get inside the car. Instead, Ladd hopped on his bike and rode, at top speed, in the opposite direction. Several moments later, and apparently having given the situation additional thought, a still gloomy Ladd lazily pedaled in the same direction the car had traveled.

NINETEEN

S heriff Clemson Reade in his black SUV, and followed by Clayton and a dozen other officers in marked cars, pulled his vehicle to a halt in one of the marked parking spots along Main Street, just outside the Greek revival façade of Town Hall.

The crowd was boisterous but, for the moment at least, respectful. At the sight of Reade exiting his vehicle, they became animated and overtly antagonistic.

'Bull should hang!' shouted one woman.

'Death to Bull,' a group of middle-aged men chanted in unison.

Meanwhile, young people representing a Richmond tabloid distributed red signs emblazoned with the words 'Kill the Killer' in bold white lettering against a bright red background and bearing the newspaper's logo displayed prominently across the top of the sign.

A young officer emerged from one of the squad cars and held his phone aloft for the sheriff to see. 'Sennette's been Tweeting again.'

'William Bull is guilty of murder. SEE THAT JUSTICE IS SERVED!' urged Tripp Sennette's post.

'You want us to go on ahead and quiet things down so you can get into the building?' Clayton offered before they approached the crowd.

'Thanks, Clayton, but no thanks. This is my job, not yours.' Reade cut through the crowd and stood on the front steps of Town Hall to address those assembled there. He was both shocked and disheartened to see Hobson Glen residents he had once considered to be friends holding signs calling for William Bull's death.

'Are you here to arrest us?' a voice in the crowd jeered.

'Arrests were made yesterday because the crowd assembled on private property,' Reade answered. 'Also, certain members of that crowd became violent and committed acts of vandalism. Town Hall is a public building and it is your right – every resident's right – to protest here, so long as you do so peacefully. My officers will be here to ensure that everything remains peaceful; that includes protecting your right to protest against those of differing opinion who might attempt to retaliate against you. I must admit, however, that the reason for your gathering both saddens and alarms me. See, when I ran for the office of sheriff, I was under the impression that the people of this county believed in the same things I did. The belief that decent people should be able to go to sleep at night knowing that they're safe and secure in their own homes; that everyone – no matter their religion, creed, skin color, gender or sexual orientation – should be treated equally in the eyes of the law; that every person deserves a fair trial, and that people should be considered innocent until proven guilty. Given the signs you're holding and the words you're chanting, it seems I was wrong about the last two.'

An uncomfortable silence fell over the crowd as Reade continued.

'When I was sworn in as sheriff, I took an oath to protect every citizen in this county and to carry out the laws of this town, county, and the Commonwealth of Virginia. That oath has become engrained in my very being. It's an oath that I have upheld, no matter the crime, no matter the situation, no matter the individual. So far, my office hasn't found a single shred of evidence connecting William Bull with Royce Behrens's murder. Not one single connecting thread,' he emphasized. 'Meanwhile, we've identified a half-dozen other suspects with a motive to want Behrens dead. Of course, everything we've found can change at any moment because it is an open investigation and we are still analyzing clues and reviewing witness testimony and statements. That is what we do when a crime is committed – we investigate every single clue, every possibility. We let the facts lead us. We don't lead the facts. I promise that we will find Royce Behrens's killer, just as we've found every other individual who has threatened the safety of our community, and when we find this person, we will make sure that our investigation has been thorough and the evidence plentiful so that the individual can be prosecuted to the fullest extent of the law. Not *beyond* the law, not *above* the law, but *to* the fullest extent of the law. Because if we abandon the law, then we abandon civility and decency. We abandon ourselves and each other.'

Reade turned his back on a now-silent crowd, walked between Town Hall's tall, bleached columns, and used his security card to gain admittance through its centuries-old carved wooden doors. Once inside, he walked up a pair of terrazzo steps to the second floor and entered the third office on the left. There, Tripp Sennette, in his usual workday attire of dark blue suit, white shirt and red tie, sat behind the desk in his office.

'Sheriff.' He addressed Reade without standing. 'I must say I'm surprised you asked to meet me here today.'

'It was either here or at my office. I figured we'd have more privacy here. In hindsight, that was a mistake. If you were at my office, you probably wouldn't have had a chance to post this.' Reade placed his phone on the desk in front of Sennette. The councilman's Tweet filled the display.

'Just telling my constituents what they need to hear. The things that other officials don't have the courage to say.'

'And what you Tweeted yesterday, William Bull's location – I suppose you think that was courageous, too?'

'He wasn't supposed to come near Hobson Glen or Royce Behrens again. Those were the conditions of his release. He violated those terms,' Sennette asserted. 'By visiting Glory's, he was breaking the law.'

'If you were so concerned about the legality of the situation, why not call my office? Why not tip us off? Why not just turn him in? No, you weren't concerned about justice being served. You were out for blood. Your Tweet this morning proves that you still are. Last night, I started to wonder why. Could it be that William Bull knew something about you – something you're desperately hoping he's forgotten? Or is it something else? Maybe you're insisting that Bull murdered Behrens because you're the actual killer.'

Sennette gave an obnoxious snort. 'How many days have gone by on this case and that's the best theory you have to offer? Son, you'd better stop working on the Sabbath and get praying. Pray for insight and guidance.'

'Oh, I have insight . . . and receipts. We know that you and Gavin Sheppard were partners. We know that you've been trying to get in on the Hobson Meadows deal since February. We know that in order to woo Sheppard to your side, you started paying the rent on his building. We know that once your partnership was forged, you and Sheppard were trying to edge Royce Behrens out of the picture for good.'

'That's preposterous,' Sennette sputtered, although his reaction made it clear that Reade's assertions were not quite as preposterous as Sennette would have other people believe.

'Yeah, it was preposterous,' the sheriff agreed. 'A man like Royce Behrens wasn't about to roll over and let you horn in on a good business deal. Not you. Not someone who's been bypassed as mayor how many times?'

Sennette's pallid face turned a bright crimson.

'You needn't answer,' Reade instructed. 'Your face says it all. Behrens stood between you and everything you've ever wanted: to be mayor of Hobson Glen and to continue to control the area's construction and real-estate market.'

'Control? I never—'

'Didn't you? In your emails to Sheppard, you bragged about your connections with area contractors and your ability to, not just navigate, but circumvent the whole permit system. Your words, not mine.'

Sennette went from irate to amused within seconds. 'Sheriff,' he chuckled, 'you know what it's like when you want to impress someone. You say anything that comes to mind.'

'Then you admit that you were trying to become Gavin Sheppard's new partner?'

And back to irate again. 'No! I admit no such thing.'

Reade, meanwhile, was unflappable. 'That's OK. We have the emails you sent Sheppard and pretty soon we'll have all your emails, as well as all the paperwork from the many projects you approved during your time as head of the planning commission and beyond.'

'This is absolutely absurd! Why are you wasting your time on me when you should be out there looking for Behrens's killer?'

'I am looking for Behrens's killer. I might even be looking at him right now.'

'What? Me? Have you lost your mind?'

'No, just wondering why you paid Gavin Sheppard ten thousand dollars the day before the shooting.' Reade still didn't believe it was a down payment on a killing, but while he had the councilman alone, he was going up against him with everything he had.

'I didn't!' Sennette was spluttering now, his sizeable jowls quivering as he shook his head. 'Why would I pay anyone that amount of money?'

'Technically, you didn't. Your foundation did – the same foundation that's been paying Sheppard's rent the past four months.'

Tripp Sennette leaned back in his chair and clasped his hands across his broad chest. 'Foundations transfer money all the time.'

'And they transfer it to pay the leases of sketchy young real-estate developers who are living out of their offices?'

Sennette smiled. 'I'm in politics. I'm not familiar with the workings of trusts.'

'Seriously? Next thing I know, you'll be telling me you have no idea how to work "the Twitter." We have Sheppard's emails, bank records and text messages – even without your cooperation, we have enough to prove that the two of you had a partnership.'

Sennette rose from his seat to retaliate, but then thought better of it. 'OK,' he started as he sat back down. 'OK. You got me. It was a down payment.'

A down payment? Reade nearly leapt out of his seat. Had Clayton been correct all along? If so, he sincerely wished his junior officer could be present to listen to Sennette's confession. 'Go on,' Reade urged calmly.

'Go on? What else is there for me to say? I just told you it was a down payment. Gavin nearly didn't make it to the planning commission meeting because of that old jalopy he's driving. I swear, that boy's father might have given him money, a business, and a college education, but he didn't provide him much in the way of common sense. In any event, I felt sorry for the young man—'

'You mean you were trying to get into his good graces,' the sheriff interjected.

'—so I promised him the down payment on a new vehicle. It would, however, be his responsibility to keep up with the monthly payments, so he could boost his credit, which is a shambles right now.' Sennette pasted on a broad smile. 'You see, Sheriff? That's what my trust is designated for – helping people.'

'The same way you helped William Bull?' Reade challenged.

'That's different. Bull murdered Behrens.'

'There's absolutely no evidence that Bull murdered Behrens. As I'm sure your sources can corroborate, Bull was with his sister in Lynchburg at the time of the shooting.'

'My sources?'

'The same sources that informed you that Bull got on a train to

Hobson Glen. No, as I said earlier, there's a reason you're trying to frame Bull for the murder and I know precisely what it is.'

'Do I really have to sit here and waste my time listening to more of your ridiculous conjectures?'

It was Reade's turn to lose his temper. 'First of all, how dare you! How dare you complain about the waste of your time when this shooting has this entire town – this community – hurting. Thankfully, no one other than Royce Behrens was wounded at Colonial Springs, but the psychological damage inflicted in those few brief minutes is something that cannot be undone. Citizens of this town are having trouble sleeping, thinking, concentrating. They're wondering if it's safe to send their kids to school – to leave their homes to visit distant relatives over the holiday weekend. They've seen their lives pass before their eyes and are reflecting on their past and future actions. Their sense of security has been shaken to its very foundation, and you're on Twitter stoking their fears and pitting them against each other to cover your own tracks. You're stoking fear in order to increase your hold over them and your authority in this town and it's absolutely pathetic.

'Second,' Reade continued, 'what I'm about to say isn't conjecture. Just as I had regarding your partnership with Sheppard, I have receipts. In this case, transmission receipts from the fax machine William Bull used to send his bids – not to Royce Behrens – but to you.'

'You're mistaken. Royce handled—'

'No, councilman. I'm not mistaken,' Reade interrupted. 'The fax number on the transmission printout matches the fax number you once had for your office, and the cover sheet lists you as the recipient. I'd show you the images, but I'm afraid that pulling them up on my phone might accidentally stop the voice recorder.'

Once again, the color drained from Sennette's face. 'You've been recording me?' he shouted.

'Of course. When I called you to arrange for our meeting, I made it clear that this was a formal interview in compliance with established Sheriff's Office protocol.'

Sennette rose from his chair. 'You never said you'd be recording me,' he bellowed.

'As a councilman, you should be aware of the laws that govern this town and county. It's your duty as an elected official. If you didn't understand what I meant, then you should have—'

'Understand? Of course I understand, but I never imagined you'd be recording our conversation. Your predecessor never would have.'

'My predecessor also arrested William Bull without even asking to see the bid documents.'

'Are you implying—?'

'I'm implying nothing. I'm stating quite clearly that my findings, once substantiated by further evidence, are more than enough for me to request your resignation. That's on top of the criminal investigation you might face.'

Sennette became absolutely apoplectic. 'I-I'll have your badge before that happens! You'll learn better than to mess with me.' With that final threat, Sennette grabbed Reade's phone from the table and smashed it down on the hard, tile floor, shattering it to bits.

TWENTY

With the café in Celestine's capable hands, Tish decided to make a quick trip to the market before their early Sunday closing to procure the additional ingredients needed for Thursday's newly expanded Thanksgiving dinner. She had just turned onto Main Street when she saw a crowd of approximately eighty people gathered outside Town Hall, angrily shouting and bearing signs calling for all manner of harm and imprisonment to befall upon one William Bull.

Spying the figure of Clemson Reade standing amid the police presence at the scene, Tish pulled her van into the parking lot behind Town Hall and walked around to the front of the building to meet him.

'Hey,' he greeted in surprise. 'I didn't expect to see you here.'

'I didn't expect to see them here.' She gestured toward the mob of protestors.

'Yeah, there's twice as many people as there were earlier this morning and a good chunk of these people seem to be from out of town.'

'Out of town? Why would people outside of Hobson Glen be protesting?'

'Because Sennette's been fearmongering again. He Tweeted that what's happening here could happen anywhere in Virginia.'

'Someone really needs to break that man's phone,' Tish remarked.

'Yeah, in retrospect I probably should have swapped his phone for mine instead of letting him smash that old burner we had at the station.'

'Smash? Sennette smashed a phone?'

Reade summarized his conversation with the councilman.

'Do you think he could have killed Behrens?'

'Killing him and then pinning it on Bull would have eliminated Sennette's problems, for sure, but I just don't see how he could have pulled it off, unless he hired someone. Clayton and our forensic accountant are looking through his bank records as we speak, to see if he might have hired someone, but it still doesn't feel right. What about the bloody T-shirt? How does that fit into the contract killing scenario?'

'I'm as puzzled as you are, but a thought did occur to me while talking to Celestine this morning. We haven't considered Annabelle Behrens as a suspect.'

'Ms Annabelle? Royce's mother?'

'Yes, it's not as crazy as it sounds. Just hear me out.' She recounted Celestine's experience living as Royce and Amanda's neighbor.

'That's what she screamed at him?' Reade confirmed after Tish had told the tale. 'That she'd brought Royce into the world and she'd take him out of it?'

'That's what Celestine overheard.'

'Mothers say all sorts of things when they're angry.'

'Of course they do, but they typically issue a statement like that to a child who's been misbehaving, not to a grown man with a wife and, at that time, a child of his own. Annabelle must have been ridiculously angry with her son.'

'Or she was still trying to establish control over her child's life,' Reade suggested.

'If Royce was having an affair, either option gives Annabelle a strong motive for "taking out" her own son.'

'Particularly after what Clayton and I discovered. At the time of Behrens's death, Lucy Van Gorder was at a women's clinic. She spent several hours there and paid eight hundred dollars for the visit.'

'You think she had an abortion?'

'Don't you? She also made a deposit of twenty thousand dollars just before Behrens was killed.'

'Implying that Behrens paid her for the abortion and a little extra to keep her quiet,' Tish inferred.

'Once again, Clayton is trying to find the documentation.'

'If this is true . . . if Annabelle knew about Lucy and the baby, she would have been beyond furious. Royce had been kicked out of the house and left without a red cent once before due to his bad behavior. But fathering a child with another woman? Annabelle would have been livid. Not only would Royce have ruined his own marriage – and possibly his career – had word gotten out, but he would have defied his family's and his grandfather's legacy.'

'Murder is a pretty steep penalty.'

'It is, but Annabelle has spent all of Royce's life trying to get him to toe the line. According to Judson Darley, she even suffered physical abuse at his hands when he was younger. Everyone has that proverbial straw, Clemson. Maybe this was hers.'

Tish rang the doorbell of Lucy Van Gorder's Ashton Courthouse cottage and listened to the sound of feet gently padding across hardwood flooring as she waited for the door to open.

'Ms Tarragon,' a surprised Lucy exclaimed. 'I've already told you and Sheriff Reade everything I know.'

'Not quite everything,' Tish replied. 'May I come in?'

Lucy held the whitewashed door open wide to allow Tish admittance. 'So what bit of undisclosed business brings you here?'

'The police have learned where you were at the time of Royce Behrens's death.'

Lucy, dressed in yoga pants, tunic-length sweatshirt and socks, flopped onto a white slipcovered sofa. 'And I suppose they also figured out what I was doing there?'

'The clinic wouldn't share any details and the sheriff's office didn't press for them, but an eight-hundred-dollar charge at a women's clinic for a procedure that required several hours? We all have an idea – whether it's correct or not is up to you to tell us.'

Lucy picked a throw pillow up from the opposite end of the sofa and hugged it to her torso. 'If you thought that I had gone to the clinic for an abortion, you'd be right. I did.'

'I'm sorry to pry,' Tish apologized.

'No, I'm glad they sent you instead of . . . well, some gigantic officer. Why that should matter, I don't know, but it does.'

'Did Royce know?'

'Yes, I told him. As you could imagine, he wasn't happy. Even though he romanced me by telling me that his life would have been so different if he had met me before Amanda, and how he wished I were the mother of his children instead of her. Just like everything else, it was a lie. It was all a lie.'

'So the abortion was Royce's idea.'

She nodded. 'He couldn't even say the word. He just told me to "take care of it." I knew exactly what he meant. I was looking into local providers who accept my insurance when I received the call.'

'The call?'

'Royce's mother, Ms Annabelle. She called me to tell me to stay away from her son.'

'How did she know about you?'

'She didn't say, but she knew. Given her timing, I assumed she knew about my pregnancy too. I was wrong. When I told Ms Annabelle I intended to have my abortion and get as far away from Royce as possible, you could have heard her shriek all the way in Roanoke.'

'So she knew about your relationship, but not about the child,' Tish confirmed, for it would imply that Annabelle didn't learn about the affair from Royce.

'That's right. She was hysterical when she found out. She told me that her son had enough kids already and warned me that if I went public with the relationship, the pregnancy, anything, it would ruin Royce's career, marriage and reputation. I agreed with the first two, but the last? Half the town knew him for what he was.'

'Did you tell Ms Annabelle that?'

'I did.'

'How did she react?'

'Surprisingly, she concurred. She told me that Royce had always been something of a disgrace.'

'That's the word she used? Disgrace?'

'Yes. A disgrace. She went on about how sweet Royce was as a little boy and how much she loved him, but as he grew up it seemed his sole objective in life was to disgrace his family.'

'When she said these things, was she angry?'

'Definitely. I'd even say she was furious – at first with me, then with Royce, and then with me again. She ended the conversation by hanging up on me. You can imagine my surprise when, a few days later, my bank notified me that Ms Annabelle Behrens had deposited twenty thousand dollars into my bank account.'

'Annabelle?' Tish was genuinely surprised.

Lucy pulled her legs up beneath her and grabbed a plush throw from the back of the sofa. 'Yeah, I know, right? If I expected money from anyone it was Royce, maybe wanting to pay for the abortion, but nope. Annabelle.' She wrapped the throw around her shoulders. 'The day before Royce was killed, she called to clarify that the cash was to be used for an abortion and to start a new life – elsewhere.'

'She wanted you out of town?'

'Immediately. She said there were enough Behrenses in this town and the world didn't need any more.'

'I'm sorry you had to deal with that,' Tish responded, as she wondered about Annabelle's curious message. 'It couldn't have been easy given what you were about to face the next morning.'

'It was . . .' Lucy cast her eyes heavenward as if attempting to find the appropriate word to describe the situation. 'Weird. It was weird, but I'm glad it happened.'

Tish's face was a question.

'When she hung up, I started thinking about the baby. I'm in my late thirties, with zero prospects of finding a mate within the next year or so. Every year I wait to have children puts me at greater risk of birth defects or complications. I'm financially stable and can afford to give a child a good life. Apart from some stomach trouble in the months before he was killed, Royce was healthy, intelligent and athletic. And, in response to Annabelle, I would never raise my child as a Behrens anyway.'

'You're having the baby,' Tish deduced.

'I made the women's clinic appointment with the intention of going there for an abortion, but as I got closer to my appointment, the more my pregnancy made sense. I'd always wanted children, so why not? When I arrived at the clinic I spoke with a fertility expert about the odds of me becoming pregnant naturally over the next few years, had a full physical, talked to a counselor about my relationship with Royce and the emotional baggage that could influence my relationship with my child, and scheduled a whole bunch of tests. I've kept Annabelle's money, for now, so she knows I'm going and stays out of my hair, but once I find a place up north, closer to DC, I'll wire it back to her. Until then, don't tell anyone that I'm still pregnant, please?'

'I don't see any need for us to tell, but—' Tish started.

'No, you don't understand. I really don't want Annabelle to know. I'm leaving – leaving just as soon as I can – but I don't want her to know about the baby. I don't want my child to have any contact with any of them – ever.'

Sensing Lucy's fear, Tish sat down beside her and took her hand.
'I won't say a word. I promise.'

Located on the outskirts of Coleton Creek, Lobelia Court was a
1920s Georgian-style structure constructed with entertaining in
mind. Its inlaid wood flooring, wall murals and intricate woodwork
must have set quite the backdrop for the lavish parties of the era.
Today, however, it was host to a flurry of activity of a different
variety.

'Welcome to Lobelia Court,' Ms Annabelle greeted her guests as
she swanned down the central staircase and into the wood-paneled
entrance hall where Tish and Reade stood waiting. In the other
rooms of the house, Annabelle's servants were busy packing boxes
and covering furniture with drop cloths. 'My apologies for the mess.
I'm preparing to move to Amanda's house, and everything that isn't
coming with me is being put into storage.'

'Is this a permanent move?' Reade asked.

'No, just for the winter, perhaps a little longer. We'll see how
things progress, but I hope to be back here by springtime. I just
couldn't bear the thought of missing the anemone, the Dutchman's
breeches, and lilies blossoming. Then there's the willow out back
– my parents planted it when I was a girl. I love to see the new
yellow-green leaves burst open every March.' She smiled. 'This
whole place is filled with such lovely memories, but never so much
as in the warmer months. My granddaddy built this house for my
grandmamma and named it for her favorite flower – lobelia – which
he planted in the front yard and court, because she was the queen.
The lobelia he planted had offshoots and now, in the summer, the
front yard becomes an endless field of deep, deep blue. We had to
thin them out last year so that the gardeners could mow the lawn.
I gave some to Royce and Amanda for their place and now their
backyard is covered. Amanda dries them and keeps them around
the house in winter, but it's not the same as when they're fresh.'

'You said you need to see how things progress. You're not ill,
are you?' Tish inquired.

'No, the doctors assured me that the incident the other day was
just an incident and not any cause for concern,' Annabelle stated as
she smoothed the skirt of her mid-length brown sweater dress about
her hips. 'Still, he would like to see me rest a little more.'

'Ah, so that's why you're going to Amanda's.'

'I don't know. Personally, I'd rest much easier here, amongst my own things, but as soon as I was discharged from the hospital, Amanda called me and insisted I stay with her. She didn't say why, she simply insisted. I suppose part of her feels she's looking after me. I suppose another part of her misses Royce, even though he was never home much except for morning coffee – which she made for him, naturally,' Annabelle added with a chuckle. 'Still, it will be a difficult holiday for all of them and a long, bleak winter.'

'It will be good for you to spend more time with your grandsons,' Tish offered on a positive note.

'It will. I'm only a fifteen-minute drive from them, but they're always so busy; getting them out here for a visit or scheduling a time for me to go there is difficult. I might as well live three states away! Being there at the house will eliminate some of that, although Amanda has those boys on a fairly tight schedule what with school and extracurricular activities. Well, she tries with Ladd, but he's been a little bit lost these past months – those early teen years are difficult, aren't they? I remember,' she said with a chuckle, 'when both boys were little. Just as soon as Ladd was able to crawl, he followed his brother everywhere he went. That's how Chase got his nickname – Ladd would always follow after him saying 'chase, chase,' wanting to chase his brother, yet struggling to keep up. Ladd doesn't follow his big brother as readily as he used to, but he occasionally trails behind him.'

Tish recalled the image of Ladd on his bicycle zooming off in the opposite direction and then, moments later, reluctantly turning around to follow the car which contained his brother.

'Mrs Behrens,' Reade addressed the older woman, 'would it be possible to speak with you in private?'

'Yes, but there's no need for that. My staff has been with me forever. Whatever you have to say—'

'Private would be best,' the sheriff asserted.

'All right.' Annabelle capitulated and led them upstairs and down the hall to a master bedroom resplendent in floral chintz. Once they were inside, she promptly shut the door. 'What is this all about? Have you found my son's killer?'

'Not yet, ma'am. We're working hard on it.'

'Oh, I heard all the talk about William Bull and thought maybe he was your top lead.'

'I'm sorry, no. William Bull has an alibi for the time of your son's death.'

Annabelle threw her hands up in the air. 'There goes that idea, then. So what do you want to see me about?'

'I don't know any other way to say this, than to just say it. We know about your son's affair with Lucy Van Gorder.'

The color drained from Annabelle's face as she plopped down onto the bed. 'How did you find out? Who else knows?'

'Judson Darley was the one who suggested we look into it.'

'Oh.' She sighed in obvious relief. 'Judson is an old friend. A good old friend. You haven't told anyone else, have you?'

'No, ma'am. We try to conduct our investigations with as much discretion as possible.'

'That's much appreciated. Very much appreciated.'

'When did you find out about Lucy?'

'I'd suspected that there was someone new in Royce's life for some time now. Royce had an intense personality – focused on work and success – but I ran into him back in the spring while I was out running errands and I nearly didn't recognize him. He was whistling, carefree. It was most unlike him. I kept my suspicions to myself, but I contacted Darley and asked him to keep an eye on things.'

'Did you often ask Mr Darley to keep tabs on your son?'

'Keep tabs? Look, I never asked him to spy! I asked him to watch for odd things. Signs. People. I never once asked him to follow my son. And, yes, I've relied upon Darley for help with odd jobs since Royce was a boy. He's always been kind enough to oblige. I imagine Darley was in love with me at some point, but he never acted on it. Nor did I. Now that I'm old and gray and withered, I wish that we had.' She stared down her nose at them. 'And before you judge me, there's a big difference between me being tempted to cheat on a man who was never faithful to me and Royce cheating on a woman who'd do anything to make sure he and her family were happy.'

'Neither of us are here to judge,' Tish assured her. 'We only want to get to the truth.'

'The truth? If that's anything like the meaning of life, let me know when you've found it, because I've been searching a long time,' Annabelle replied wearily. 'Until then, I'll tell you everything I know.'

'We would appreciate that,' Reade said.

Annabelle nodded. 'Within days of my calling him, Darley came up with the names of three different women with whom Royce might have been involved. Lucy was at the top of the list, most likely because she's beautiful and accomplished, but I knew that Royce didn't always punch above his weight when it came to his "leisure time" activities. Like his daddy, he made his choice based on vulnerability as much as physical attractiveness. Nor did he always limit himself to one playmate.'

'So, Royce was involved with all of the three women Darley told you about?'

'Yes, in some capacity. Two of them were dalliances, one-night stands, whatever you want to call them, but Lucy was different. Much different. I heard from our family's lawyers – firms we'd worked with for decades – and learned that Royce had severed his contracts with them and hired Lucy Van Gorder to take their place.

'I try not to cling to the past and accept change,' Annabelle continued self-consciously. 'Or I try to convince myself that I accept change, but when a man shrugs off the loyal service of attorneys that his family has retained for ages – at no cost to him, mind – it sends a distinct message.'

'And that message was?' Tish prodded.

'That he'd found someone who he thought could temporarily replace the other people in his life. In politics, Royce planned his every move, but his personal life was all about the here and now. Whatever made him happy or got him ahead in the immediate future, he did, with little thought to the long-term ramifications of his actions. Royce never sought permanence in relationships. When he grew tired of something or someone he would cast them aside with little to no notice.'

'But he'd been married for – what? – nearly twenty years.'

'With my help. I guarded his marriage and family life with every fiber of my being. Amanda was sick when she learned of one of Royce's first affairs – physically sick and couldn't get out of bed. Since then, I've done my best to keep Royce on the straight and narrow, and when I couldn't I did my best to keep Amanda from finding out Royce's foot had slipped again. I did an excellent job, too. That's why when Lucy Van Gorder took over his affairs, I knew we were in trouble.'

'We?' Reade questioned.

'His family. Me, Amanda, the boys. It was crystal clear that Lucy was more than a passing fancy. I didn't know what to do about it at first, so I asked Darley to hush things up as best he could while I confronted Royce.'

'How did that meeting go?'

'Ha!' Annabelle gave a sardonic laugh. 'About as well as one might expect. Royce told me he was in love with Lucy. In love! As if he'd ever loved or cared for anyone or anything other than himself. I know that sounds harsh, but it's true, Sheriff. I don't delude myself as to who or what my son was. I'd been hurt by him too many times – emotionally, financially, and even physically – to pretend otherwise. I gave him chance after chance to turn his life around – to change – but he didn't. Maybe he couldn't. I raised him with the belief that if I showed him kindness and understanding, nurture would win out over nature, but I was a fool. And yet when I look at . . .' Annabelle was about to cite a specific example but abandoned it.

'In any event,' she went on, 'when I confronted Royce and he told me that he intended to see more of Lucy – rather than less – because she could help his career, I lost control of my senses. After all Amanda had done for him, after all of her sacrifice – I just couldn't see straight. I told Royce that I had disowned him before and that I'd do so again and then I told . . .' Her voice cracked. 'I told him that I was sorry that I ever gave birth to him. It was terribly cruel of me to say it, but that was how I felt at the time. Those were the last words I ever said to him.' Annabelle broke into gentle sobs.

'I'm sorry, Mrs Behrens,' Reade said as he handed her the tissue box from her bedside table and then waited for her to compose herself. 'You and your daughter-in-law seem quite close.'

'Close? Not really. We don't spend much time together. Nor do we chat a lot on the phone, but I sympathize with Amanda. She suffered from seizures when she was a young girl. Her peers and family's social network were quite unkind to her. They referred to her as the awkward sister when speaking about her family and, when she was older, they claimed she didn't want to marry, not because it was true but because they didn't think she would or could ever find a potential suitor. She was easy fodder for my Royce. When he first told me he was engaged to her, I couldn't believe my ears. Then I recalled her father's position in Virginia politics and that Amanda's sisters wouldn't have given Royce a second glance. No, like his father, Royce preyed upon perceived weakness to further his own ends.'

'Would you say your husband preyed upon you as well, Mrs Behrens? Was your marriage a means to an end?'

'You're very perceptive, Sheriff. Yes, that vulnerability applies to me as well. I was born and raised in this house. Growing up, I never saw any reason to leave this place for anything. Here were my books, my music, my pets, my art supplies – all the things that brought, and still bring, me joy. I left for school, naturally, but was always thrilled to return. I'd resolved early on that nothing would ever take me from this place. When I was a young adult, I learned the price of keeping the things I love: marriage. Being an only child and a girl, it was my job to marry and marry well. Taking up a profession wasn't quite as common for women back then, and even less common for women of social standing. University wasn't a place for educating my mind, but catching a husband.

'I did, however, enjoy my time there. I majored in art history – when you're not thinking of finding a job, why not? – and, again, immersed myself in things that brought me joy. I was so naive, so young, and, as some would say, lost in my own little world. It was my second year when I met Royce's father at a dance and was completely swept off my feet. That such a handsome, dark-haired and popular young man should be interested in the likes of me was like a dream! He proposed to me while I was in my third year of school and my parents approved of the marriage. We had a good name and reputation, of course, but a mayor's salary doesn't support a house the size of this one, so the Behrens fortune came in handy. Just like my name and breeding came in handy to them.

'I'd only been married two years when I realized that I wasn't the only woman in my husband's life. That I had *never* been the only woman in his life. It was devastating. My entire adult life felt like one gigantic lie, but I was trapped. I couldn't divorce. I'd signed a contract – a contract wherein I got to keep Lobelia Court and my husband got a well-mannered, well-educated, reasonably attractive wife from a good family to host business dinners and fundraising luncheons. So, like Amanda, I threw all my efforts into starting a family and, eventually, raising a son. We know how that turned out,' she scoffed. 'So yes, I can sympathize with Amanda. I've also done my best to protect her and the children. She has a contract with Royce, just as I had with his father, but she needn't have the sordid details of his behavior aired in public so she can't walk down a street without hearing whispers behind her back. I know how that feels.

'When I was a girl and my daddy first became mayor, I used to walk through Hobson Glen, Coleton Creek, Ashton Courthouse – even Richmond – with my head held high. Everyone knew who I was. I was the daughter of a well-loved mayor. Then, when I got married, all that changed. The whispers started. I was still my father's daughter, but I was also the poor, unfortunate, helpless little wife.'

'Is that why you paid Lucy Van Gorder twenty thousand dollars?' Reade asked. 'To protect your daughter-in-law?

'What? Lucy told you? That horrible little—'

'No, we saw the bank transaction,' Reade interrupted.

Annabelle relaxed. 'I had to,' she said softly. 'I had to do *something*. I couldn't let that woman and her unborn child interfere with Royce's family. I just couldn't. You've met Amanda, she's frail enough as it is. And Lucy, she's not a pushover. She wouldn't have walked away like some other women would. She's a lawyer, for heaven's sake. Just the type to demand child support, hospital fees, a share of the Behrens fortune – you name it. I had to get rid of her somehow.'

'And Royce?'

Annabelle looked up at the sheriff with tears in her eyes. 'Are you suggesting . . .? Of course, that's why you're here, isn't it? You want to know if I killed my own son – if I killed my boy. I'm not going to lie to you, Sheriff. I was disappointed, disgusted, and absolutely furious with him. Not only did I tell him that I wished he'd never been born, but I was prepared to never see him again. Now that I can't see him, even if I wanted to, my heart is full of pain and longing. I long to see the little boy I once knew and stroke his hair and I wonder what I'm to do now. My whole life's ambition was to be a mother and now that's gone. Is a mother whose child is dead still a mother? Perhaps I was never a real mother at all. If

I were, Royce might have been a kinder man, a nobler human being. He also might still be alive, which I so wish was the case. So, no, Sheriff, Ms Tarragon, I did not kill my son. I may have been an unsuccessful mother, I may have enabled his behavior with my efforts to conceal it, but I am not a murderer.' She rose from the bed, opened a dresser drawer, and tossed a thin, light-colored blouse into an open suitcase. 'I am, however, still a grandmother. So, if we're finished with this conversation, I'll bid you adieu so I can continue packing.'

TWENTY-ONE

'Do you honestly believe that Amanda Behrens had absolutely no idea of what her husband was up to?' Tish proposed as the SUV headed toward the home that the younger Behrens woman shared with her late husband and children.

'I believe that Amanda probably noticed changes in her husband's routine and behavior, but that without either evidence or confirmation that Royce was being unfaithful, she probably chose to ignore the signs and go on with life as usual,' he opined as he followed the driving directions on the vehicle's navigational system.

'Denial isn't just a river in Egypt, huh? Seems plausible. Annabelle described her as being frail and we both witnessed the terrible physical and emotional state she was in after Royce's death. I'm sure she copes with her situation any way she can.'

'She also has an ironclad alibi for the time of the murder. She'd dropped Chase off at the rec park for his usual afternoon run and was in her car, reading a book, waiting for him to finish at the time the shots were fired. Nor could she have paid someone to murder her husband. All of her assets were shared with Royce. Had she made a withdrawal from a bank account or taken a cash advance in order to pay the killer, Royce would have noticed it.'

'Then we're just speaking with Amanda to confirm Annabelle's earlier statements,' Tish surmised.

'Pretty much. And to see if we can get any new information from her now that she's under less stress than she was the day of the murder.'

'Hm, I was just thinking about Annabelle and some of the phrasing she used.'

'What about it?'

'Well, for starters, Annabelle told Lucy that "we don't need any more Behrenses in this town." Don't you find that a little strange?'

'After the way her son and husband treated her? No.'

'Yeah, but her daughter-in-law and grandsons are Behrenses as well, and she harbors no ill-feeling toward them. It seems strange to me that she'd bundle the two bad apples with the rest of the lot. Plus, her statement makes it sound as if the town is overrun with members of the Behrens family, which it isn't. Then, just now, she made that strange comment about Lucy Van Gorder not fading away like other women.'

'Is that strange, though? Considering how many women he'd been involved with, Royce was extremely lucky none of them went public, especially given he was in public office.'

'Yeah, I suppose you're right, but there's something she's not telling us.'

'That she murdered her son?' Reade guessed.

'No, I believed her when she said she didn't. No, there's something else.'

'Maybe Amanda will be able to help,' he stated as they pulled into the driveway of the stately wood-shingled home at the end of a tree-lined cul-de-sac overlooking the community golf course.

An older man of slight build, who had been raking leaves from the front lawn of the house next door, approached them. 'May I help you?'

Reade held his badge aloft. 'We're here to speak with Mrs Behrens.'

'Oh. I'm afraid she's out for the day. Amanda always takes her older son, Chase, to practice on Sunday. Don't ask me what he's practicing for – I have a tough enough time keeping my own schedule straight.'

'Thanks. And you are?'

'Hank Fairchild. My wife and I have lived next door to the Behrenses since they first moved in.'

'Do you know when they might be back?'

'They usually don't get home until after dark, although they have Ladd with them this time, so they might be earlier. I'm not sure how enjoyable Ladd finds their family outings. He tends to go rogue fairly often, skipping classes, taking off on his bike during family meals. What with that father of his, it's not surprising.' Fairchild glanced worriedly at his visitors. 'Sorry to speak ill of the dead.'

'That's OK, so long as it's the truth. What was Mr Behrens like as a father?'

'Absent. I think that's why Amanda tries extra hard to be

omnipresent in her sons' lives. Her parenting style works for
Chase, but Ladd rejects it totally. My wife and I have an open-
door policy with him – if things get tough at home, he can hang
out at our house, no questions asked.'

'That's very kind of you,' Tish noted.

'Eh, we're retired and our kids are grown, so we have extra time
and plenty of space. If we can help the kid out, we do.'

'Has Ladd ever taken you up on your offer?'

'A couple of times. The first was when Amanda put the boys on
a strict vegan diet. Ladd smelled us grilling burgers in the backyard
and pretended to go out on a bike ride before doubling back and
sneaking through the gate. Man, did he eat. I'd forgotten how much
food teenage boys can put away.'

'And the second time?'

'The day his father died,' Fairchild said with a frown. 'Chase
called my wife and me to give us the news and ask if we could
pick Ladd up from school. Naturally, we said yes. When we arrived,
Ladd was quiet, despondent.'

'Well, his father had been murdered.'

'That was before we gave him the news.'

Reade and Tish glanced at each other.

'He was cold, shivering,' Fairchild continued. 'When we told
him his father had passed, he started shaking uncontrollably. We
got him back here and my wife wrapped him in a heavy blanket
and made him cocoa. Ladd drank it all down in front of the fire I'd
started. We nearly took him to the hospital, but the shaking subsided.
The whole time, he never said a word.'

'Shock,' Reade ventured.

'Yeah. My wife and I tried to engage him in conversation a few
times, but he didn't respond. We didn't want to push him to talk,
so we just did our best to make him comfortable. We made some
fish for dinner – it was Friday night – with coleslaw and a salad.
My wife baked a couple of potatoes to bulk up the meal for Ladd
– she and I are low carb these days. He devoured everything on
his plate and went back for seconds. After dinner, he took a long,
hot shower. I gave him an old pair of my sweats to change into
and a clean pair of socks. He seemed a bit better – he wasn't
cold and shivering any longer – but he still didn't say a word. He
watched a little TV with us – again without reacting – and then

went to bed in our son's old room. He didn't wake until nearly one o'clock the next afternoon.'

'What did you do with his dirty clothes?'

'I bagged them up and he took them home with him.'

'And what happened when Ladd got up the next day?'

'He wanted to head back home right away, but we – my wife, really – persuaded him to stay and have some breakfast before he left. He still didn't say much of anything and we didn't push. We just wanted him to feel safe and secure, you know?'

'Did Mrs Behrens – Amanda – know that Ladd was here?' Tish asked.

'We called her when we first got home with Ladd, but she didn't answer, so we left a message. We tried again when Ladd was in the shower and the next morning while he was asleep. Same thing. No answer.'

'I know you said Mr Behrens was frequently absent from his children's lives, but apart from that, how did he and Ladd get along?' Reade questioned.

Fairchild shrugged. 'Same as he got along with his mother. There were rules galore in that household, but otherwise, Ladd was pretty much ignored. Again, I don't wish to speak ill of the dead, but that's just the way it was.'

Tish and Reade drove back to town in troubled silence.

'Poor Ladd,' Tish finally uttered. 'You think he killed his father, don't you? That's why you asked about his clothes.'

'I think it's a distinct possibility. The emotional neglect Ladd endured, his lack of interest in school and friends, and finally his reaction on the day of the murder. Why was he displaying symptoms of shock before he even learned that his father had been killed?'

'Because he already knew he was dead,' Tish filled in the blanks.

'A kid ignored by his community and his parents finally lashes out in a very public shooting. It's straight out of a police academy textbook.'

'Or a Lifetime movie. Would a kid Ladd's age have the self-control to shoot his father and no one else? Oh, and what about his clothes? Mr Fairchild didn't mention any blood splatter being on

Ladd's clothing. If it had been there, you'd think he would have mentioned it.'

'Not necessarily. Fairchild is highly sympathetic to Ladd.'

'He was also extremely honest about his feelings regarding Royce Behrens,' Tish pointed out.

'Feelings which might make him even more sympathetic to Ladd,' Reade proposed. 'I don't want to put a fourteen-year-old kid in jail, hon, but we both have to admit that Ladd's behavior is highly suspicious. I'm going to put in a call to Clayton to bring him in for questioning, but it's not going to be as simple as that. We need Amanda's permission to speak with him and I doubt she's going to grant that without consulting with a whole team of attorneys. Heck, Annabelle will probably get her family lawyers on the case too. It could be days before we speak with him.'

'Can you work around that?'

'If I can prove Ladd is a danger to the community, yes, but it will take some finagling. Behrens's legacy looms large in this town. In the meantime, I need to meet with the lord mayor about forcing Tripp Sennette to resign from the town council.'

'Schuyler isn't going to do anything to punish Tripp Sennette. The scandal would be a mark against his administration.'

'If Sennette and his cronies were defrauding the town with his building scheme, Schuyler can't let him stay in office either. It would look as if he condones Sennette's behavior. Also, let's not forget that Sennette ultimately wants Schuyler's job.'

'Well, good luck with all of that, because I know firsthand that Schuyler's middle name is "Resistant."'

'I thought it was something a little harsher than that,' he replied with a grin.

'It's Sunday. I'm trying to keep things PG,' she joked.

'Are you heading to the market?'

'No, it's a little late in the day and I want to take my time. Instead, I think I'll pay a social call of my own.'

TWENTY-TWO

Reade arrived at Schuyler Thompson's condo to find the mayor in an uncharacteristically casual ensemble of blue chambray shirt, jeans, and a pair of slip-on house slippers. He opened the door and, without a word of greeting, moved into the living room, leaving Reade to close the door behind him.

'I hope you're here to tell me you've arrested Royce's murderer,' Schuyler said from behind the laptop computer he'd set up on the counter that separated the living area from the kitchen.

'Not yet, no,' the sheriff replied as he followed Schuyler into the living room. 'But we have some very strong leads.'

'"Leads?" I thought the killer was already sitting in the county jail. All you need to do is charge him for the crime.'

'William Bull didn't murder Royce Behrens.'

'Really? People seem to think he did.'

'Just because people believe something, doesn't make it true.'

'Maybe, but what are those folks going to think when you don't charge Bull with murder?'

'When I explain that he has an alibi for the time of the murder, I'd like to think they'll be glad that I upheld the law.'

'If you were upholding the law, you'd have charged William Bull by now. The man is a hazard to our community.'

'The man served his time without incident. He was a model prisoner who completed the court-ordered therapy sessions and was, upon release, deemed fit and able to contribute to society.'

'And as soon as Bull was released, he hightailed it back here to stir up trouble at Glory Bishop's place.'

'He came back to see his daughter. The only ones stirring up trouble were the people Senette called upon to see that "justice was done."'

'This is why crime is so high. Our law enforcement officials make excuses for the criminals.'

Reade couldn't help but laugh. 'I'm not one of your constituents,

Thompson. I know the crime stats in this area. Hobson Glen has the lowest crime rate in the county.'

'That's a pretty low bar, Reade.'

Reade scanned the mayor's face for a sign of mockery, but found none. 'Are you delusional? You know that Hobson Glen is below the state average for both violent and property crimes. You're the mayor – you received the same report I did. You must have.'

Schuyler didn't answer. 'Why are you here if it's not to announce that you've solved the Behrens case?'

'To tell you to ask Sennette to resign.'

It was Schuyler's turn to laugh. 'Why should I do that?'

'Sennette incited a mob with his false rhetoric – a mob that did extensive damage to Glory Bishop's inn yesterday. He tried to fuel another mob today.'

Schuyler continued to smile.

'Doesn't this bother you?' Reade grilled.

The mayor poured himself a glass of lemon ice water from a nearby pitcher. He offered none to his guest. 'Why should it bother me? I've already told you – people want William Bull punished.'

'Only because Tripp Sennette told them that they should want him punished. He misrepresented the facts of the case, just like you, he and Behrens have been misrepresenting Hobson Glen's crime rate ever since you started running for office.'

'No one has misrepresented anything. If crime wasn't a problem here, you wouldn't have hired Tish to be a consultant – whatever that means.'

'First of all, leave Tish out of this. Secondly, you're a great one to talk about crime rates when you're the one who did everything within his power – including making threats – to deter me from taking on the Honeycutt murder case.'

'As mayor, I have to protect the interests of this town.'

'*Special* interests, you mean,' Reade corrected. 'Well, we'll soon see whose side you're really on.'

For the first time since their conversation, Schuyler appeared concerned. 'Now who's making threats?'

'No threats. I'm just advising you that, in addition to the incitement charges I'm referring to the DA, my office is launching an investigation into Mr Sennette's time on the planning commission.'

'This is an abomination. Tripp Sennette has faithfully served this community for years.'

'If my suspicions are correct, he also served himself. Oh, and a few local contractors.' Reade flashed a smug grin. 'But, hey, I get it. You support the guy and he supports you – even though he as much as told me that he wants your job. Rumor has it he's also a shoo-in to become the next deputy mayor.'

'What about it?'

'Nothing, except that I hope I'm wrong about my suspicions. Having it come out that your deputy mayor has been skimming a little off the top of town building contracts is going to be a little more difficult to deal with than if the guilty party is a simple councilman. Even worse when the townsfolk realize that the majority of that money came from their taxes. But you seem to have a good handle on things, so as they say, "You do you."' With a fake salute, Reade exited the condo via the door through which he had entered and quietly closed it behind him.

Tish pulled up in front of the gray-shingled, single-story ranch house a stone's throw from the center of town just as Celestine's daughter, Lacey, had sat down on the front stoop to watch her seven- and nine-year-old sons engage in a game of touch football on the front lawn.

Lacey issued a friendly wave before meeting Tish at the van's driver side door. 'Hey, Tish. What brings you this way? I thought you'd be flat-out with the new café and the Behrens case.'

'Yeah, it's been a bit nuts lately. It would be nice to be able to put this case to bed. The shooting has really cast a pall over this town.'

Lacey nodded. 'I saw what happened over at Glory's yesterday. You OK?'

'Fine. This was the worst of it.' Tish pointed to the bandage on her forehead.

'I'm glad. This is seriously scary stuff. As if the shooting wasn't bad enough, now it's like half this town has gone crazy.'

'With members of the town council leading the charge.'

'Hmph,' Lacey grunted in agreement. 'So what brings you here? If I couldn't already guess.'

'Your mother stayed at our house last night. She's at her wits' end about how rapidly things have deteriorated between the two of you.'

Lacey closed her eyes and shook her head. 'No, Tish. No. If she sent you here, I have absolutely nothing to say.'

'Your mother has no clue that I'm here. If she did, she'd be extremely angry with me.'

'Would she? I'm sure she's on cloud nine with her new boyfriend.'

'No, Lacey, she isn't. The last time I saw her, she was heading off to see Daryl to explain the situation and, most likely, break things off with him.'

Lacey took a step back and threw her hands up in the air. 'No, don't do this, Tish. Don't try and make me feel guilty.'

'I'm not trying to make you feel guilty and I'm not here to make you upset.'

'Then what are you here for?'

'I want you to know that I understand your reaction to your mother dating Daryl. You're still grieving the loss of your father and figuring out how to move on without him in your life. Suddenly, your mother begins to act like a single woman. It's jarring and disruptive and – well, I went through it when my mother passed, only my father didn't wait until my mother was gone to line up a replacement. I had assumed that he was going through the same emotions I was, but he wasn't. He had moved on. Only, your mother hasn't moved on, Lacey. I know it seems to you as if she has, but she hasn't. She still loves your father. She always will. Daryl Dufour has always been a friend to her, ever since they were children. It's perfectly normal that she should seek companionship with him.'

Lacey stared at the ground.

'Your mother didn't plan on this happening,' Tish continued. 'In fact, a few days ago, she told Mary Jo that she didn't have the bandwidth for a new relationship. All that changed the moment those shots rang out at Colonial Springs. She – we all thought we were going to die. It's difficult to find reasons not to live life to the fullest when you realize just how precious and short it really is.'

'But why so soon? Can't she just wait a decent amount of time?'

'What is a decent amount of time, Lacey? How long would it take until you deem her relationship with Daryl to be acceptable?'

Lacey had no answer.

'I didn't know your father very well, but from what I did know of him, I can say that he would want your mother to be happy. I also know that he'd be pleased that she's chosen an upstanding man who genuinely cares for your mother and for your whole family. I'm not saying that you need to be OK with Daryl being in your mother's life right now, I'm simply asking that you don't block her from your life. She'd never block you or the rest of the family from hers, no matter what any of you might have done.'

Lacey looked her in the eyes. 'I can't do that right now, Tish. I just can't. Now, I'd best get back to my boys and you'd best get back to your café.'

With a frown, Tish nodded and got back into her van. As she drove home, she prayed she hadn't made the situation worse.

TWENTY-THREE

Tish and Reade had arrived home within minutes of each other and were sharing the details of their meetings when a familiar car pulled in the driveway.

'Don't look now,' Reade quipped. 'But it looks like our eldest has returned to the nest.'

'Poor Jules. Poor Celestine. I wish there was something more we could do for them both,' Tish remarked as she watched Jules extract several medium-sized brown shopping bags from the back of his Mini Cooper.

'We've done what we can,' he replied as he set about starting a fire to ward off the evening chill. 'We've been here for them and will continue to do so for as long as it takes.'

'Thanks for that, Clemson. I'm so glad you consider my friends to be your friends, too.'

'Celestine's always been a friend of mine and Jules – well, you really can't hold that guy at arm's length, can you?'

Tish laughed. 'He can be rather all-encompassing. Speaking of which . . .'

Through the sidelights of the front door, Tish could see that Jules, with Biscuit in one arm and the bags in another, had made his way to the front stoop and was struggling to ring the bell. She rushed to his aid.

'Hey, what's all this?' she asked, taking the bags from his arm.

'Bombolini,' he answered as he placed Biscuit in the office and secured the gate.

'I thought Bombolini was closed on Sundays.'

'They are, but because I arranged for a lovely review for them in our lifestyle segment, which is basically free advertising, the owner and cook is willing to whip up my favorites whenever I ask.'

'Um, OK, but shouldn't you reserve that sort of favor for a special occasion?' Reade questioned from his spot in front of the fireplace.

'I did! Today *is* a special occasion. Maurice and I are back together!'

'Jules!' Tish rushed forward and embraced her friend. 'That's wonderful news!'

Clemson stood up and moved into the entryway to shake Jules's hand. 'I'm really happy for you, but shouldn't the two of you be enjoying Bombolini together?'

'Oh, he's working tonight but, before his shift, he stopped at my apartment with Cassius. He explained how the shooting and the possibility of losing me scared him and that he broke things off as a way of protecting himself but, in reality, he was being cowardly. After a few days alone and some very sage advice from you two, he came to realize that he'd rather take the risk of losing me than live without me altogether.'

'Oh, this is wonderful!' Tish gushed. 'I can't even tell you how happy I am.'

'Thanks. I am, too. We really had a great talk – I mean we discussed everything, including the holidays. We're both cancelling our respective trips back home and spending the holiday together with Cassius. Maurice's mother is expecting a whole slew of people at her table, so she won't be alone and my mama – well, I'm a chip off the old block so you know she has dozens of invitations all around town. We also said we'd visit both of them over Christmas. The only downside of our new plan is, of course, that I didn't tell Maurice that I've never cooked a turkey before . . .' Jules slid his eyes toward Tish.

'It's easy. I'll give you my recipes and I'll coach you,' she offered.

'That's very sweet of you, honey, but . . .'

Tish's mouth became a small 'O' as she understood what Jules was really asking. 'The three of you are welcome to join us for dinner, if you'd like.'

'Really? Oh, no, we couldn't. Not after all you've done for us.' Jules looked away as if he hadn't already anticipated the invitation and his eventual acceptance.

'You can bring the wine,' Reade stated drily, cutting to the chase.

'And a high chair for Cassius,' Tish added.

'But I haven't accepted yet,' Jules argued, prompting Tish and Reade to cross their arms and stare at him. 'Ha! You two *do* know me well, don't you?'

Tish peered into the brown paper bags. 'How much stuff did you buy, Jules?'

The journalist snatched the bags from her and brought them into the kitchen. 'Oh, this isn't just for us. I invited Clayton, Celestine, and Mary Jo over, too. Celestine couldn't make it – she was with Daryl and I didn't want to pry. I mean I did want to pry, but I resisted temptation. The others should be here any—' His voice was interrupted by the sound of the doorbell.

'Clayton,' Tish and Reade responded in unison.

'Hey,' the young officer greeted them as Reade held the door open for him. 'Jules said we were celebrating. What's going on? Do you know who Behrens's killer is?'

'If I did, I'd be sending you to pick them up, not hosting you for dinner,' the sheriff replied.

'Oh, I know! You popped the question and Tish said "yes,"' Clayton guessed.

'I may not be the most romantic guy on the planet, but I'd like to think I'd know better than to propose marriage during a murder investigation.' Reade hiked a thumb toward the kitchen. 'Jules is the one celebrating.'

'Yes, Maurice and I are back together,' Jules called from the kitchen, having overheard Reade and Clayton's conversation.

'That's great news. Congratulations. And thanks for the food.' Clayton turned to the sheriff. 'I left McCarthy in charge at Town Hall and told her to call us if there were any problems.'

'Good call,' Reade said approvingly. 'She's tough, but she's also smart and balanced. She'll be great at keeping tempers from flaring.'

'That's what I thought. Although she shouldn't have too much trouble out there. Two-thirds of the crowd left once the sun started going down.'

'Maybe, but as we saw last night, dusk is when the crazy ones sometimes take over. Better make sure our phones are fully charged. And, stay off the beer – just in case.'

'It's too bad Maurice is working,' Tish lamented. 'It would great to have him with us.'

'Oh, I know,' Jules said with a frown. 'But we've scheduled a date night for after Thanksgiving to make up for it. Dinner in Richmond, maybe a movie, a drink down by the river, and everything awash in the glow of Christmas lights. We've already reserved the sitter and the Uber.'

'Sounds magical. And if your sitter cancels, let me know. I'm happy to take Cassius for the evening.'

'I will, honey, but you'll have to take a number and wait in line. Mary Jo already volunteered.'

'I should have known.' Tish pulled a set of cloth napkins out of the drawer and placed them on the table, while Jules uncorked the bottle of champagne.

'MJ and Kayla will have that baby so spoiled he'll want to be carried everywhere. We may never get him to walk. Speaking of which, I hope she gets here soon so we can eat dinner. I promised I'd watch Maurice's piece on the six o'clock news. I know I can watch on catch-up, but it's not the same as watching it live.'

'It's almost six o'clock now,' Reade said, unloading the contents of the bags.

'His is a puff piece so it won't air until the end of the broadcast, so we have plenty of time,' Jules explained.

'What's it about?'

'It's a lead-up to the Rod and Gun Club event next Saturday. Under normal circumstances, I wouldn't give it a moment of my time, but it's Maurice's first foray into editing. He put together a little segment outlining the history of the event to play before the live interview, which he'll be shooting. It's a great opportunity for him.'

'Another reason to celebrate,' Tish stated, adding utensils on top of the napkins she'd just placed on the table.

'Yeah,' Reade chimed in. 'I look forward to watching it.'

'Who is he interviewing?' Clayton asked.

'Oh, I have no idea. Some stuffed-shirt politician or event organizer, most likely. They're all the same to me,' Jules dismissed.

'I don't recall this much hype for the Rod and Gun Club event in previous years,' Reade recollected.

'Because there wasn't. The organizers and the town are in a panic. Not only was this year's event supposed to be a boon to tourism, but it was an opportunity to introduce our area to some very wealthy donors. If they like what they see – outdoor recreation, easy commute to the city and points north – they might put some money down on a house in Hobson Meadows. Hosting a – let's just call this what it really is – a shooting competition one week after the deputy mayor is shot and killed isn't a good look.'

'That gives Connie Ramirez a whole new motive, doesn't it?' Clayton noted.

'You mean, she killed Behrens with the hope of shutting the

whole event down? That's an interesting angle,' Reade remarked. 'It's also yet another reason for Sennette to want to pin the crime on William Bull. With the case open, he's losing potential donors.'

'The shooting's impact on the Rod and Gun Club event also throws a spotlight on anyone who might have wanted the event to fail or who wanted to hinder progress on the Hobson Meadows development,' Tish pointed out. 'Leonard Pruett happens to come to mind.'

'You've checked their backgrounds, Clayton. Do either Ramirez or Pruett own an AR-15?'

'No. As far as I can see, neither of them own any firearms,' the officer replied. 'That doesn't mean they didn't have access to one via a friend or a loved one.'

'I can't imagine someone borrowing something like that from a friend,' Jules thought aloud as he poured the champagne and passed the glasses around. '"Hey, girl, can I borrow a cup of sugar and an assault rifle, please?"'

'It's more likely that the gun was taken without the owner's knowledge or permission,' Reade explained.

'Oh. That does make more sense, doesn't it?'

'Hello,' came a woman's voice from the entryway. It was Mary Jo, dressed in a long black overcoat and looking more than a little flustered than usual. 'Hope you don't mind me letting myself in. I saw the cars outside and figured y'all were sitting down to eat already.'

'That's fine,' Tish said, taking her friend's coat and hanging it in the hallway closet. 'Are you OK?'

'Yeah . . . no. My Thanksgiving plans just went into the dumper.'

'What happened?' She led MJ into the kitchen, where Jules presented the new arrival with a glass of bubbly.

'I WhatsApped Gregory this afternoon and he informed me that he's spending the holiday in upstate New York. Apparently Kevin – his roommate – has free lift passes and his family owns a cabin near the resort, and they invited Gregory to join them for dinner and a weekend of snowboarding – in between studying, of course. Kevin's parents are picking the boys up after classes on Tuesday.'

'How kind of them. I bet Gregory's excited.'

'Yeah, he's thrilled and I'm happy for him but . . .'

'But you're going to miss him?' Tish guessed.

'It's the first Thanksgiving that we'll be apart,' MJ cried. 'And I know it's just the first of many more holidays I'll spend without him. And that's normal and what should happen but it's – it's not easy letting go.'

Tish wrapped a comforting arm around her friend. 'I'm sorry, MJ. It happens to every parent eventually, but that doesn't make it any easier.'

'It's OK. I'd only just got used to him not being around the house and wasn't expecting to have to adjust to him not being here for holidays too.'

'Well, the end-of-term break is right around the corner,' Reade offered optimistically.

'That's right,' Jules agreed. 'In the meantime, you and Kayla can have Thanksgiving dinner here.'

Reade and Tish glared at the weatherman.

'What?' the confused weatherman asked. 'You were going to invite her, weren't you?'

'Yes,' Tish replied. '*We* were going to invite her.'

'What? Oh – oh! I'm sorry, I was so excited to have the gang together for another holiday that I forgot my manners.'

'Just for that, you'll need to bring some beer to go with the wine,' Reade teased.

'Consider it done.' The weatherman raised his glass in a toast for friendship and then distributed the dinners. 'Tish, here's your favorite smoked salmon with peas and fusilli. MJ, the chicken marsala with linguine. Reade, I didn't know what you might like, so I went for a classic carbonara.'

'I love carbonara,' the sheriff replied.

'And, Clayton, I guessed you might like the meatballs and spaghetti.'

The officer accepted his meal greedily. 'I'm always down with a good meatball.'

'Good. And, for me, the chicken Alfredo with tortellini. Cheers, everyone!'

The group consumed their pasta, stopping only to "ooh," "aah" and to converse about the day.

'What are you doing for Thanksgiving, Clayton?' Tish asked.

'I signed up for duty that day.'

'You did? I thought you'd want to be with your family.'

'I usually do, but this year's weird. My sister's getting married and her future in-laws are coming over for dinner. My sister's stressed out that my parents are going to embarrass her. My father's stressed out because my mother's requiring him to wear something other than his college football jersey. And my mother's stressed out because she thinks our usual menu is too low class, so she's cooking a bunch of dishes from her *Food and Wine* magazines from the Eighties and Nineties.'

'Oh, noooo!' Tish sang. 'All those complicated recipes.'

'Yeah,' Clayton confirmed. 'We're starting with tuna tartare and finishing off with pumpkin tiramisu. Somewhere in between, Mom's deboning a turkey and rolling it up with a stuffing made with sausage and pistachios. Blech! Anyways, I figured I'll stay out of trouble and fill in for some of the people whose families are cooking normal things.' He gave his boss a nudge with his elbow.

'Well, if you'd like we can bring you a plate during your break,' Tish offered. 'Or you can come by here after your shift for leftovers. Choice is yours.'

'Really? That would be so awesome.'

'You bet,' Tish replied before whispering to Reade. 'Good thing I didn't make it to the market today. Between Clayton's appetite, the addition of Maurice, the possible addition of Daryl, the plate for Enid Kemper, and the desire for leftovers, we need a bigger bird. And more of everything else. Looks like we're at the complete opposite end of a romantic holiday for two.'

'This year, it seems fitting that we're all together. I'm grateful and relieved that everyone is alive and well,' he stated. 'When those shots rang out, I was certain we'd be missing a number of people around the holiday table. Thing is, lately I've been feeling as if . . .'

'As if the Behrens murder isn't going to be the only one?'

'Exactly.'

'Oohh, it's time!' an excited Jules announced as he flew into the living room and switched on the TV.

'Time for what?' MJ asked, her mouth full of pasta.

'Maurice edited his first segment for the news.'

'How exciting!' She picked up her aluminum take-out dish and fork and brought them to the coffee table, where she finished her supper. Clayton, after delivering MJ's champagne glass, plopped down beside her on the sofa and did the same.

Jules's time estimate was accurate, for only a minute or two after switching on the television, the segment in question started. 'Here it is! Shh! Quiet!'

The camera switched from a view of the anchor desk to a shot of an Asian woman in warm outerwear standing outside a sign advertising the Rod and Gun Club event. 'The Annual Rod and Gun Club competition holds a special place in the hearts of many residents within the Channel Ten viewing area. With less than a week until the event, we're taking a look back at past highlights as well as competitors to watch in the future.'

The picture segued to Maurice's segment, recounting the history of the event via antique black-and-white photos and voiceovers from local historians. Tish watched and sipped the remainder of her champagne. Suddenly a familiar face flashed across the screen. Dark-haired and smiling, the teenager in the faded color photograph held a trophy in one hand and a rifle in the other. 'In 1996, sixteen-year-old Royce Behrens set the record for biathlon—'

Jules interrupted the voiceover. 'Boy, Royce looked waaaaaay different back then.'

'Didn't we all?' MJ quipped.

'Not *that* much different.'

Tish watched as the segment closed and Chase Behrens appeared on the screen. 'Now Royce's son, Chase Behrens, seeks to beat his father's record—'

'You know, apart from his dark hair, Chase doesn't really look that much like his father,' MJ said between bites of chicken. 'He's more a blend of his parents with a little of his great-grandfather, the former mayor, mixed in for good measure.'

Tish had no idea what Annabelle's father looked like, but Mary Jo was right. Everyone had been so quick to equate Chase's dark good looks with his father, that they hadn't analyzed the rest of his features, the most of which were, indeed, inherited from his mother.

Much unlike another young resident of Hobson Glen.

'Your observations are spot on, Mary Jo,' Tish replied as she stared at the television. 'Chase Behrens doesn't resemble his father as much as I thought he did, but, surprisingly, Ethan Wheeler does.'

TWENTY-FOUR

'Yes, Royce was Ethan's father,' Faye Wheeler confessed from within the confines of her dimly lit kitchen. She did not dare speak to her visitors in the living room lest she awaken her mother who, after a rough few hours, had finally fallen asleep. 'When Royce was first elected councilman, he was like a breath of fresh air. He was dynamic, energetic, and he promised to make life better for everyone in this town. I was enamored with his looks, his charm, but mostly his passion. He had such a forceful, dynamic personality – it was difficult to say no to him.

'He'd been on the council less than a year when he asked me to have lunch with him. I thought for certain that it was a business lunch. He'd had some issues with some of the other clerks in the office, so I assumed he was asking me to handle his files and schedule exclusively. He did ask for that – and more.' Faye closed the collar of her fluffy blue chenille robe tightly around her neck, as if to either protect herself from the memories of Royce or defend herself from the judgment of Tish and Reade. 'I wasn't about to get involved with a married man. At least that's what I told myself, but Royce was persistent. He kept telling me how I was unlike any woman he'd ever met. How his wife was focused on their children and was no longer interested in him or their marriage. The same old story. I *knew* it was the same old story and I swore I wouldn't weaken, but he wore me down. He wore down my defenses by telling me how special I was, how efficient, and yes, how beautiful. After months of lunch dates, I finally agreed to meet him after work at a restaurant out of town. It was a magical night. He surprised me with flowers and a candlelit dinner by the James River. He told me to order whatever I liked – I'd never been with a man who did any of those things. It was . . . dazzling. He promised me that if I stuck with him, my life would get easier. He was going places in politics and he would take me with him. Needless to say, that night ended in a hotel room. So did all the other nights afterward.

'Unfortunately, it didn't take very long before I realized that

Royce wasn't what he claimed to be. He started voting against measures that would help the working people of Hobson Glen and bringing business people from outside of Hobson into council meetings to see "what they could offer" our town. What they offered were schemes that never came to fruition – schemes our tax money paid for. But the biggest change arrived in the amount of time he spent with me.

'When Royce and I started out, we'd meet for lunch at least twice a week and after work at least once. After several months had passed, we were seeing each other less and less and, when we did, Royce seemed distracted, less interested in talking to me about my life or my views of the job he was doing. He simultaneously was spending more time elsewhere – out of the office. I finally discovered that he had found someone else.'

'Someone else?' Tish questioned.

'Yes, another woman. A councilwoman from Staunton. Younger than I was, thinner, more attractive. If he had gone back to his wife, I'd have understood,' Faye said, her voice trembling with emotions, despite the passage of time. 'But I couldn't and wouldn't put up with that, so I broke up with him. He was relieved. Said that I'd "let myself go" since our relationship started and that I was also less effective in the office. His words pierced through me as sure as any dagger. A few weeks later I discovered I was pregnant with Ethan. Only, of course, I didn't know it was Ethan and yet . . . something in me *knew*. Having him was the best decision I ever made.'

'Did you tell anyone that Ethan was Royce's son?' Reade asked.

'Only Royce, who wanted nothing to do with him, and my mother. My mother was so supportive of me – never once did she tell me that I'd messed up or ruined my life. We decided that I'd go out of town on an extended vacation – I told everyone it was a singles cruise, but in reality I visited my aunt in Florida. I was tempted to abort the baby. Seriously tempted, but as I said, something in me *knew* who Ethan was. So, I came back to Hobson Glen and went ahead with the pregnancy. If anyone asked, it was the result of a fling on the high seas. My mother was brilliant at covering up Ethan's paternity. She's been a blessing to me in so many other ways, too. I only hope I can be as much of a blessing to her during her last days.'

'Those are the only people who knew?'

'No, Annabelle Behrens knew as well. Royce must have told her. She came knocking on my door shortly after I found out I was pregnant, threatening me to keep quiet. I told her I wanted nothing at all from Royce or the Behrens family. I was embarrassed to have anyone know that I had ever cared for Royce, that I had fallen for his lies, that I became pregnant by him. I had been at the top of my class in high school. I was seen as the glue holding the Town Hall offices together, and then I allow myself to be so blatantly used. How could I have been so stupid?

'There were times when I wished I could have lived elsewhere. When I wished I could raise Ethan away from Royce and Annabelle's prying eyes, but where else was I going to go? I'd never worked anywhere other than Town Hall and my mother, when she was well, ran a beauty parlor out of our garage. My dad had fixed it up for her. She had lots of faithful clients, but as they were older, none of them were going to travel too far out of Hobson Glen for a weekly wash and set or a monthly dye job. We were stuck.'

'The night of the planning commission meeting – the night that cost you your job – you'd been arguing with Royce. Were you arguing about Ethan?' Tish asked.

Faye broke into tears. 'Things have been so hard this past year. So hard. I've been trying to keep things going here with the house and Mom and paying for Ethan's room, board and transportation, but I've been falling behind on bills. So, I asked Royce if he could help in some way. It was crazy of me to think he'd say yes, but I was desperate. His reaction was even worse than I'd anticipated. He called me a loser and a dumb whore and Ethan . . . well, I lost my temper completely. I couldn't see straight. You know the rest.'

'Ma'am,' Reade addressed Faye, 'is your son aware that Royce Behrens was his father?'

'No,' Wheeler denied. 'I never told him. My mother never told him either. Even in her state now, she wouldn't. Couldn't.'

'Do you happen to know where Ethan was at the time of Royce Behrens's shooting?'

'He was at school,' Faye replied. 'Where else would he be? And why are you asking these questions about my son?'

'If Ethan knew Royce was his father, he's a prime suspect in this case.'

'He didn't know and he was at school. Thanksgiving isn't for a few days yet,' she insisted.

'So then you wouldn't mind us calling Old Dominion to confirm,' Reade presumed.

'That won't be necessary,' came a young man's voice from just outside the entrance to the kitchen. It was Ethan Wheeler.

'Ethan!' his mother nearly shrieked. 'What are you doing?'

'I'm telling the truth. I have nothing to hide.'

'But Ethan—'

'Mom, I'm not a little boy anymore. I'm eighteen years old. I can handle myself. Why don't you go and check on Grandma?'

Faye rose from her seat and, after touching her son gently on the face, moved to the other room. At Reade's invitation, Ethan sat in the chair his mother had vacated.

'Where were you Friday at noon?' the sheriff asked.

'I was here,' the young man answered. 'I drove here immediately after my Friday morning class.'

'What time did you arrive?'

'A few minutes after eleven. My class started at eight and ended at nine thirty. I got on the road right away and drove straight here. Route 64 is always clear sailing, but even 295 was a breeze.'

'Don't you have classes next week?' Tish questioned.

'Yes, tomorrow and Tuesday, but I spoke with my professors and explained that my grandmother's health condition had deteriorated since my departure and that my mother was having trouble caring for her on her own. I asked if I could attend class virtually, so that I could spend the whole week here. They very kindly agreed.'

'What did you do once you got here?' Reade continued.

'My mother was surprised to see me, so we hugged and talked and then we had lunch. She said I looked thin,' Ethan added with a weary smile. 'Then I had a brief visit with my grandma.'

'Did either of you go out? To the store or to run an errand?'

'My mother went out for a little while. I persuaded her to take some time to get a coffee or take a drive. You know, some "me" time. There's not much to do in this town, but I felt she needed to get out of the house.'

'What time was that?'

'Oh, it was later.'

'Later than?'

'Later in the afternoon,' Ethan clarified. 'Maybe two or three?'

'So, you were here the entire day?'

'Yeah, I texted a few of my friends to see what their plans were for this coming week, but none of them are home yet, so there was no one in town to hang with, so I just kinda hung out here. Did my laundry, ate, slept, studied.' Ethan shrugged. 'That kinda stuff.'

'Are there any witnesses who can vouch for you?'

'Just my mother. And my grandmother, but she doesn't always recognize me.'

'Do you know that Royce Behrens was your father?'

'Yes.'

'When did you find out?' Tish asked.

'When I was a junior in high school.'

'I'm surprised it was that late. Weren't you ever curious?'

'Oh yeah. When I was little, I asked my mom why other people had dads and I didn't. She told me that she'd met my father on a cruise in turquoise waters and had fallen in love at first sight, but that he, sadly, wasn't ready for the awesomeness that was me.' He laughed. 'I probably annoyed a lot of kids on the playground repeating that, but it made me feel good.'

'As it should,' she agreed. 'You never asked again?'

'No. I was a happy kid. I had a good life. My mom, grandma and I would take trips and go camping and play board games. I guess I didn't see what a father would add to my life. It was already good the way it was.'

'What happened in your junior year?'

'I was on the school newspaper covering one of our team's football games. Mr Behrens showed up, for a photo-op probably. It was election season, so he was going for parents' votes. I remember asking him a question so that I might include it in my write-up of the game. He looked right at me and stared, as if he'd seen something that frightened him. He then left before answering my question. The whole thing was creepy, but I'd kinda forgotten it until a few days later when I was working on an article about the Thanksgiving Rod and Gun Club event, when I saw a photo of Mr Behrens when he was young. It was like looking in a mirror. From that point, everything kinda clicked into place. I was never allowed to visit my mom at Town Hall. When "Bring Your Kid to Work" day rolled around, I hung out with my grandma in the garage while she did hair. I didn't mind – all her customers would give me money or candy – but it was weird until I figured out why.'

'What did you do?'

'I asked my mother if Mr Behrens was my father and told her everything that had happened. She admitted that he was.'

'Did she explain why she didn't tell you?'

'Yeah, she didn't want me to grow up with his values, which I totally get. I know he's dead now, but he was a real . . . jerk.' It was abundantly clear that Ethan longed to call Behrens something stronger than a jerk. 'I'm glad he wasn't in my life.'

'So you weren't angry with Behrens at all?'

'No. I mean, maybe, at how he treated my mom. He left her to raise me alone and then, this past summer, he got her fired. It's not right that just because a guy has money and is in a position of power, he can do whatever he wants to a woman and is never punished.'

'I think he's paid his dues now, don't you?' Reade prodded.

'Yeah, I guess he has,' Ethan replied, but his body language suggested he was uncomfortable with the answer he'd given. 'I'd prefer if he'd been forced to apologize first, but, yeah, at least he's paid.'

'Well?' Tish asked as she slid into the passenger seat of Reade's SUV.

'Interviewing a family caring for a dementia patient isn't my idea of a relaxing Sunday evening,' he said with a sigh as he locked his seatbelt into place. 'That said, Ethan had the motive and the opportunity to kill Royce Behrens, but so far, I don't see that he had the means. Clayton just texted and no firearms have ever been registered to Ethan, Faye or the grandmother.'

'I'm not surprised, are you?'

'No, just frustrated. I'm going to get a warrant to search the house and I've already asked Clayton to look into Ethan's friends and acquaintances at Old Dominion. One of them might have provided the firearm.'

'A search warrant? Ugh.' Tish grimaced.

'I hate it too. I really hate it. An eighteen-year-old kid forced to think like an adult, a sick old woman, and a mom working to hold things together. It stinks all the way around, but I have no choice. Ethan is still a suspect – one of our key suspects.'

'I know. But I can't believe Ethan did it. He seems so happy and well-adjusted. Far better adjusted than Ladd Behrens.'

'Ethan is older than Ladd and, as such, could be much better at hiding his feelings,' Reade suggested, although Tish got the impression that he was trying to convince himself more than anyone else. 'Speaking of which, Clayton and I have an appointment to speak with Ladd tomorrow morning at eleven. Care to join us?'

'Sure. You mean Amanda agreed?'

'Yes, so long as she and her attorney are both in the room. Which might be a deterrent to Ladd confiding in us, but we'll take what we can get for now, right?'

TWENTY-FIVE

Tish awoke at seven thirty a.m. to find Clemson showered, shaved and waiting for her in the kitchen. 'Sorry for sleeping so late,' she apologized with a yawn.

'No worries. You'll be getting up before I do soon enough.' He poured her a cup of coffee and handed it to her with a kiss. 'The way you didn't budge when my alarm went off said to me that you needed the sleep.'

'I guess so, although I was hoping to get up a little earlier so I could get some work done before our meeting with Ladd Behrens.' She added some milk to the coffee mug and then drank it.

'You have all the time in the world to work at the café,' Reade announced as he refreshed his own cup. 'Amanda Behrens's attorney called. They've cancelled for this morning.'

'Oh no! Why? Did they reschedule?'

'No reschedule yet. It seems Ms Annabelle took sick in the middle of the night.'

'Sick? Is she OK?'

'Just a stomach bug, but from the lawyer's tone of voice it sounds as if she's got it pretty bad. Like it-might-warrant-a-trip-to-the-hospital bad.'

'I hope she's OK. Given her age and her state of mind, a simple virus could be very serious,' Tish noted, as she placed two slices of wholegrain bread in the toaster.

'I know. That's why I didn't push to reschedule immediately. Once I find out she's in the clear, however,' Reade stipulated as he plucked an avocado from the fruit bowl and tossed it to Tish, 'we'll be on their front doorstep.'

Tish sliced the avocado in half and removed the pit. 'Anything else on tap for today? Anything I can help with?'

'No, just reviewing paperwork and reports and making sure statements jive with each other. We're also expecting the report from Connie Ramirez's clothing and a full tox screen of the victim's blood and a few other reports, but it's all a waiting game. Might as well use that time to get the café in order.'

'A whole day at the café,' she said dreamily as she scooped the avocado into a bowl and mashed it with the back of the fork. 'With Celestine's help, I should be able to get everything done that needs to be done, which means I can be nice and relaxed while prepping Thanksgiving dinner.'

'Just remember I live here too. I'm happy to help with the prep or whatever you need me to do,' Clemson offered.

'I know you are,' Tish purred as she slathered a bit of avocado onto a slice of toast and took a bite. 'Don't worry, sweetie. I already have plans for you.'

'I'm sure you do,' he said as he kissed her before heading out the door. 'I'm sure you do.'

Tish arrived at the café to find Celestine and Jules behind the counter giggling. 'Hey. You two are in a good mood this morning.'

'Hey, honey,' Celestine greeted.

'Hey, Tish,' Jules echoed. 'We've got good men in our lives, so we're happy.'

'It's just the other people in my life I need to straighten out,' Celestine completed the thought.

'So you and Daryl are—?' Tish pushed her right index and middle fingers together and held them aloft.

'Still together, yeah.'

'That's great news! What happ—' Tish looked up to see that the moose hanging above the counter had been decked out in a gray wig, wire-framed spectacles, and a hand-knitted shawl. 'What. On. Earth. Is. That?'

'Oh, Celestine and I have been texting back and forth about your moose problem,' Jules explained.

'My moose problem?'

'Yeah. When someone knows a guy who can do a job, it's never good.'

Celestine shook her head.

'We both thought,' Jules continued, 'that instead of paying money for it to be removed – money that could be better spent elsewhere – you should keep the moose but make it a mascot for the café.'

'Do cafés need mascots?'

'Of course they do. Everything should have a mascot or a spirit animal, or something that encapsulates the essence of its being. With your love of books, your newly discovered sleuthing abilities, and your weakness for a good – or bad – pun, I introduce you to . . .' Jules fluttered his arms in the direction of the head in question, '. . . Moose Marple!'

Tish couldn't help but laugh. 'Moose Marple? The two of you may have found great men, but you've completely lost your minds.'

'Well, yeah, but what do you think of Moose Marple?'

That during such a difficult time, something so simple, so silly could bring her friends such joy seemed remarkable. 'When did you find time to do all this? How? And how did Mary Jo not find out?'

The question had no sooner left Tish's lips when Mary Jo came bounding down the stairs, a lavender pillbox hat in her hands. 'I've got it ready, Jules. I think the glue should hold— Oh, hi, Tish.'

Tish folded her arms across her chest in mock anger. '*Et tu*, Mary Jo?'

'I think it's cute,' MJ asserted. 'So does Kayla.'

'It *is* cute. It's also very sweet. And, it's provided the first good laugh we've had all week.'

'So?' Jules prodded.

'Moose Marple stays.' Her friends gave a cheer. 'But let's make it clear that we're not going to pay tribute to any other fictional detectives. I don't want another animal head on the wall.'

'Oh, no worries, honey,' Jules promised. 'The only other names we came up with were Purrlock Holmes and Hercule Poi-roo, but I think a cat and a kangaroo probably wouldn't go over too well with your customers.'

'No, probably not. Hey, let's get that hat on there and then let's have a toast to our new mascot, Moose Marple,' Tish suggested.

Jules scurried up the ladder to place the hat on the moose head, while MJ set to work brewing some coffee.

'I'm sorry I got distracted, Celestine,' Tish apologized to her baker. 'What happened with Daryl yesterday?'

'He was wonderful, Tish. I'm so glad I told him what's been goin' on. He said we could break up if that's what I really wanted, but he thought we should schedule a family meetin' just him, me and the kids. That would give them a chance to say how they felt about us bein' together and give us a chance to explain how we feel. You know, talk things out.'

'I think that's an excellent idea.'

'Yeah, we're gonna try to schedule somethin' soon. We'll see if Lacey goes for the idea. Johnny, too. As the oldest, Lacey leads the others, but since Lloyd's passin', Johnny considers himself the "head of the family" – the one to take his papa's place and watch over things.'

With the words 'head of the family,' Tish was transported back to the day of the shooting. So much had transpired since that day – mobs, protests, breakups, reconciliations – and yet nothing of substance had actually occurred, at least not until today.

'I hope you can change their minds,' Tish replied absently.

'Wait. You have that look on your face again,' Celestine observed. 'What is it? What did I say? Did I help the case?'

'More than that, Celestine,' Tish answered, extracting her phone from her handbag. 'You may have just saved a life.'

Tish pulled up outside the High Ridge residence of Amanda Behrens just as Reade, Clayton and two uniformed police officers were approaching the front door. She hopped from behind the steering wheel of the van and, slamming the door behind her, ran to join them.

'Mrs Behrens,' Reade addressed Amanda when she'd opened the door. 'Is your mother-in-law in the house?'

'Yes, but I told you – my lawyers should have told you – she's ill and we're all much too upset to answer your questions.' Amanda endeavored to close the door, but Reade's foot blocked the way.

'This isn't an interview request, Mrs Behrens. This is a wellness check. We have reason to believe your mother-in-law is in danger.'

'Danger? Don't be ridiculous! She has a stomach bug, but she's as strong as an ox.'

'We'd like to see for ourselves.'

'This is all so absurd! I-I-I don't know who you've been speaking to, but—'

'We need to see her now, ma'am.' Reade's tone was stern.

'She's up here!' Ladd shouted from the upstairs landing.

Reade, Clayton and Tish rushed toward his voice, while the uniformed officers stayed behind to prevent Amanda, who was calling for help from her eldest son, from following. There, in the bedroom at the top of the stairs, they found Annabelle Behrens sitting up in bed, a hot cup of tea in her hand. She was wan, frail, and looked as if she'd aged several years since their meeting the previous day.

'Clayton, grab that cup and have its contents analyzed,' Reade directed.

Chase barged into the room. 'Get out of my house!'

Ladd, overwhelmed with the situation, hopped up on the bed and sat beside his grandmother, who embraced him and pulled him close to her.

'What's this all about, Sheriff?' a weakened Annabelle asked as Clayton took the cup and saucer from her hand and dumped its contents into a re-sealable bag.

'We don't think you have a stomach bug. We think you're being poisoned.'

'Poisoned?'

'Yes,' Tish replied. 'Lucy Van Gorder told me that your son, Royce, was experiencing stomach trouble before he passed away. Is this true?'

'Yes, it is,' Annabelle answered. 'I thought it was due to job stress, and maybe a side effect of his lifestyle – you know, all those darn pills he took, combined with those business dinners and their rich food. I was positive he was working his way toward an ulcer.'

'We don't think it was an ulcer, Mrs Behrens. We think it was lobelia poisoning.'

'Lobel . . .' She stopped mid-word as a thought occurred to her. 'That's why Amanda was drying the flowers I gave her.'

'We believe so. I know before she married your son, Amanda worked in science. In what field?'

'She was a pharmacist with a specialty in homeopathic and herbal remedies.' Annabelle's jaw dropped open. 'My God . . .'

Tish nodded. 'In low doses, lobelia causes nausea, diarrhea, vomiting, profuse sweating and dizziness. In large doses, it induces coma and eventually death.'

'You think – you think, Amanda . . .?'

'Amanda wanted to kill Royce and had planned to do it via lobelia poisoning.'

'That's all a lie!' Chase shouted. 'My mother would never hurt anyone.'

'Once we get your grandmother's tea analyzed, we'll see if that's true,' Reade responded as he called for an ambulance.

Chase's reaction changed from angry to panicked.

'When she couldn't kill Royce quickly enough without arousing suspicion, Amanda devised "Plan B," didn't she, Chase?' Tish asked the young man.

'What does Chase have to do with this?' Annabelle demanded as first responders entered the room to check her vitals.

'Nothing, I thought, until I saw his interview on Channel Ten News last night. I was so fixated on the photo of your son, Mrs Behrens, that I didn't pay attention to what your son won a trophy for at the Gun and Rod Club event when he was sixteen. It was only when I checked the transcript of the broadcast on the web this morning that I found out it was for the biathlon.'

'That's right,' Annabelle confirmed. 'The same event Chase hopes to win on Saturday.'

'Yes, only Chase hasn't been training for a biathlon.'

'That's not true,' Chase cried. 'Grandma knows I've been training for months. Ladd too. Everyone knows.'

'Indeed, you have been training,' Tish verified. 'Training not just to unseat your father's record, but training to murder him. All those hours spent running through the woods – you knew that trail like the back of your hand. You knew the best spot on the Turkey Trot route. You knew the best shortcut out of there. You knew precisely where to lie in wait.'

Chase broke down in tears.

'You buried the gun somewhere along the trail early that morning, didn't you? Somewhere only you would find it. Ladd, did your brother and mother leave for school early that morning?'

Ladd, also in tears, nodded his head.

'Later, after your half-day of classes were over, your mother drove you to the rec park for your usual after-school run,' Tish continued. 'No one suspected a thing. You were always running. Always training. Your mother waited in the car, as she always did, reading a book. Everyone imagined that you were on the rec park trail, but you weren't. You'd retrieved your rifle and cut through the woods to Colonial Springs. And there you waited. Waited for the precise moment your father approached and you had a clear shot. Your father was a runner, had been since his youth. You knew he'd overtake Mayor Thompson. You knew he'd want to be seen as finishing first.'

'You . . . you have no proof.' Chase, suddenly defiant, challenged.

'Yes. Yes, I do. Your brother, Ladd, skipped school that day, hopped on his bike, and did what he's been doing ever since he could crawl: he followed you.'

'Is this true, Ladd?' Annabelle asked.

Ladd let out a loud wail. 'Yes. I went there. I saw everything.'

'Would you care to tell the story?' Reade offered the young man.

'No. No.' He curled into the fetal position and rested his head on his grandmother's shoulder.

'I'll recount it then, and you can correct me if I'm wrong,' Tish said softly. 'The ride from the school to the rec park was a long one and Ladd had worked up a sweat, so he removed his sweatshirt and decided to surprise Chase in the woods. He hid in a spot on the opposite side of the trail. Both Mayor Thompson and Connie Ramirez heard him crackling the underbrush. Only Chase surprised Ladd – he was there, behind a copse of trees, with an automatic weapon aimed at their father.'

Tish turned to the older brother. 'Did you choose the spot, Chase? A place known as The Cathedral, where the trees signify eternal life, sorrow, and renewal through purification?'

Chase nodded. 'It was a favorite spot of mine, but my father never saw the beauty in it.'

'How poetic of you. Your mother said that evening that you were a much better student of English than your father. When the shots rang out, desecrating the sanctity of The Cathedral, they killed Royce Behrens and splattered blood everywhere, including over the T-shirt Ladd was wearing – a T-shirt similar to the one he's wearing now.' Tish gestured toward Ladd's black T-shirt, emblazoned with a different Nirvana album cover.

'After the shooting, Chase ran, like lightning, back to the rec park, where Amanda texted him when it was safe for him to emerge from the woods with the gun and place it in the trunk of the car. Although, to be fair, no one would have thought much of seeing a young man training for the biathlon carrying a weapon. Ladd, meanwhile, terrified by what he'd seen and not wanting you or him to be implicated in the crime, removed his bloody T-shirt and snuck it into a trash can at the fringe of the woods behind my catering table, before hopping back onto his bike and pedaling, as quickly as he could, through the woods and along one of the many secret trails, back to school.'

'You – you don't understand,' Chase sobbed. 'My father was going to leave us with nothing. Nothing!'

'That's not true, Chase. Your father had ended things with Lucy Van Gorder.'

'That's right, Chase,' Annabelle confirmed as she held a trembling Ladd close to her.

'Lucy? Who's Lucy? I'm talking about his other son. My mother overheard my father and some woman arguing at Town Hall this summer. She was asking for money for "their child." I didn't believe it when she told me, but then we were out one day and she pointed him out to me. He looked just like the photos of my dad when he was young. He looked a little like . . . me. My mother and I couldn't let him leave us penniless. We couldn't. We had to stop him.'

'Chase,' Annabelle said softly, tears streaming down her cheeks, 'I would never have let you or your brother be penniless. You should have known that.'

'And what about my mother? Why didn't she inherit Lobelia Hall when my father died?' an irate Chase questioned. 'Why wasn't this place put in her name? Why are we still squatting here? Wasn't my mother good enough to own the house she lived in?'

Annabelle drew a hand to her face. 'My God . . . is that why—?'

'That's why Amanda invited you to stay here. To poison you,' Tish explained. 'When you finally passed away, everyone would have assumed it was because you were broken-hearted over Royce. She wanted the money, this house, Lobelia Hall, all of it. She'd been destitute before, and she wasn't about to let it happen again. Royce had prohibited Amanda from even having her own bank or credit card account. With him – and you – out of the picture, the money and both properties would have been split between her and the boys. She would have preferred to have all the money herself, but Amanda could control the boys. They were the only things in this world she could control.'

While the paramedics lifted Annabelle onto a gurney, Clayton placed Chase in handcuffs and escorted him downstairs. At the sight of her son being arrested, Amanda, also handcuffed, began to shriek.

'My boy! No, not my beautiful, most darling boy! He only did it to save us. He only did it to save us all from my abusive husband. Oh, please,' she implored Reade as he made his way down the steps. 'My husband used to beat them. He used to beat me. That's why Chase did what he did.'

'Stop lying!' Ladd screamed from his spot beside Annabelle's gurney. 'You're always lying! Dad never touched us. Never! He wasn't always here, but he never would have hurt us. You're a liar! A liar!'

Amanda's face turned an unearthly shade of gray. 'Ladd? Wha . . . what's gotten into you? That's no way to speak to your mother. You know about all the ways your father hurt me. *All* the ways!'

'And what about all the ways *you* hurt *me*? You know why I followed Chase around? Because I hoped you'd love me the way you love him. You know what? Now I'm glad you didn't love me because I would have believed your lies and I'd be heading off to jail, too. So, thanks, Mom. Thanks for hating me. I hate you too!' Ladd's face twisted in anguish.

Reade directed the uniformed police to take Amanda to the car while Annabelle, despite the tubes and wires in her thin white arms, extended a hand to console her younger grandson. Ladd took hold of it and didn't let go.

'Her pulse is thready and she's dehydrated, but she'll be OK,' the chief medic informed Reade when the scene had settled down. 'Good thing you got to her before she took another dose.'

Ladd, tears in his eyes, had been forced to wait with the Fairchilds outside the ambulance while his grandmother was being treated.

'Mind if the boy travels with you to the hospital?' Reade asked the medic.

'Tell him to hop in. I'll request a cot gets put in her room.'

'Thanks. The neighbors are going to follow in their car. He might want to stay with them tonight, he might not.'

'Either way, he'll be covered.'

The medic directed Ladd into the back of the ambulance and instructed the Fairchilds to follow. Reade put his arm around Tish's waist and they watched the vehicles depart from the hospital. 'You OK?'

'Better, now that the case is behind us.'

'Me too. How'd you know it was Amanda and Chase?'

'Celestine mentioned the words "head of the family" today and it reminded me of our initial interview with Amanda. Faye Wheeler never referred to Ethan as the head of the family, yet he acted like one when he left school early to help his mother care for his grandmother, and again when he stepped forward to speak with us. Chase Behrens, on the other hand, wasn't permitted to get his driver's license, had no friends, rarely visited Grandma, and was even forced by his mother to go on a vegan diet. So how, precisely, *was* he the "head of the family?" In what way was he being treated or expected to behave like an adult?'

Reade shook his head. 'God . . . I feel sorry for both those boys.'

'Me too. At least Ladd has Annabelle – she might help him heal.'

'And at least Annabelle has him. She needs some healing, too.' He extracted his phone from the back pocket of his jeans and began tapping at the screen.

'Who are you texting?'

'Jules. I'm giving him the scoop.'

'That's very kind of you.'

'It's more than kind. I trust Jules to break the story with tact and discretion.'

'You're right, of course. But it does seem weird to rely upon Jules for tact.'

'I know,' he chuckled.

'Oh, um, he may not reply right away, by the way. Last I saw him, he was on a ladder in the café, placing a pillbox hat on Moose Marple.'

'Moose Marple,' Reade repeated in disbelief. 'Do I want to know?'

'No,' Tish answered decisively. 'Probably not.'

TWENTY-SIX

T hanksgiving Day was bright and sunny with just enough crispness in the air to add to the seasonal festivities. Daryl and Celestine sat on the back patio, sipping hot apple cider and enjoying the late November afternoon. Indoors, Kayla was in the living room lounging on the sofa, watching the National Dog Show with one eye and checking text messages from friends with the other, Mary Jo was setting the dinner table in the dining room, and Reade and Tish were in the kitchen tending to various tasks.

Reade took a break from peeling potatoes to give Tish a kiss on the cheek as she sat at the kitchen table, prepping Brussels sprouts for a roast in the oven while the turkey rested. 'What's that for?' she asked.

'For making this house a home. I never realized how much I missed the smell of turkey in the oven and the anticipation of spending a day with a table of people I care about. Thank you.'

'Thank you for providing me with a place to turn into a home. Although, I'm wondering if you're currently swept away with me or the smell of turkey permeating the house.'

'Maybe a little of both,' he confessed before returning to his potato peeling.

The doorbell rang. 'Jules,' Tish and Reade announced in unison.

Kayla sprung from her spot on the sofa to answer the door. 'Hi, Uncle Jules,' she greeted, and then, with a squeal, she took a fleece-clad Cassius out of his arms. 'Who is such a cutie? Who's a cutie? Is it you?'

Jules placed Biscuit in the gated office, as per usual, and ducked into the kitchen with a shopping bag of bottles. 'Happy Thanksgiving, y'all. And a very happy Thanksgiving it will be with the goodies I've brought along. Reade, I got you some beer from Legend Brewery – I think you like them.'

'I do,' Reade confirmed, filling his pot of cut, peeled potatoes with water. 'Thanks, Jules.'

'*De nada.* Then, for dinner, I got a few bottles of this year's

Beaujolais Nouveau and a couple of Riesling to go with or after dessert.'

'That's terrific!' Tish got up from her seat and thanked her friend with a hug and kiss.

Mary Jo arrived from the dining room and followed Tish's greeting with her own. 'Happy Thanksgiving! Hey, aren't you missing something – or someone?'

'Oh, Maurice got called down to cover the press conference at Town Hall. He'll be here after it's over.'

'Press conference?' Reade asked with narrowed eyes. 'My office didn't get a call for security.'

'That's because, since Behrens's shooting, our mayor has his own private security.'

Tish rolled her eyes. 'Figures. What's the conference about?'

'It's about to start. Why don't we watch and see for ourselves?'

The foursome moved into the living room, where they usurped the remote from Kayla. 'Hey, I was showing Cassius the doggies,' she whined.

'Well, now you can show him a snake,' Jules quipped as he changed the channel to the local news. Meanwhile Celestine and Daryl had come inside to join the party.

'Hey, what's everybody watchin'?' the baker asked.

'Schuyler's press conference,' Tish replied.

'Schuyler?' Daryl scoffed. 'Why ruin a perfectly good holiday?'

'Probably talkin' up the big shootin' fest this weekend – again.' Celestine cackled with glee and the pair went into the kitchen to freshen their mugs of cider.

Schuyler Thompson's mood was somber as he took to the podium. 'Good afternoon. Thank you all for being here. I apologize for taking everyone away from their families on a holiday, but there are important changes to our town government which I need to announce.'

'Were you informed of any changes?' Tish whispered to Reade.

The sheriff shook his head. 'I expect I'll receive the official email after the press conference.'

Schuyler drew a deep breath before speaking again. 'Last Saturday, at approximately 3.48 p.m., Councilman Tripp Sennette posted an inflammatory Tweet falsely accusing one William Bull of murdering Deputy Mayor Royce Behrens. Because of the Tweet, an angry band of civilians descended upon the Abbingdon Green Bed and Breakfast where Mr Bull had arranged to meet his daughter. This mob sought to extract vengeance for the death of the deputy mayor. In seeking that vengeance, they injured another civilian and caused thousands of dollars' worth of property damage. Despite the damages incurred, the next day, at 9.32 Sunday morning, Councilman Sennette once again posted an inflammatory Tweet demanding that the residents of Hobson Glen ensure that justice was done. What he meant by this statement was clear: Councilman Sennette wanted our citizens to demand that an innocent man be sent to prison.'

In the distance, the cameras picked up the sound of a group of people booing the mayor and shouting, 'Bull is Guilty! Amanda's been framed! Free the Behrenses!'

'Because of these reckless, irresponsible actions,' Schuyler went on, despite the background noise, 'I have demanded that Tripp Sennette resign from the Hobson Glen Town Council. Mr Sennette tendered that resignation to me at six o'clock this morning. This resignation is effective immediately. Also, as a show of good faith, I have recommended to the district attorney that Mr Bull be released from prison and all charges against him be dropped. I have also dropped all charges against Connie Ramirez, pursuant to her promise that she will no longer protest within the Hobson Glen town limits.'

At the news about Bull and Ramirez, the dissenters' boos grew louder. 'This is an outrage! Disgrace!'

Schuyler cast a side-eye in their direction and persisted. 'Following an emergency council meeting later this morning, Judson Darley was elected as our new deputy mayor. Councilman Darley is no stranger to most of you in this town. He's been a member of the Hobson Glen Town Council for over twenty-five years and is recognized, by all, for his loyal service and his balanced, impartial approach to governing. I look forward to working closely with Deputy Mayor Darley to make Hobson Glen a top-notch place to work, live and raise a family.'

A smattering of applause just barely overpowered the sound of the hecklers.

'To replace Tripp Sennette as senior council member, the council and I have elected Edwin Wilson. Edwin's vast business experience will be essential as we move to increase jobs and help local businesses.'

Tish gave a cheer. 'I'm so glad Edwin has a larger role to play on the council.'

Jules agreed. 'Maybe he'll stick around instead of resigning at the end of his term.'

'As for the now-vacant council seat,' Schuyler added, 'an election will take place in late February. For anyone wishing to throw their hat into the ring, applications will be available in Town Hall on Monday. And, finally, in one last announcement, the Rod and Gun Club event has been cancelled for this Saturday. In light of recent events, organizers and the council thought it in bad form to continue. We'll address, in future council meetings, whether the event will continue in its current form next year or be refashioned into something more befitting modern audiences. Thank you again for being here today. On behalf of myself and the town council, I wish you and yours a very happy Thanksgiving.'

'That's the first speech he's given that didn't make me want to throw a shoe at the television,' Mary Jo said.

'He's still a jerk,' Kayla added.

'Yep,' Reade agreed. 'The only reason Schuyler made Sennette resign is because of the investigation Sennette is facing. If he didn't cut ties with Sennette now, he'd go down with him. And as for Bull, Schuyler knew the town was looking at a lawsuit after Sennette intentionally put his life in danger.'

'I, for one, don't care why he did what he did,' Jules stated. 'I'm just glad the whole thing's over and Sennette's gone. Now if only the people who acted on his Tweets would be gone, or at the very least wise up.'

'That might take some time. "Those who can manage to make people believe absurdities, can make people commit atrocities."'

'Is that from CNN?'

'Nope. Voltaire. Misinformation has a long, long history.'

'Hey, look at that.' Tish pointed at the corner of the TV, where Maurice's camera happened to capture Leonard Pruett walking with Faye and Ethan Wheeler. It was a smile-filled and easy conversation that culminated in Faye gesturing to Leonard to follow them. 'Pruett might just have gotten a Turkey Day invitation.'

'Good for him,' Celestine replied, having just returned from the kitchen with a full mug. 'Those veggie deliveries finally paid off.'

'Good for her. Now that Ethan is grown, it would be nice for

Faye to have some companionship and maybe a little happiness for herself.'

'Yeah, that's all any of us want,' the baker responded with a frown.

Tish placed a comforting arm around her friend and announced, in an effort to keep the mood elevated, 'I have to get that turkey out of the oven to rest. Clemson, put those potatoes on and I'll get the sprouts roasting.'

'Anything I can do to help?' Mary Jo asked.

'You want to make the gravy? You make a great one and it would clear the decks for us to do other things.'

'You've got it!' MJ followed Reade into the kitchen.

'I'll tend bar,' Jules volunteered.

'I knew you would.'

While Jules opened two bottles of red to allow them to breathe, Kayla, Celestine and Daryl played with Cassius in the living room. Amid the laughter, chitchat, and clanking of pots and pans, there was a knock at the door.

'Wow, Maurice got here fast!' Jules said with a laugh. 'After I went on and on about how good your turkey dinner is, Tish, he probably flew here.'

Tish rushed to open the door, expecting to welcome Maurice. Instead, she was greeted by another familiar face. 'Lacey, Happy Thanksgiving. So good to see you.'

'Hi, Tish. Happy Thanksgiving. Is my mother here?'

'She sure is.' Tish led Lacey into the living room, where an astonished Celestine couldn't believe her eyes. 'We'll just give you some privacy.'

'No, that's OK, Tish. I don't mind speaking in front of y'all.'

'Lacey, honey, what are you doin' here?' the baker finally managed to ask.

'We had an early supper, like we always do, and the kids said what they were thankful for, like they usually do, and we started talking about Christmas like we always do. But nothing was like it usually was because Daddy wasn't there – which was bad enough – but you weren't there either.' Lacey's eyes welled with tears. 'I got to thinking about what Tish said the other day—'

At the mention of her visit with Lacey, Tish silently sidestepped toward the kitchen. Celestine, however, spied her movements from the corner of her eye and sneered, forcing the café owner to stop dead in her tracks.

'It's true. I've been – we've all been – grieving Daddy, and when I saw you with Daryl in *that* way, it was if Daddy suddenly never existed. And I felt alone in my love for him and my belief that the two of you had a good marriage and I wondered if I needed to stop grieving for him too.'

'Oh, Lacey, no,' Celestine cried. 'Never. I'd never expect you to stop grievin' or stop lovin' your daddy. Neither of us would.'

'Yeah, I figured that out when Daryl stopped by to tell me that he had the utmost respect for Daddy and that he never wanted us or you to forget him.'

Celestine gave a side-eye to Daryl, prompting Tish to whisper to the librarian, 'You're in trouble, too.'

'Then,' Lacey continued, 'when he told us about y'all's idea about the family meeting, it showed he wasn't making promises he wouldn't keep. He wanted us to all be together and was willing to work at things. I didn't accept the offer for the meeting right then and there, and I'm sorry I didn't because maybe we could have had dinner together today, but I needed to talk to the rest of the family first. All of us agreed that we'd love to have you both over for dessert.'

'Dessert? Today? We would.' She glanced at Daryl, who smiled and nodded his head. 'We would love to. You mean even Johnny agreed?'

'Oh yeah. He didn't have much choice when we girls ganged up on him. Why he thinks he's the head of the family is beyond me.'

Celestine let out a hoot. 'That's my girls! We'll, uh, we'll be over after dinner.'

'Sure. Take your time and enjoy.' She opened her arms wide to embrace Celestine. 'I'll see you later, Mama.'

Celestine, with tears streaming down her face, engulfed Lacey in her embrace. 'Child, I will be there with bells on.'

'I can't wait. The kids can't either. Enjoy your dinner everyone. Happy Thanskgiving.' Lacey turned toward Tish before she headed for the door. 'And good luck with the opening tomorrow. We always put up our Christmas decorations the day after Thanksgiving – the kids won't let me do it any other day – otherwise I'd stop by.'

Tish nodded and smiled as she escorted Lacey to the door.

'Thanks and no worries, I totally understand. I just hope I don't need to delay that opening, because I think your mother might be about to kill me.'

'I'm not gonna kill you, but you're sure gonna hear it from me,' Celestine commented upon Tish's return. 'What were you thinkin', meddlin' in my business? You think you're me?'

Tish raised an eyebrow. 'You do kinda meddle, don't you?'

'Darn tootin'. The key is not to let anyone know you're doin' it. You almost succeeded.' She turned to Daryl. 'And *you,* why I oughta . . . I oughta kiss you for bein' so sweet.'

'Please do,' Daryl urged, and the pair shared a sweet peck on the lips.

'Aww, y'all look good together,' Jules gushed. 'I'm so happy everything worked out for you, Celestine.'

'Thanks, sugar. I am mighty pleased myself.'

'But I do have to ask, when you go to Lacey's later, you *are* going to leave the pies here, right?'

'Jules,' Tish and Mary Jo cried in unison, with a backing "Uncle Jules" from Kayla.

'*Jules,*' he mimicked. 'Go on and yell at me for asking the question, but you know y'all were thinking it. Two chocolate bourbon pecan pies might be about to fly out that door and y'all are going to tell me you're not in the slightest bit concerned?'

As Mary Jo countered Jules about his pie comment, Kayla sang to baby Cassius, and Celestine and Daryl reminisced about Thanksgivings when they were kids. Tish led Reade into the kitchen to get on with the dinner preparations. 'Still grateful for a big, old-fashioned Thanksgiving?'

'Oh yeah! I wouldn't trade this for anything, but,' Reade added, putting his arm around Tish's waist, 'I'm also grateful that everyone is getting along again because that means everyone will be going home at the end of the night. No one camping on the office sofa bed or in the guest bedroom. Not that it bothers me, but you and I have some celebrating to do.'

'Oh? I thought we were doing that.'

'We're celebrating the holiday. I'm talking about celebrating the opening of your new café tomorrow. Later on, how about I draw you a nice, hot bath and give you a massage?'

'That would be bliss!'

'And then tomorrow morning, I'll make you breakfast.'

'Really?'

'Yep, the post-Thanksgiving special: pie and coffee.'

'And if Celestine takes her pies with her?'

'Um, my undying love and affection and coffee?'

'Sounds good to me, but what will you have?'

'Well, your undying love and affection and coffee, of course.'

'Uh huh,' she deadpanned as she stirred the gravy MJ had started. Clemson had been talking about having pie for breakfast all week and had mentioned it no fewer than three times the previous evening.

'You know, I, um, I should probably go out there and show Jules some support,' he stated nervously.

'Uh huh.'

'And maybe check in with Ms Celly.'

'Uh huh.'

'Make sure her drink is to her liking.'

'Uh huh.'

'I'll, um, I'll be back in a few minutes.'

'Uh huh.'

Alone in the sun-dappled kitchen, filled with the sights and aromas of a beautiful Thanksgiving feast and the sounds of a baby cooing and her friends laughing in the other room, Tish sighed contentedly and, with an eye cast heavenward, whispered, 'Thank you.'

Bread, Onion, Celery, and Sage Stuffing

Yield: Enough to stuff a 12-pound/5.5 kg turkey

Ingredients

1 x 20 oz/567 g loaf sliced white or stuffing bread (stuffing bread
is typically found in supermarkets in November and December)
1 stick unsalted butter, softened
4 tablespoons/60 ml vegetable oil
1 large sweet onion, finely chopped
4 stalks of celery, finely chopped
2 teaspoons poultry seasoning (I use Bell's Poultry Seasoning)
Salt and pepper to taste
32 oz/950 ml chicken or turkey broth

Spread bread slices on a large baking tray, cover with a tea towel
and allow to dry overnight. Alternately, you could toast them in a
low oven for fifteen to twenty minutes.

Cut bread into ½ inch/1 cm cubes.

In a large Dutch oven or stockpot, melt butter over medium heat.
Add oil.
Cook onion and celery until soft, being careful not to allow vegeta-
bles to brown.
Season with poultry seasoning and stir to combine.

Stir in bread cubes until evenly coated with butter/oil mixture.

Moisten with broth one cup at a time, mixing well in between, until
stuffing is desired consistency. You will use far less broth for a
stuffing that is going inside the turkey. If baking in a casserole dish,
you will most likely use the entire amount of broth.

Allow mixture to cool completely before stuffing the turkey. Otherwise, turn into a casserole dish and bake at 350°F/180°C for 30 minutes until top is browned and crunchy and interior is hot.

Baked Brie with Fig and Pear

Yields approximately 6 to 8 servings

Ingredients

1 x 6–8 oz/170–225 g wheel of cream Brie, Camembert, or other soft cheese, chilled
2 tablespoons/30 g fig jam
1 tablespoon/15 g unsalted butter
1 pear, cored and diced
1 teaspoon/5 g sugar
1 sheet of all-butter puff pastry
1 egg, beaten

In a small saucepan, melt the butter. Add the diced pear and sugar and stir to combine. Cook until pear is just soft and has surrendered its juices. Allow to cool.

Preheat oven to 375°F (190°C). Place Brie or other cheese in the center of the puff pastry sheet. Spread the fig jam on top of the cheese. Top with the cooled pear mixture.

Fold the dough up and over the top and pleat together to enclose cheese and toppings. Set the pastry parcel on a baking sheet lined with parchment paper and brush with beaten egg.

Place baking sheet in oven and bake until pastry is golden and crisp, approximately 30 minutes.

Remove from oven and allow to cool for five minutes before slicing into wedges and serving.